Christy® Juvenile Fiction Series

VOLUME ONE

Christy® Juvenile Fiction Series

Christy® Juvenile Fiction Series
VOLUME ONE

The Bridge to Cutter Gap
Silent Superstitions
The Angry Intruder

Catherine Marshall
adapted by C. Archer

Tommy nelson™

A Division of Thomas Nelson Publishers
Since 1798

www.thomasnelson.com

VOLUME ONE
The Bridge to Cutter Gap
Silent Superstitions
The Angry Intruder
in the *Christy*® Juvenile Fiction Series

Copyright © 1995
by the Estate of Catherine Marshall LeSourd

The *Christy*® Juvenile Fiction Series is based on
Christy® by Catherine Marshall LeSourd © 1967
by Catherine Marshall LeSourd © renewed
1995 by Marshall-LeSourd, L.L.C.

The *Christy*® name and logo are officially registered
trademarks of Marshall-LeSourd, L.L.C.

All characters, themes, plots, and subplots portrayed in this
book are the licensed property of Marshall-LeSourd, L.L.C.

Published in Nashville, Tennessee, by Tommy Nelson®,
a Division of Thomas Nelson, Inc.

ISBN 1-4003-0772-4

Printed in the United States of America

05 06 07 08 09 BANTA 9 8 7 6 5 4 3 2 1

The Bridge
to Cutter Gap

The Characters

CHRISTY RUDD HUDDLESTON, a nineteen-year-old girl.
Her father, mother, and brother George.

CHRISTY'S STUDENTS:
ROB ALLEN, age fourteen.
CREED ALLEN, age nine.
LITTLE BURL ALLEN, age six.
BESSIE COBURN, age twelve.
VELLA HOLT, age five.
SAM HOUSTON HOLCOMBE, age nine.
SMITH O'TEALE, age fifteen.
RUBY MAE MORRISON, age thirteen.
JOHN SPENCER, age fifteen.
CLARA SPENCER, age twelve.
ZADY SPENCER, age ten.
LULU SPENCER, age six.
LUNDY TAYLOR, age seventeen.

SCALAWAG, Creed Allen's pet raccoon.

ALICE HENDERSON, a Quaker mission worker from Ardmore, Pennsylvania.

DAVID GRANTLAND, the young minister.

IDA GRANTLAND, David's sister.

DR. NEIL MACNEILL, the physician of the Cove.

JEB SPENCER, a mountain man.
FAIRLIGHT SPENCER, his wife.
> *(Parents of Christy's students John, Clara, Zady, and Lulu)*
> Their toddler, LITTLE GUY.

BOB ALLEN, keeper of the mill by Blackberry Creek.
MARY ALLEN, his superstitious wife.
> *(Parents of Christy's students Rob, Creed, and Little Burl)*

AULT ALLEN, Bob's older brother.

MRS. TATUM, the boarding-house lady.

BEN PENTLAND, the mailman.

JAVIS MACDONALD, the train conductor.

DR. FERRAND, a medical missionary in the Great Smoky Mountains.

❧ One ❧

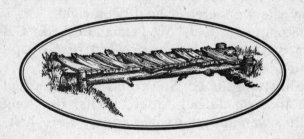

It was her worst nightmare come true. She couldn't cross. She couldn't cross the bridge, not if her very life depended on it.

Christy Huddleston managed a grim smile. Bridge! It was not a bridge at all, just two huge, uneven logs with a few thin boards nailed across them here and there. A deadly layer of ice coated the logs and boards. Far below, frigid water swirled past and around and over jagged chunks of ice and razor-sharp rocks.

Christy took a step closer to the bridge. The whole contraption swayed in the biting wind. Her stomach swirled and bucked. She had never liked heights, but this . . . this was impossible.

She looked across to her guide, Ben Pentland, on the other side of the swollen creek. The mailman gazed at her doubtfully. He'd told her she wouldn't be able to make this seven-mile journey through rough, snowy terrain. "Too hard a walk for a city-gal," he'd said, and now she wondered if he'd been right.

"Stomp your feet," Mr. Pentland called. "Get 'em warm. Then come on—but first scrape your boots, then hike up your skirts."

Christy hesitated. She could no longer feel her toes inside her rubber boots. Her long skirts, wet almost to her knees, were half-frozen.

Mr. Pentland shook his head. "Can't get to where you're goin' without crossin' this bridge."

His words hung in the brittle air. Not for the first time that day, Christy wondered if she'd made a terrible mistake coming to this place. What was she doing here, deep in the Tennessee mountains in the middle of winter, heading off to a world she'd never seen before? Teaching school to poor mountain children had seemed like a fine idea in the cozy warmth of her home back in Asheville, North Carolina. But now . . .

Christy fingered the locket her father had given her before she'd left Asheville. Inside was a little picture of her parents and one of Christy and her brother George. No one in her family had understood why she'd felt she had to come to this wild and lonely place to teach at a mission school.

And now, she wasn't so sure herself.

"Guess you ain't crossed a bridge like this before," said Mr. Pentland.

"No," Christy agreed, forcing an unsteady smile.

She took a deep breath, then put one foot on a log. It swayed a little. Her boot sent a piece of bark flying. She watched it as it twirled down, falling the dozen feet to the water. The water snatched at the bit of wood and sped it away.

Another step, and she was on the bridge. The sound of the water became a roar in her ears. There was no turning back now. "You're doin' fine," came Mr. Pentland's soothing voice. "Keep a-comin'. Not far now."

Not far now? It seemed he was a hundred miles away, safe on the far side.

The logs swayed and tilted. Christy stared at her feet as she struggled with her heavy wet dress. Another step, another. With great effort, she forced herself to look at Mr. Pentland.

She was halfway there. She was going to make it.

Another step, and another. The far side was—

Her boot slid on a crosspiece! She clutched at empty air for support that was not there, slipped and landed hard on her knees. She clung as best she could to the icy log.

Mr. Pentland was shouting something and coming out to her. She crawled another few inches toward him.

Why am I here, risking my life to get to a place I've never seen? some sensible part of herself kept asking. *Why is teaching so important to me?* Had it only been yesterday that she'd stepped aboard the train to Tennessee, so confident and full of hope? Christy's mind raced as she slowly crawled toward Mr. Pentland.

Then her right knee hit a slick spot on the log. Her weight shifted. Slowly, terrifyingly slowly, she slid over the side of the bridge.

"No!" she cried. She clawed for support, but her fingers lost their grip. She was falling, falling, toward the icy water below. The roar of the water and the sound of her own screams filled her ears, and as she fell she wondered why she had to die now, die here—when she was trying to do something so good.

As the icy waters rushed over her, the events of the last two days flashed across Christy's mind. *Was this the way it would end?*

❧ TWO ❧

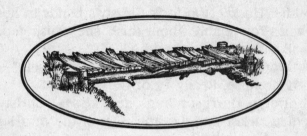

O*ne day earlier.*

"Now, you watch your step going out to the car. With all that snow last night, the walk's bound to be icy." Mrs. Huddleston fussed with the bow of her crisp white apron. Tears glistened in her eyes.

Christy took a deep breath to keep herself from crying, too. The look of love and longing in her mother's eyes was hard to bear. "I'll be careful," she promised.

Slowly, Christy took in the smells and sights around her, all the things she was leaving behind for who knew how long. The smell of starch in her mother's apron, the hissing of the pine resin in the big iron stove in the kitchen, and the sleepy half-smile on her brother George's face. He had stumbled out of bed just in time to see Christy off.

"We have to go," Mr. Huddleston repeated from the doorway. "The engine's running. I had a time cranking the car in this cold."

Mrs. Huddleston took Christy's hands in her own. "You're sure about this?" she whispered.

"Positive," Christy said.

"Promise me you'll take care of yourself."

"I promise. Really I do."

After a flurry of hugs and kisses, Christy settled at last into the front seat of the car. Her father drove silently, intent on navigating the icy roads. Asheville was a hilly town, and driving took all his concentration as he made his way in the pre-dawn gloom to the railroad station.

In the gray light, the station had a ghostly look. Black smoke billowed from the engine smokestack. Mr. Huddleston parked the car and they climbed out. The slamming of the car doors seemed unnaturally loud and final. Christy began the walk to the train, keeping pace beside her father.

She tensed, waiting for what she knew would come. She'd battled long and hard with her parents for the chance to leave home like this. They considered her far too young, at nineteen, to be going off alone on a wild adventure like teaching school in the Tennessee mountains.

She'd told them that she was grown-up now. That this was, after all, 1912, and that women could take advantage of all kinds of exciting opportunities. Her life in Asheville was nothing but teas and receptions and ladies' polite talk, dance-parties and picnics in the summer. A good enough life, certainly, but she knew in her heart that there had to be more than that waiting for her somewhere. All she had to do was find it.

Her parents had argued with her, pleaded, bargained. But Christy was stubborn, like all the Huddlestons, and this time she was the one who'd gotten her way. She'd been thrilled at her victory, too—that is, until now, looking at her father's worried, gentle face, and his too-gray hair.

"My hand's cold," she said suddenly, sticking her hand into the pocket of his overcoat. It was a childish gesture, but her father understood. He paused, smiling at her sadly.

"Girlie," he said, using his favorite nickname for her, "do you really think you have enough money to get you through till payday?" His breath frosted in the crisp January air.

"Plenty, Father."

"Twenty-five dollars a month isn't going to go far."

"It'll be good for me," Christy said lightly. "For the first time in my life, I probably won't have the chance to shop."

Reaching into his other pocket, Mr. Huddleston retrieved a small package. It was wrapped in blue paper and tied with a satin bow.

"Father!" Christy exclaimed. "For me?"

"It's nothing, really," he said, clearing his throat. "From your mother and me."

Christy fumbled with the wrapping. Inside was a black velvet-covered box. She opened it to discover a heart-shaped silver locket.

"Great-grandmother's necklace!" Christy cried.

"Go ahead," her father said. "Open it."

With trembling fingers, Christy opened the tiny engraved heart. Inside were two pictures. One was a carefully posed photograph of her parents: her mother with a gentle smile, her father gazing sternly at the camera, with just a hint of a smile in the creases of his eyes. On the other side was a picture of Christy and her brother, taken last summer at their church retreat.

"That's so you won't forget us," her father said with a wink.

"Oh, Father," Christy said, wiping away a tear, "as if I ever could!"

Her father helped her put on the necklace, then led her to the steps of the train. She climbed aboard and gazed with interest at the brass spittoons, at the potbellied stove in the rear, at the faces of the other passengers. It was only a few hours to El Pano, the stop nearest to Christy's new job, but it felt as if she were about to embark on a journey around the world. She had taken train trips before, of course, but never alone. This time everything seemed new, perhaps because she was going away without knowing when she would return.

Christy sank down onto a scratchy red plush seat and smiled up at her father, who had followed her on board. He placed her suitcase on the floor beside her. The whistle blew shrilly.

"Don't forget now," her father said. "Soon as you get there, write us." He gave her an awkward hug, and then he was gone.

Out on the platform, Christy saw her father talking to the old conductor. Mr. Huddleston pointed in her direction, and Christy sighed. She knew what he was saying—*take good care of my girl.* It was so embarrassing! After all, if she was old enough to go off on this adventure, she was old enough to take care of herself on the train. And the train was going to be the easy part of this trip.

"All a-boarrd!" the conductor called. The engine wheezed. Chuff . . . chuff . . . chuff. The train jerked forward, and a moment later, the telephone poles outside were sliding past.

Before long, the conductor was making his way down the aisle, gathering tickets. *Please,* Christy thought desperately, *don't humiliate me in front of the other passengers. I'm a big girl. I can take care of myself.*

"Ticket, please," came the old man's voice. "You're Christy Huddleston, aren't you?"

Christy nodded, trying her best to seem like a dignified adult.

"I'm Javis MacDonald. I've known your father a long time," the conductor said as he punched her ticket. "So you're bound for El Pano, young lady. I understand you'll be teaching school there?"

"No, actually I'll be teaching in Cutter Gap," Christy corrected. "It's a few miles out of El Pano."

Mr. MacDonald rubbed his whiskers. His expression grew troubled. "That Cutter Gap is rough country," he said. "Last week during a turkey shooting match, one man got tired of shooting turkeys. Shot another man in the back instead."

Christy felt a shiver skate down her spine, but she kept the same even smile on her face. *Is Cutter Gap really such a dangerous place?*

The conductor gazed at Christy with the same worried look she'd seen on her parents' faces this morning. "I suppose I shouldn't be telling you that sort of thing. But you'll be seeing it for yourself, soon enough. It's a hard place, Cutter Gap."

"I'm sure I'll be fine," Christy said.

"If you were my daughter, I'd send you home on the first train back. That's no place for a girl like you."

A girl like me, Christy thought, her cheeks blazing. What did that mean, anyway? What kind of girl was she? Maybe that was why she'd started on this trip, to find out who she was and where her place was in the world.

14

As the conductor moved on, she opened her locket. The sight of her parents brought tears to her eyes. George gazed back at her with his usual I'm-about-to-cause-trouble grin. But it was her own picture that caught her attention. The slender, almost girlish figure, the blue eyes beneath piled-up dark hair.

What was it in her eyes? A question? A glimmer of understanding? Of hope? Of searching?

That picture had been taken at the end of the church retreat last summer. By then, she'd decided that she had to go to Cutter Gap. The answers to her questions lay somewhere in the Great Smoky Mountains.

It seemed strange that she'd found a clue about where her life might go from a perfect stranger, rather than from her own family or her church back in Asheville. But the little, elderly man who'd spoken to the retreat group with such passion had reached her in a way no one else ever had.

Dr. Ferrand was a medical doctor doing mission work in the Great Smokies. He'd spoken of the need for volunteers to help teach and care for the mountain people, or highlanders, as he'd called them. He'd talked of desperate poverty and ignorance. He'd told the story of a boy, Rob Allen, who wanted book learning so much that he walked to school barefoot through six-foot snow.

Listening to his moving words, Christy glanced down at her pointed, buttoned shoes with their black, patent-leather tops, the shoes she'd bought just the week before. Thinking of the barefoot boy, she felt a shudder of guilt. She'd known there was poverty in places like Africa and China, but was it possible that such awful conditions existed a train's ride away from her home town?

Dr. Ferrand went on to talk about someone who shared his passion to help the mountain people—Miss Alice Henderson, a Quaker from Ardmore, Pennsylvania, a new breed of woman who had braved hardship and danger to serve where she saw need.

I would like to know that woman, Christy thought. *I would like to live my life that way.*

By the time they sang the closing hymn, "Just As I Am," Christy felt herself coming to a very important decision. Her heart welled up so full she could hardly sing the words.

When the benediction was over, she made her way down the aisle to Dr. Ferrand. "You asked for volunteers," Christy said. "You're looking at one. I can teach anywhere you want to use me." She was not the most well-educated girl in the world, but she knew she could teach children to read.

A long silence fell. The little man gazed at her doubtfully. "Are you sure, my child?"

"Quite sure."

And so it was done. There had been plenty of arguments with her doubtful parents. But for the first time in her life, Christy Rudd Huddleston felt certain she was about to take the world by storm. Even her parents' disapproval couldn't change her mind.

After all, she'd told herself, *throughout history, the men and women who have accomplished great things must have had to shrug off other people's opinions, too.*

Suddenly the train screeched to a halt. The conductor's gruff voice broke into Christy's thoughts. "A snowdrift has flung two big rocks onto the roadbed, folks," he said. "There's a train crew comin' to clear the tracks. Shouldn't take long."

At the rear of the coach, the potbellied stove was smoking. Across the aisle, a woman was changing the diaper of her red-faced, squalling baby.

A little fresh air couldn't hurt, Christy thought. She buttoned her coat, reached for her muff and headed outside. Snowflakes as big as goose feathers were still falling. As far as she looked, Christy could see nothing but mountain peak piled on mountain peak. It was a lonely landscape, lonelier still when the wind rose suddenly, making a sad, sobbing sound. It was a wind with pain in it.

Christy shivered. Was she going to be homesick, even before she reached her destination?

She returned to the coach. A long time passed before the train once again chugged slowly toward its destination. Outside, as the sun sank, the world glittered with ice, turning every bush and withered blade of grass to jewels—sapphires and turquoise, emeralds and rubies and diamonds.

Darkness came suddenly. For what seemed like the thousandth time, Christy imagined her welcome at the train station.

Someone would, of course, be sent to meet her—a welcoming committee of some kind.

"Miss Huddleston?" they would ask. "Are you the new teacher for the mission?" They would look her over, and their eyes would say, "We were expecting a young girl, but you're a grown woman!"

At last the train began to slow. Mr. MacDonald announced that they were coming into El Pano. As he lit the railroad lanterns on the floor in front of the coach, the engine's wheels ground to a stop. Christy reached for her muff and suitcase and started down the aisle. She was certain she could hear the nervous beating of her own heart.

"Let me help you with that suitcase," the conductor said. "Easy on those steps. They may be slippery."

Christy stepped down to the ground. Her eyes searched the dark. There wasn't much to see—just the tiny station and four or five houses.

Where was the welcoming committee she'd imagined? A few men came out of the little station and began to unload boxes from a baggage cart. Now and then they paused to stare at Christy, muttering and laughing under their breath.

"You're a mighty pert young woman, Miss Huddleston," said the conductor. "But land sakes—watch yourself out there at Cutter Gap."

"Thank you," Christy said, trying to sound confident despite the fear rising in her. She spun around, searching again for some sign that she was not about to be left completely alone. But no one was coming. The snowy landscape was deserted.

"It's not too late to change your mind," Mr. MacDonald said as he climbed the train steps.

Christy just gave him a smile and a wave. Slowly the train began to move. The smaller it grew, the greater the lump in Christy's throat. Far away, the engine whistle blew. Her heart clutched at the sound, and then there was nothing but emptiness. She was alone, all alone.

The men finished unloading the baggage cart. She could feel their eyes on her, and she could hear their whispers.

With a firm grip on her suitcase, Christy strode toward the little station. Whatever happened, from this moment on, this was *her* adventure.

She was not about to let anyone see how afraid she really was.

❧ Three ❧

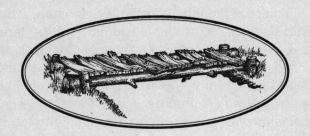

Inside the little station, a group of men stood near the stove. They fell silent as Christy headed toward the grilled window where the ticket agent stood.

"Sir?" Christy said to the old man. He did not look up. "Could you tell me if there's somewhere in town where I could spend the night?"

There was no answer.

"Sir," Christy repeated loudly. "Could you tell me—"

"Young woman, you'll have to speak up."

This time Christy practically shouted her question. The men near the stove laughed loudly.

"Well, now," said the ticket agent. "Let's see. Maybe Miz Tatum's."

"Where is that?"

"Oh, close. You just—guess it's easier to show you."

Christy followed the man into the stinging cold. He pointed across the tracks. "Can't quite make it out, but it's that big house, second one down. You'll find it."

Christy nodded, peering into the velvety darkness.

"Just tell Miz Tatum that I sent you. You'll get plenty to eat and a clean bed." He chuckled. "Mind you, Miz Tatum can talk the hind legs off a donkey."

Christy soon discovered that carrying a heavy suitcase wasn't easy, not while holding up long skirts at the same time. Halfway to the boarding house, she slipped and fell. The snow churning up over her shoe tops was bad enough, but the laughter coming from the old ticket agent was even worse.

Mustering as much dignity as she could, Christy struggled to her feet and made her way toward the Victorian frame house the agent had pointed out. Yellow lamplight glowed from several windows, and smoke poured out of both chimneys. The cozy sight filled her with a sudden, desperate longing for her own home back in Asheville. Her parents and George would be sitting down to supper right about now. She could almost hear her father's soft voice saying grace.

Christy set her suitcase on the porch, shook out her snowy skirts, and twirled the bell. Once more she glanced around her, hoping for a sight of the welcoming committee she'd imagined in such detail. But the street was empty and perfectly silent. The whole world seemed to be holding its breath.

A tall, big-boned woman opened the door. "Yes?"

"Mrs. Tatum?" Christy asked.

The woman nodded, arms crossed over her chest.

"I'm Christy Huddleston from Asheville. The station man told me you take in roomers. Could I rent a room?"

"Sure could. Come on in out of the cold. Bad night, ain't it?"

"Yes, it is," Christy agreed, filled with relief. For tonight, at least, she would have a place to stay.

As Christy stepped inside, the woman looked her over carefully. "You come from Asheville-way?" she said, taking Christy's suitcase. "Not many women come through here on the train. Where you bound?"

"I—" Christy began.

"Oh, but listen to me!" Mrs. Tatum interrupted. "There's time enough for questions. Let me show you to your room, child." She pointed to a lamp. "Bring that lamp over there."

The room upstairs was plain and clean. A shiny brass bed sat in the center. "Now, you make yourself to home," Mrs. Tatum instructed, setting down Christy's suitcase. Once again she gazed at her, eyes full of questions. "I'll build up the fire downstairs, and you can eat by the stove."

Before Christy could respond, Mrs. Tatum was bustling out the door. Christy changed clothes quickly, shivering in the unheated room. A nice, hot fire would be a welcome relief. Her toes were practically numb.

Christy picked up the lamp and groped her way down the dark stairs to the kitchen. Mrs. Tatum had put on a large calico apron. "Here's your supper," she said as Christy sat at the kitchen table. "Spareribs and pickled beans. And there's some sourwood honey and some apple butter to put on the biscuit bread. I saved the sourwood honey for something special."

"Thank you," Christy said, suddenly realizing how hungry she was.

"So tell me now," Mrs. Tatum said, watching Christy as she began to eat, "where exactly are you bound?"

Christy swallowed a piece of biscuit bread. "I've come to teach school at the mission. You know—out at Cutter Gap."

Mrs. Tatum practically gasped. "Land sakes, child. You, teaching? At Cutter Gap? What does your mama think about that?"

"Oh, it's all right with my parents," Christy said, not wanting to discuss *that* whole thing. "After all, I am nineteen."

Mrs. Tatum settled into a chair next to Christy. "Have they *seen* Cutter Gap?" she asked, eyes wide.

"No," Christy admitted. *Do all middle-aged people think this way?* she wondered silently.

"Look," Mrs. Tatum said sincerely. "I just don't think you know what you're getting yourself into. I'm a pretty good judge of folks, and it's easy to tell you come from a fancy home—your clothes, the way you talk."

"My home isn't that fancy," Christy protested. "Besides, I'm not afraid of plain living."

"Mercy sakes alive! You don't know *how* plain. Did you ever have to sleep in a bed with the quilts held down by rocks just to keep the wind from blowing the covers off?"

Christy smiled. Surely Mrs. Tatum was exaggerating.

"The thing is, I know those mountain people." Mrs. Tatum lowered her voice. "They don't take much stock in foreigners."

"What do you mean, *foreigners?*" Christy cried. "I'm an American citizen, born in the Smoky Mountains."

"Now, don't get riled," Mrs. Tatum soothed. "The folks in Cutter Gap think anyone who's not from there is a foreigner. They're mighty proud people. It's going to be well-nigh impossible for you to help them."

Christy pushed back her plate. As much as Mrs. Tatum's words bothered her, she didn't want to show it. *"She could talk the hind legs off a donkey,"* the station man had said. Was this just so much talk?

"That was excellent," Christy said, hoping to change the subject. "Thank you, Mrs. Tatum. I was starving."

Mrs. Tatum reached for Christy's plate. Her brow was furrowed. "Look, maybe you don't like somebody like me that you never saw before tonight butting in. But my advice is that you get yourself on the next train and go straight back to your folks."

How could I run away like that, before I've even seen Cutter Gap? Christy wondered as she pushed back her chair and stood.

"Mrs. Tatum," she said gently, "I've given my word about teaching school. A promise is a promise." She reached for the lamp. "How far is the Gap from here, anyway?"

"Seven miles, more or less."

"How can I get out there tomorrow?"

Mrs. Tatum clucked her tongue. "My, you are eager, aren't you?" She sighed. "Ben Pentland carries the mail out that way, but he ain't been there since the snow fell."

"How could I talk to Mr. Pentland?"

"At the General Store most likely, come morning."

"Thanks again for the supper, Mrs. Tatum. And please don't worry about me."

Christy glanced over her shoulder as she

started up the stairs. Mrs. Tatum was staring at her, shaking her head in disapproval.

Back in her cold bedroom, Christy stared out the window at the little village beyond. The houses were roofed with silver, the railroad tracks a pair of shining ribbons. Where was Cutter Gap from here? Was it really such an awful place? What if her parents were right? Her parents, and the conductor, and Mrs. Tatum . . . What if they were *all* right? Didn't anyone think she was doing the right thing, coming here?

They need a teacher, Christy told herself. Dr. Ferrand had said they were desperate for help. But then why hadn't anyone been here to greet her? Had he forgotten to tell them she was coming? No, she had a letter from him. It couldn't be that.

Cold air was seeping through the window. Christy retreated to the dresser and began to pull hairpins from her hair. She stared at her reflection in the mirror. Staring back at her was a face too thin, too angular. For the millionth time, she wished she were beautiful, like her friend Eileen back in Asheville. She sighed. Her eyes were too big for the rest of her face, but this time she saw something new in them, something she'd never seen before.

She saw fear.

Christy opened her suitcase. Digging through the layers of clothing—she hadn't been sure what to bring, so she'd brought a little of everything—she found what she was looking for.

Clutching the leather-bound diary to her chest, she leapt under the covers, grateful for the warmth of Mrs. Tatum's old quilt.

She opened to the first, crisp page, yellow in the lamplight. Her fountain pen poised, she waited for the perfect words to come to her. This was, after all, the beginning of her adventure. She'd promised herself she would write it all down—good and bad, highs and lows.

> *January 7, 1912*
> *My trip to El Pano was uneventful.*

Christy wrote in her pretty, swirling handwriting. She stared at the words, then smiled at herself. *Be honest, Christy,* she told herself.

She tapped the fountain pen against her chin.

> *I have begun my great adventure this day, and although things have not gone exactly as I had hoped, I am still committed to my dream of teaching at the mission.*
> *The day began with a heavy snowfall, which has made for difficult travel. Last night when it began to snow, Mother said, jokingly, that perhaps I should take it as an omen.*

I don't believe in such things, of course. Neither does Mother. (I suppose she was just hoping to convince me not to go, although she knew in her heart that was not to be.)

Still, upon my arrival in El Pano, no one was here to greet me, and I cannot help but wonder if that is not a bad sign. I want to be wanted, I suppose, to feel that my coming here is a good thing.

The truth is, I have not been this afraid before, or felt this alone and homesick. Leaving everyone I love was harder than I thought it would be. But I must be strong. I am at the start of a great adventure. And great adventures are sometimes scary.

Christy set her pen and diary on the night table. She lay back with a sigh and pulled the covers up to her neck.

It was a long, long time before she finally fell into a restless sleep.

❧ Four ❧

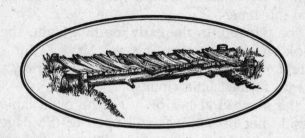

She was having that dream again. She knew it was a dream, because she'd had it so many times.

Christy was standing on the railroad trestle, two hundred feet above the French Broad River. She and some friends had been on a picnic, and now they were heading home across the bridge. Her friends urged her on, but every time Christy looked down at the open spaces beneath her feet, her stomach began to somersault, and her head turned to rushing noise like the river raging far below her.

She looked down, down through the hole to her certain death, and her knees became liquid. Someone screamed, and then she was falling, falling, falling. . . .

Christy's eyes flew open. A dream. It was just a dream, the same dream she'd had a million times before. She tried to swallow. Her throat was tight, her skin damp with sweat.

If it were just a dream, why did it feel so real this time?

She blinked. In the early morning light, she took in the surroundings of Mrs. Tatum's guest room. It was so cold that Christy's breath formed little clouds.

She glanced at her diary on the night table beside her bed. It was still open to the page where she'd begun writing. *I have not been this afraid before*, she read.

Well, no wonder her dreams were getting the better of her. Yesterday *had* been quite a day. She stared out the window at the snowy, mountainous landscape. Somewhere out there, Cutter Gap was waiting for her.

Today, she vowed, would go more smoothly.

When she pushed open the door to the General Store, Christy was greeted by the smells of coal oil, strong cheese, leather, bacon fat, and tobacco. A group of men sat by the stove, whittling and rocking and talking among themselves.

At the nearest counter, a woman was arranging spools of thread in a cabinet under curving glass. "Excuse me," Christy said. "I was told I might find Mr. Pentland, the mailman, here."

The woman's eyes swept the men. "Ben," she called loudly, "come here, will you?"

A man looked up from the high boots he was lacing. When he stood, he unfolded like a jackknife to a height of over six feet. He was wearing overalls, covered by a frayed and unpressed suit coat. But it was his face that caught Christy's attention—long and slim, creased by wind and weather, with bushy arching eyebrows and deep-set eyes that sparkled.

"This here's Ben Pentland," said the woman. "Miss—"

Christy stuck out a mittened hand. "Christy Huddleston from Asheville."

"Howdy." He took her hand so firmly that she winced.

"You're the postman, aren't you?"

"Yep."

Obviously, Mr. Pentland was a man of few words. Christy glanced back at the circle of men watching her and Mr. Pentland with clear curiosity.

"Could I talk with you a minute?" Christy asked. "Back there, maybe?"

Mr. Pentland followed Christy toward the back of the store where the hardware and the harnesses and saddles were kept. "Mr. Pentland, I need help," she said. "I've come to teach school in Cutter Gap. I thought someone would meet me at the station yesterday, but nobody did. So I'm trying to find a way to get there.

Mrs. Tatum said you could help me, since you carry the mail out that way."

"Yep," he said proudly. "Carry the letters regular. But ain't nobody been in or out of Cutter Gap in a couple days. Snow's too deep."

"When are you going next?"

"Startin' now. That's why I was gettin' my boots on. Letters are piled up somethin' fearful."

"Do you ride?"

The mailman looked astonished at her question. "No critter could make it in this snow!"

Christy felt her heart sink a little. Mrs. Tatum had said it was seven miles from here to Cutter Gap. Christy had *never* walked seven miles at one stretch in her entire life. But what did that matter? She couldn't exactly sit here, waiting for the snow to melt and spring to come.

"Could I walk out there with you today?" Christy asked.

"Nope. Too hard a walk for a city-gal. These here mountains make for tough walking, and the deep snow makes it near impossible, even for mountain people. And, besides, you're just a runt of a girl. You'd never make it."

He did not sound like he was going to change his mind. "Mr. Pentland," Christy said forcefully, "you don't understand. I'm strong, honestly I am, and the snow may last for weeks."

"Sorry, Miss. It just wouldn't be right for a woman to go along with the U-nited States mail." He took a step backwards and placed his hand over his heart, as if he were about to salute the flag. "'Neither rain . . . nor snow . . . nor heat . . . nor gloom of night . . . will stay these couriers from the swift completion of their appointed rounds.'"

Christy stared at him in amazement. She had never heard that slogan before. Was Mr. Pentland making fun of her?

"Beautiful, ain't it?" Mr. Pentland asked. "The government in Washington wrote it up for us. Anyway, I figure if rain or snow can't stop us from getting the mail where it needs to go, then I surely can't have no city-gal getting in the way." He turned to rejoin his companions by the stove.

Now what? Mr. Pentland was Christy's only chance to get to Cutter Gap. She couldn't give up, not yet.

"Mr. Pentland, *please*," Christy begged, running after him. "That's a *wonderful* slogan. I promise I won't interfere with the mail one bit. I won't even slow you down. Please? At least consider it?"

The mailman looked her over doubtfully. "Look, I don't want to discourage you, but it's for your own good. It ain't easy, walkin' in the snow. And what about your things?"

So he was weakening—at least a little. "I only have one small suitcase," Christy said hopefully. "The rest of my things are being shipped in a trunk. May I—" she smiled her most winning smile— "May I come with you?"

33

Mr. Pentland smiled, shaking his head. "Can you be ready in a hip and a hurry?"

"Ten minutes," Christy vowed.

She ran back to Mrs. Tatum's and quickly gathered her belongings together. As she said goodbye on the front porch, Mrs. Tatum took Christy's face between her hands, kissing first one cheek and then the other.

"That's for your mother, since she ain't here," she said. "And you let her know that I did my level best to send you home to her." She shook her head. "You're a sight on the eyes," she said. "They've never seen the likes of you before, out at the mission." She thrust a brown paper bag into Christy's hand. "No use walkin' on an empty stomach."

Christy turned to see Mr. Pentland, waiting impatiently by the edge of the road. "Women!" he muttered under his breath, clearly embarrassed by all the female fuss. "Always cacklin' like hens!"

"I must go," Christy said. "Thank you again for everything, Mrs. Tatum."

"Mind you watch that slippery, log bridge over the creek!" Mrs. Tatum warned. "The Lord bless you and keep you, child."

Mr. Pentland walked at a brisk pace, but Christy managed to keep up with him. She was feeling much more hopeful this morning. The world looked fresh and welcoming, coated with glistening snow. Over the far mountains a soft smoky-blue haze hung like a cloak, but in the valley where she was walking, the sky was clear blue.

Things were definitely looking up, Christy decided. Not only was Mr. Pentland letting her tag along—he had even offered to carry her suitcase, along with his mail bag. Out here, surrounded by the beauty of the mountains, the warnings she'd been hearing about Cutter Gap seemed silly.

After a while, Mr. Pentland turned and gave Christy a smile. "Maybe I should whittle down my walk a bit," he said. "Women's skirts ain't the best for snow."

Christy smiled back. There was something courteous and dignified about Mr. Pentland that she liked. His speech was full of odd expressions she had never heard before. The sun was a "sunball." Twilight was "the edge of dark." A mountain lion was a "painter." The words were beautiful, but very strange to her ears.

"Mr. Pentland," Christy asked as they began to walk more slowly, "how many families are there in Cutter Gap?"

He thought for a moment. "Maybe 'bout seventy in the Cove," he answered at last.

"The Cove?" Christy repeated.

"A cove is like a holler."

Christy shook her head, still confused.

"You know, a valley, between them mountains."

"Oh!" Christy nodded, understanding dawning at last. Would it always be so hard, she wondered, communicating with these people? "Most of the people farm, don't they?" she asked. "What crops? What do they raise?"

"Raise youngsters, mostly," he answered dryly.

Christy couldn't help smiling. "And do most of these children go to the mission school?"

"Well, now, that depends. Not all of them has got religion. Course, most everyone seems to like the new preacher, David Grantland."

"Has he been at the mission long?"

"Three months or so."

"What else can you tell me about him? Is he married?"

Mr. Pentland looked at Christy and chuckled. "Nope," he said.

Christy felt a blush rising in her cheeks. "Tell me," she said, quickly changing the subject, "do you know Miss Alice Henderson?"

"Everybody in Cutter Gap knows Miz Henderson."

"What's she like? What does she look like?"

The mountaineer shifted Christy's suitcase to his other hand, considering her question. "Well, she's a smiley woman. All her wrinkles are smile-wrinkles. Keeps busier than a honeybee 'round a rosebush. Started two schools and churches before comin' to Cutter Gap, she did. She rides a horse all over the mountains by herself. Sidesaddle, longskirt. Teachin', preachin', nursin' the sick, comfortin' the dyin'." He smiled. "She has a heap of hair. Wears it in braids 'round her head, like a crown. And she sits in that saddle like a queen."

Christy considered the picture he'd painted for her. Because of his speech and the fact that he hadn't had much formal education, she'd jumped to the conclusion that Mr. Pentland was a simple man. Clearly she'd been wrong. That was something she needed to remember.

Mr. Pentland stopped at a small, rustic cabin, calling out, "Mornin'! U-nited States mail!"

A woman rushed out to retrieve her two precious letters, waving happily at Mr. Pentland.

"How many more stops will we have?" Christy asked as they headed on.

"Four more letters. Ain't that a wonder!"

"But back at the store you said—" Christy stopped in mid sentence, trying to understand this mountain world where six letters meant "piled-up" mail.

Soon the trail grew so winding and narrow that they had to walk single-file. After a couple of hours of walking in Mr. Pentland's footsteps, the cold had begun to creep into Christy's bones. Her eyes stung. Her skirts were wet from snow and were beginning to stiffen in the cold. Her eyelashes were beaded with wet snow.

As she trudged along, she began to wonder if she really *could* make it all seven miles. She hadn't imagined that the trail would be so steep. And what was that Mrs. Tatum had said about the "slippery, log bridge"? Whatever she'd meant, it didn't sound easy.

Gradually the path grew almost vertical. The trail seemed to have been sliced out of the side of the mountain to their right. To their left, the ledge dropped off into space. Before long, it was five hundred feet to the valley floor below. Christy's breath came in short, hard gasps.

"This here's Lonesome Pine Ridge," Mr. Pentland called back. "There's another way that's shorter. But that way is so up-tilted, you could stand up straight and bite the ground."

Struggling for breath, Christy wondered silently if any piece of land could be more up-tilted than this. The wind grew more fierce, a gale from the north with a howl that stood her hair on end. The closer they got to the top of the ridge, the more certain she was that she would be blown right over the cliff, falling to a rocky death.

The memory of the falling dream, the one she'd had last night, came back to her suddenly. She shivered, but she couldn't tell if it was from fear or from the never-ending, bitter-cold wind that seemed to sneak its way inside her coat.

Christy studied her feet. One foot in front of the other. One dainty boot into each of Mr.

Pentland's great footprints. She was beginning to see why the mailman hadn't wanted her to come. This morning seemed like days and days ago.

Don't think about the wind, Christy told herself. *Don't think about how high you are. You are having an adventure, a great and wonderful adventure.*

Mr. Pentland must have sensed she was afraid. He called back over his shoulder, "Not much farther now to the Spencers' cabin. They live just on the other side. Guess we could stop and sit a spell by their fire and let you warm yourself."

"I'd like that," Christy called back wearily.

"You must be mighty tired out," Mr. Pentland called. "It's just another step or two."

At last, when Christy didn't think she could go another step, they came upon a cabin made of rough logs chinked together with mud. In the cleared place enclosed by a split-rail fence sat an immense black pot, a tall pile of logs for firewood, and some squawking chickens pecking in the snow.

A man wearing overalls and a large, black felt hat appeared on the porch. "Howdy!" he called. Hounds raced toward Mr. Pentland and Christy, wagging their tails and yapping happily.

"Howdy," Mr. Pentland called back. "Jeb Spencer, this here's Miz Huddleston. New teacher from Asheville."

"Howdy-do, Ma'am," the man said respectfully. He led them through the doorway into the gloomy little cabin. At first Christy could see nothing but the red glow of firelight. Then she noticed several beds piled high with quilts. In the shadows to one side stood a tall woman and an assortment of children, all of them with white-blond hair.

"Come and see the new teacher," Mr. Spencer said to the children. He nodded at the woman in the shadows. "This here's my wife, Fairlight," he explained to Christy. "And that's Zady, Clara, Lulu." He pointed to a tiny boy. "And that there is Little Guy. The oldest boy, John, he's out huntin'."

Would these children soon be some of her students? Christy wondered. She smiled at them and held her hand out to Mrs. Spencer. But the pretty woman didn't seem to know what to do. She touched Christy's fingers shyly. "Would you like to sit a spell?" she asked softly in a sweet, musical voice.

Christy could scarcely take her eyes off Fairlight Spencer. She was beautiful, in a plain, simple way. She had on a worn calico dress, and her feet were bare, despite the cold.

The Spencers, Christy realized, were watching her just as closely. As she took off her coat, the children seemed to be fascinated with the red sweater she was wearing underneath.

Mr. Pentland handed Mrs. Spencer the

lunch Mrs. Tatum had prepared. "You must be starvin'," the woman said softly. "Dinner'll be on the table right quick. You two rest up."

While Christy held her hands close to the fire, she had a better chance to look around the cabin. It was just two rooms, side by side. This one, she guessed, judging from all the beds, must serve as both the living and sleeping quarters. The other was the kitchen.

The children's bright eyes were still watching Christy. The littlest girl, the one named Lulu, had the fat-cheeked cherub look of a china doll. The tiny toddler—the one his father had called Little Guy—came up and touched his shy fingers to Christy's red sweater.

After a few minutes, Mrs. Spencer called everyone to dinner. The whole group gathered around a plank table set in a corner near the kitchen. Mr. Spencer began asking the blessing in a loud, clear voice. "Thank Thee, Lord, for providin' this bounty. Bless us and bind us. Amen."

Just then, out of the corner of her eye, Christy noticed a small gray pig. As soon as the "Amen" had been spoken, the older girl named Clara spoke up eagerly. "That there's Belinda, our pet pig," she said proudly. She picked up the pig and set it in her lap.

Christy tried not to show her surprise. But she couldn't help thinking that a smelly pig at the table was probably just the beginning of what she'd have to get used to here in the mountains. And after all, her mother had always insisted that a lady should be poised under all circumstances. If only her mother could see— not to mention smell—this house! Were all the homes in Cutter Gap as primitive as this one?

Mrs. Spencer placed a big black pot of steaming cabbage on the table, and the men broke up cornbread to sop it up. It looked awful to Christy. Longingly she gazed at Mrs. Tatum's ham sandwiches, which Mrs. Spencer had placed on a tin plate. The children were staring at them with total fascination.

"Would you like one of my sandwiches?" Christy asked, and within seconds, the ham sandwiches had disappeared. Even Belinda the pig sneaked a small bite.

Taking a piece of cornbread, Christy gazed at the unscrubbed faces around her. There was something strong and serious about them— something that reflected a spirit and attitude of a time long ago. It was as if one of those old tintype photographs of pioneers had come to life. Well, these *were* pioneers, in a way, she thought. It certainly had taken strength and courage to journey hundreds of miles through wilderness to settle here. And it would take strength indeed to live and try to keep house in a cabin like this one.

Sitting there with these people, Christy had a strange feeling. It was as if, in crossing the mountains with Mr. Pentland, she had crossed into another time, back to the days of the American frontier. Was she still Christy Rudd Huddleston from Asheville, North Carolina—or was she somebody else? It was as if the pages of her history book had opened—as if, by some magic, Daniel Boone or Davy Crockett could walk into this cabin at any moment. But this was no storybook. This was real.

"Are you likin' the food all right?" Fairlight Spencer asked nervously.

Just as Christy opened her mouth to answer, a little red-haired boy rushed into the cabin. He leaned against the chimney, gasping for breath.

"Creed Allen!" Mrs. Spencer cried. "What on earth is it?"

"Mighty sorry, Miz Spencer," he gasped. "But Pa's been hurt bad! It was a fallin' tree. Hit him on the head!"

"Where is he?" Mr. Spencer asked.

"They're carrying him here." The little boy's eyes fell on Christy. "He was on his way to the station to fetch the new teacher when it happened!"

❧ Five ❧

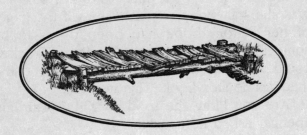

Christy gasped, the boy's words whirling in her head. So that was why no one had been at the station to meet her. A horrible feeling of guilt swept over her. Someone had been hurt because of her.

A moment later, two boys carried in a makeshift stretcher made of branches. A man lay on it, limp and unconscious. His head was bloody.

Mr. Spencer took one end of the stretcher and helped the boys ease the injured man onto a bed. Mrs. Spencer removed the man's heavy shoes and covered him with a quilt.

This happened because of me, Christy thought. She stared at the breathless little boy kneeling by the bed. *"Pa,"* he'd said. This poor man, so badly hurt, was the boy's father.

"Is Doc comin'?" Mr. Spencer asked.

"Yep," one of the boys answered. "Ought to be here pretty quick."

"Who is the man who's hurt?" Christy managed to whisper to Mrs. Spencer.

"That be Bob Allen." Her voice was gentle, as if she sensed how Christy felt. "Miz Henderson asked Bob to fetch you at the station. But it probably was snowin' too heavy on Sunday for him to journey. Guess he figured the snow had you stuck there." She nodded at one of the boys who'd carried in the stretcher. He was tall and slender, about fourteen or so. "That be Rob Allen, Bob's oldest son."

Christy thought for a moment. Hadn't that been the name of the boy Dr. Ferrand had mentioned in his speech last summer? The boy who had walked to school for miles, barefoot, because he was so anxious to learn?

Christy glanced at the boy's feet. They *were* barefoot, like all the children's. Suddenly she felt self-conscious in her own expensive clothes and shoes.

"That other boy, the fair-haired one, is mine. John. He's fifteen. And that there is Creed Allen, Rob's little brother," Mrs. Spencer said. She pointed to the red-haired boy who'd run into the cabin to announce that his father was hurt. "A rascal, that one is."

At the sound of his name, Creed looked up.

"This here's the new teacher from Asheville," Mrs. Spencer told him.

Rob and Creed stared at Christy. She couldn't read their faces. Was it curiosity or anger she saw there? Were they thinking that she was . . . that she was the cause of their father's accident?

Rob nodded shyly. "Proud to know you," he said softly. "I been lookin' forward to your comin'. . . . " He turned back to his father, his voice trailing off.

His little brother ran over to eye Christy more closely. Overalls, tousled hair, lots of freckles—he looked like a character out of the book *Tom Sawyer*. His two front teeth were missing.

"Howdy-do," he said, head tilted to one side.

"I'm so sorry about your father," Christy said.

"It ain't your fault," the boy said. "Near as we can figure, Pa was cuttin' across Pebble Mountain when a high wind come up. A big tulip-poplar tree bumped him right on the head."

"How'd you find him, Creed?" Mrs. Spencer asked, running her hand over his tangled hair.

"Me and Rob and John was huntin' squirrels out thataway. Bait-em—" he turned to Christy, "that's our old hound dog—well, he nosed Pa right out. Tree was still on him."

Within minutes, a crowd began to form in the tiny Spencer cabin. Apparently word traveled fast out here in the mountains, even without telephones. Most of the people gathered seemed to be relatives of Mr. Allen.

The cabin was nearly full when Christy

46

heard the stomping of feet and the whinny of a horse. A big-boned man strode inside and the crowd parted. He had a shock of reddish, messy hair—hair that looked as if it had not seen a barber in a very long time. His features were rugged. Deep lines etched his face—or maybe it was just the long shadows cast by the kerosene lamp.

"That be Doc," Mrs. Spencer said.

"I'll be needing more light over here," the doctor said to Mrs. Spencer. His eyes fell on Christy. He stared at her for a moment, an intense gaze that seemed to go right through her, and for some reason Christy felt a blush flare in her cheeks.

"Neil MacNeill," he said in a deep voice.

"Christy Huddleston. I'm the new—"

Before she could finish, Dr. MacNeill had turned his back on her. Mrs. Spencer brought another lamp close so he could begin his examination. He took off his coat and rolled up his shirt sleeves. The figure lying on the old post-and-spindle bed had not moved.

Mr. Pentland made his way through the crowd to Christy's side. "Doc MacNeill's the only doctor in the Cove," he explained.

Christy nodded and smiled up at him. She wished she could let him know how glad she was to have a friend in this awful situation, but an eerie silence had fallen on the room. All eyes were watching the doctor. The lamp cast giant shadows, dancing like monsters ready to spring from the walls. Only the draft of cold air seeping through a crack at Christy's back told her that this was all actually happening.

The doctor slid his fingers over Mr. Allen's head, feeling and probing. He took the patient's pulse, checked reflexes, opened the eyelids and stared intently into the eyes.

Finally he spoke, his face grim. "Bob's bad off," he said to a woman near the bed.

"Who's that?" Christy whispered to Mr. Pentland.

"That's Mary Allen, Bob's wife," the mailman answered. "And the man with the beard next to her is his brother, Ault."

The woman's face was rigid with fear. "Is he goin' to die, Doc?"

The doctor's voice was gentle. "Don't know the answer to that, Mary. He's in a coma now, like a deep sleep. There's some bleeding inside his skull. If I leave the bleeding there, Bob will die."

He paused, looking around the room, as if lost in his own thoughts. For a moment, his eyes met Christy's. She thought she saw the glint of tears in them.

He probably blames me, too, Christy thought. She felt like an outsider, the cause of all this horror. If she could have left, if there were anywhere for her to go, she would have.

"There's one chance of saving Bob, though,"

the doctor continued. "I could bore a small hole in his head, to let the bad blood out and try to lift the pressure. Mary, I want to tell you the truth. I've never tried this operation. I saw it done once. But it's a risky procedure. It's up to you, Mary. Will you let me try it?"

"I say no," the bearded man who was Bob's brother exclaimed. "Life and death is in the hands of the Lord. We've no call to tamper with it."

"No, Ault, you're wrong," Mary said. Her voice was firm. "We can't let go so long as there's one livin' breath left in Bob. We've got six young'uns to feed. Will you try, Doc?"

The doctor seemed unsure for a moment. Christy could see his problem. There wasn't much chance for the injured man, with or without the operation. With a mountain cabin for an operating room, no nurses, little light, what chance did he have? Still, if Bob Allen died during the operation, it was likely that some of these mountain people would blame the doctor.

"All right then," Dr. MacNeill said at last. "We'll go ahead."

He's made a courageous decision, Christy thought. Had there ever been such an awful setting for an operation? A baby crying, the smell of chewing tobacco, a crowd of people, dirty pots and pans by the hearth. It was hardly sanitary.

"We'll use the kitchen table," the doctor said. "Fairlight, I'll need boiling water and a hammer and awl. And somebody get me a couple of saw horses and two or three boards. That will have to do for an instrument table. Those of you who aren't helping, stay out of the way, clear to one side. And no wailing or crying."

Soon the doctor's instruments were sterile, and he was prepared to operate. As some of the men lifted Bob Allen onto the makeshift operating table, Christy heard a scuffle at the door.

Suddenly Bob's wife dashed through the cabin. In her raised hands was a razor-sharp axe. She lifted the axe high over her head and gave a mighty heave. Christy clapped her hand over her mouth to stifle a scream.

With a crash, the axe bit deep into the floorboard under the table.

Christy stared at the axe in stunned disbelief. But the doctor continued his work, unconcerned. Then Mary took a string and tied it around one of her husband's wrists.

"All right, Mary," said the doctor. "That's fine. That should be helpful. Will some of you take care of Mary until this is over?"

Mrs. Spencer led Mrs. Allen to a chair in a corner. "What was she doing with that axe?" Christy demanded of Mr. Pentland. "And the string . . . Is she crazy?"

"It's to protect Bob during the operation," Mr. Pentland explained matter-of-factly, as if he were surprised that Christy didn't understand. "The axe is to keep him from bleedin'. And the string is to keep disease away."

Once again Christy felt that she'd entered a world where she didn't belong. Here people still believed in omens and witchcraft. It was as if these people had been born a century earlier.

"I'll need some help here," the doctor said, but no one moved forward in response.

He glanced over his shoulder. "You—do you have any nursing training?"

There was no answer. Christy realized that he was speaking to her.

"Me? I . . . no," she stammered. "I'm a teacher."

"That'll do just fine. Come here."

Once again, as she had been at the station and this morning at the General Store, Christy was aware of many eyes on her. She joined the doctor at the table. He was sharpening a razor on a strip of leather.

"You've got a strong stomach?" he asked.

"I . . . I don't know. I suppose so," Christy said.

The doctor gazed at her steadily, and for a moment she thought she saw a hint of a smile. "We'll know soon enough, I expect," he said. "I'm going to shave Bob's head. I just need you to hold it steady."

Carefully the doctor washed his hands in a basin. As he began shaving Mr. Allen's head,

51

Christy tried her best to hold it steady while keeping her hands out of the way. Already, watching the smooth skin of the man's skull appear, she felt woozy. She wondered how long she would last in her new occupation as nurse. She felt herself swaying. To steady herself, she looked up at the ceiling.

"You still with me?" the doctor asked as he reached for his scalpel.

Christy swallowed. Her stomach did a somersault. "I'm fine," she lied.

"Good. Now, I'm going to be making my incision. Then I'll carefully drill the hole through Bob's skull. You may not want to watch."

"You may be right," Christy said, managing a weak smile.

"Bet you weren't expecting this when you set out for Cutter Gap," the doctor said.

"I'm starting to get used to the unexpected," Christy said.

"That'll serve you well here."

Christy glanced down at the thin red line trailing his scalpel. Quickly she looked away.

She met the gaze of Mrs. Spencer, who was holding Mrs. Allen's hand. Mrs. Allen rocked back and forth, her face taut with fear.

"Steady now," said the doctor. "Keep a tight hold. Your legs holding out?"

"It's my stomach I'm worried about."

"Don't think about it," the doctor advised. "So you walked all the way here?"

Out of the corner of her eye, Christy could see the doctor setting down his scalpel and reaching for a thin, pointed, metal tool. "With Mr. Pentland," she answered.

"In those frocks," Dr. MacNeill said, "I'm surprised you made it this far."

"So am I, now."

The doctor laughed slightly, then fell silent. "No movement," he commanded, his voice tense.

The room went still. Christy held Mr. Allen's head, his skin oddly cool against hers. Dr. MacNeill's breath was labored. A baby cried, then stopped, as if it understood the importance of the moment.

Christy tried not to think about what was happening just inches from her own hands. A man's skull was being opened. His life hung in the balance. Here, in this primitive cabin in the middle of nowhere, she was helping a doctor try to save a man's life.

If he died, it would be her fault.

There was only one thing to do now.

Christy closed her eyes and began to pray.

❧ Six ❧

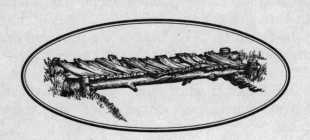

That's all, Miss Huddleston."

Christy looked up at the doctor in surprise. How long had he been working on Mr. Allen? How long had she been praying?

"I can finish up here," Dr. MacNeill said. "You get yourself some fresh air. I suspect you could use it."

Slowly Christy released her hold on Mr. Allen. "You're sure?"

"Quite sure. And thank you. You did a fine job."

Christy allowed herself a momentary glance at the patient. Mr. Allen's face was a ghastly white in the glow of the kerosene lamp. She caught sight of the incision the doctor had made, and her stomach climbed into her throat.

She reached for the wall. "I'll be . . . going then," she said, making her way dizzily through the crowd.

Outside she breathed deeply of the cold air, trying to shake off the effect of the nightmarish scene. She shivered with the realization of what she'd just done. Was it only yesterday morning that she'd hugged her mother goodbye? How she longed for just a moment in the Huddlestons' warm parlor, with its shiny piano and cozy, welcoming furniture. She'd never appreciated the cleanliness and beauty of it all. Not until now . . .

Christy sat down on the porch steps. Around the yard, people milled in small groups. From time to time they would glance at her curiously, but no one approached.

A small crowd had gathered around Mr. Spencer, who was leaning against a tall pine, singing a song while he strummed a goose quill back and forth across the strings of a box-like instrument. It had four strings, and was shaped differently from a guitar, with a slender waist and heart-shaped holes.

The simple melody seemed to wing its way into her mind and heart.

> Down in the valley,
> valley so low
> Hang your head over,
> hear the wind blow.
> Hear the wind blow, love,
> hear the wind blow;
> Hang your head over,
> hear the wind blow.

"You feelin' poorly, Miz Huddleston?" came a low voice. "You look a little pale."

Christy looked up to see Fairlight Spencer. The bare feet in the snow sent a shiver through her. But all Mrs. Spencer's concern seemed to be about Christy.

"I'm fine, thanks," Christy said. "The fresh air is doing me good. But you . . . aren't you cold?"

"Land sakes, no. This is pretty near spring-like to me. Warmed up considerable since yesterday."

"Tell me, Mrs. Spencer. What is that instrument your husband is playing?"

"That's a dulcimer," she replied. "Jeb, he loves to play."

They fell silent. Christy stared up at the tall peak nearly blotting out the winter sun. "It's beautiful here," she whispered. "I feel . . . like I'm in a whole different world."

Mrs. Spencer stared at her, as if she were trying to climb inside Christy for a moment and know what it was like. *She's only ten or so years older than I am*, Christy realized, despite all the children and the lines of worry near Fairlight's eyes.

Mrs. Spencer looked away, suddenly self-conscious. "Sorry," she apologized. "I guess I was just wonderin' what it would be like to come from your world. Is all your kin back in Asheville?"

Christy nodded. A sudden ache of homesickness fell over her like a shadow. She fingered the locket around her neck. "Would you like to see them?"

"I'd be right honored."

Christy took off the locket. Mrs. Spencer cupped it in her hand gently, as if she were holding a soap bubble.

"It opens—see?" Christy showed her how to unlock the silver heart.

Mrs. Spencer studied the pictures inside. "A mighty fine-looking family," she said. "Would that be you? There, lookin' all serious-like?"

Christy laughed. "That was at the church retreat last summer, right after I decided to come here. I suppose I was feeling pretty sure of myself."

Silence fell between them again. Gently Mrs. Spencer returned the necklace to Christy.

"Mrs. Spencer," Christy said, "I think Fairlight is such a lovely name."

The mountain woman looked pleased. "I'd be right honored if you called me by my front name."

"Good. And you can call me Christy."

A few feet away, some of the children began a wild snowball fight. "You'll have your hands full, over at the mission school, I expect," Fairlight said. "The Cove is full of youngsters." She grinned. "Some of 'em is more trouble than others, mind you."

"I'm sure I can handle them," Christy said. Even to her own ears, she didn't sound entirely convincing.

"I'm sure you can." Fairlight paused, staring up at the mountain peak bathed in shadow. "Still and all, if you ever . . ." She shook her head gently.

"What?"

"Nothin'. It was a crazy thought."

"Tell me," Christy urged. "Believe me, I've had my share of those."

Fairlight shrugged. "I was just goin' to say that if you ever need an extra pair of hands over to the school, I'd be mighty proud to help. That's a heap of young'uns for one gal. Maybe I could clean up the school after class?"

The words were spoken with a gentle dignity, as if a gift were being bestowed on Christy. Here was a mountain woman with a husband and five children to care for, living in such poverty that if she had any shoes, she was saving them to be worn somewhere special. Yet she was offering to help Christy, a girl she'd just met.

Even as Christy started to answer, she realized something else. This woman was not just volunteering to do some cleaning for her—she was also holding out the gift of her friendship. For the first time since leaving home, Christy sensed the possibility of connecting with people here, of not feeling quite so completely alone.

"Fairlight, that's a very kind offer," Christy said. "And I'll accept it, on one condition. I'm a long way from home, you know, and it would be nice to feel like I had a new friend here in the mountains. And maybe there'll be something I can do for you, too."

The pioneer face was suddenly all smiles. "That you could, Miz Christy!" she exclaimed. Suddenly she went shy again, her voice sinking almost to a whisper. "I can't read nor write. Would . . . would you learn me how? I'd like that!"

Her voice was filled with such eagerness that at that moment Christy wanted to teach this woman to read more than anything she'd ever wanted to do before.

"I'd love to do that, Fairlight. As soon as I get settled in at the mission. It's a promise."

"For sure and certain, that's wonderful to hear," Fairlight cried, her face full of hope. And immediately Christy felt encouraged about her decision to come to Cutter Gap.

— — ⁓

A few minutes later, a voice spoke from the shadows. "You must be real tired," Mr. Pentland said kindly. "Why don't I take you on out to the mission? It's not far now—"

"But what about Mr. Allen? How is he? Is he—"

"Still livin' and breathin'," Mr. Pentland said. "Doc says he found the blood clots all right and Bob has a fightin' chance now. If the bleedin' in his head don't start up again."

"Oh, I'm glad, so glad," Christy said with relief.

Mr. Pentland reached for her suitcase. "Before you go, Doc said he wanted to see you."

"Me?" Christy asked.

She stepped back into the dark cabin. The doctor was sitting by Bob Allen's side, studying him seriously. He didn't even notice Christy until she said, "Doctor? You wanted to see me?"

He looked up wearily, rubbed his eyes, then gave a smile. "There she is. The Cove's answer to Florence Nightingale. I wanted to thank you for your help."

"I didn't do much," Christy said, gazing at the motionless patient. "And to tell you the truth, my knees nearly gave out there at the end. I couldn't wait to get outside."

He gave a laugh, a deep, warm sound that filled the small cabin. "You should have seen me, my first surgery. Couldn't eat for two days afterward. And in any case, I knew you'd be fine."

"You did? How could you? *I* didn't even know."

He shrugged, then ran a hand through his messy curls. "The kind of girl who walks to the Cove in the middle of a January snowstorm has more courage than many." He looked her up and down. "You'll be needing it, too."

Christy frowned. "Why does everyone keep warning me like that?"

"You'll see, soon enough," the doctor said. He grinned. "For starters, you'll have some characters there at the mission to deal with."

"Characters? You mean some of the children I'll be teaching?"

"Actually, I was referring to the adults there." The doctor chuckled. "There's David Grantland, the new minister. His sister, Ida, is as crotchety as they come. And then there's Miss Alice, of course." He shook his head. "Now that's one interesting woman. Tough as can be."

"You didn't say anything about Mr. Grantland," Christy pointed out.

"Didn't I?" the doctor said, a glimmer in his eye. "David's a good man. Just new to these parts and still learning. He's more than a little stubborn. In any case, I have a hunch you'll manage just fine."

"I hope you're right." Christy touched Bob Allen's fingers with her own. "He'll be all right?"

"He's not out of the woods yet. The next few hours will tell the tale."

"I feel . . . so responsible. It's my fault he's here."

"Nonsense," the doctor said. "Don't you go worrying about things like that. You'll have plenty to keep you busy without taking responsibility for falling trees."

Christy turned to leave, then paused at the door. "Will I see you again?" She saw his smile and quickly changed her words.

"I mean, how will I know if Mr. Allen is all right?"

"Oh, you'll hear soon enough," said Dr. MacNeill. "Word travels fast."

Christy was halfway out the door when he added, "And yes."

"Yes?"

"Yes, we'll see each other again. I've no doubt of that." He gave a fleeting smile, then turned all his attention back to his patient.

Christy found Mr. Pentland waiting outside. She said goodbye to the Spencers, then fell into step behind the mailman. She'd had all the walking she wanted for one day—for one month, come to think of it—but she had no choice but to follow him and hope that when he said "not far" he really meant it.

As they headed from the cabin, she could hear Mr. Spencer begin to sing again. It was such a sad melody, the kind of song that seemed to belong here in this lonely and forbidding place.

They walked in silence. It was just as well, since Christy was far too tired for conversation. Questions swirled around in her head like the snowflakes blown loose from the tall trees swaying overhead.

She didn't believe in omens. She wasn't the least bit superstitious (although she had been known to avoid walking under ladders). But she couldn't help wondering if Mr. Allen's accident was some sort of signpost, trying to tell her she had made a mistake, pointing her back to the world where she belonged.

"Not much farther now," Mr. Pentland called back to her.

"We've just got the bridge to cross, and then the mission is right over the next ridge."

"Bridge?" Christy asked. Her throat tightened as she remembered waking up from her terrible dream that morning at Mrs. Tatum's—had it just been this morning?

Christy quickened her pace. "This bridge . . . is it a big one?" she asked, trying to sound casual.

Mr. Pentland considered. "Not too big. Big enough, I s'pose. Gets real slippery-like, when it ices up." He glanced at Christy's face. "Don't worry none, though."

They trudged along the snowy trail for two hundred more yards. The sound of rushing water met Christy's ears. Around a bend, the swirling waters of a half-frozen creek came into view. A creek, Mr. Pentland had called it, but it moved, even choked with ice, with the speed of a raging river.

Christy's gaze moved upward. Then she saw it.

"*That* . . . *that's* the bridge?"

"Yep."

But it was not a bridge at all, just two huge, uneven logs with a few thin boards nailed across here and there. A deadly layer of ice coated the logs and boards.

Christy joined Mr. Pentland near the edge of the bridge. The whole contraption swayed in the biting wind.

"I'll go first to see if it's too slippery," Mr. Pentland said. He shifted the mail pouch to the middle of his back and regripped Christy's suitcase. He paused, scraping his feet on the edge of the bridge.

Christy kept her eyes on his feet. Halfway across he stopped. Below him, the water sprayed over the boulders in the middle of the creek. "Ain't so bad," he called back. "Wait until I get across, though, so you won't get no sway."

Carefully he finished crossing. "Stomp your feet now," Mr. Pentland called from the other side. "Get 'em warm. Then come on—but first scrape your boots, then hike up your skirts."

As frozen and unmoving as the landscape around her, Christy stood staring at the bridge.

The sound of the water became a roar in her ears. There was no turning back now. Slowly, very slowly, she began to make her way across the log bridge.

Then it was her worst nightmare, come true. She was slipping . . . screaming . . . falling toward the icy water below.

❧ Seven ❧

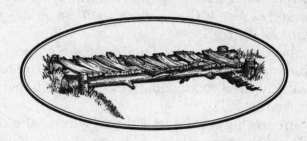

Back to the present.

Cold. The water was so cold. Instantly thoughts of the last two days were behind her, and Christy was struggling to breathe. She opened her mouth, but there was only icy water where air should be. She felt it rush inside her, into her throat, into her lungs. She grabbed for the surface with all her being, but something was pulling her down.

She was choking, she was dying, and all she wanted was air, one sweet, clean breath of air. The water in her lungs should have been cold, but it burned like she'd breathed in fire. She stroked with all her might against the current, frantically trying to propel herself toward the surface. Her hand broke through to air, and she groped for it as if she could breathe with her fingers, as if her fingers could suck in the precious oxygen she wanted so badly.

God, don't let me die here, she prayed desperately. *Not yet . . . there's still so much I want to do, Lord.*

She thought of her family, of their horror upon learning that their daughter had died this way, in a mountain creek far from home, far from love.

She thought of the school where she'd wanted to change lives. She was doing something that would really make a difference. She *had* to make it.

The current sucked her down again, but this time she groped at the frigid water with renewed fury. Her hand broke through once more, and again she felt the air. But this time someone grabbed her hand.

As if in slow, slow motion, she was pulled from the icy grip of the current. At last, she could breathe.

— — —

Someone was wrapping a blanket around her. She tried to talk, but she was coughing too hard. Violent shivers shook her whole body, as if someone were shaking her and wouldn't let go.

Strong arms lifted her into the air. Someone was carrying her. Christy blinked, tried to focus. It wasn't Mr. Pentland. Who was this man?

"Feel like anything's broken?" the man asked.

Christy shook her head.

"She's a feisty one, that gal," came Mr. Pentland's familiar voice. "Reckon she'll be fine."

They began to walk, and Christy realized that this man, whoever he was, was going to carry her the rest of the way to the mission.

"Good thing she's not any heavier," he said to Mr. Pentland with a wink.

She started to answer, but all that came out was a raw, hacking cough.

"I'm David Grantland, by the way."

"Chr—" Christy paused to cough. "Christy Hud—"

"Huddleston. Yes, I know. We've been expecting you. You really know how to make an entrance, I must say."

Christy gazed up at his handsome face. Mr. Grantland had black hair, fine white teeth, and friendly brown eyes set wide apart. And there was something about his nose—it looked a little different, as if it might have had a run-in with a baseball or a fist somewhere along the way.

"I'm sorry," Christy managed to say. "I guess I slipped—"

"You were lucky," Mr. Grantland said. "You could've hit one of those rocks."

"Lucky you came along when you did," Mr. Pentland said. "By the time I'd have gotten down to the bank, no telling where she mighta been."

"I was on my way to the bunkhouse just up the hill when I saw you two coming," Mr. Grantland explained.

"We stopped over to the Spencers' on the way," Mr. Pentland said. "Wait'll ya hear what happened to ol' Bob Allen."

While Mr. Pentland recounted the story of Mr. Allen's surgery, Christy rested her cheek against Mr. Grantland's shoulder. She felt a little embarrassed, being carried this way like a helpless child, but she was too wet and exhausted and cold and battered to much care. The steady rock of Mr. Grantland's steps and the lull of his deep voice pulled her closer and closer to sleep.

She had just shut her eyes when Mr. Pentland said, "Here we go. Told ya it weren't too far."

Christy lifted her head. Ahead of them was the mission house—a large square frame building set in a big yard with a mountain rising behind it.

"There it is," Mr. Grantland said. "Home sweet home."

The front door of the mission house opened to reveal an older woman. She was tall, almost gaunt, with angular features. "What in the world has the cat dragged in?" she demanded.

"Miss Huddleston fell into the creek," Mr. Grantland said. He stepped inside the house.

The warmth on her icy face brought tears to Christy's eyes.

"Think you can stand?" he asked.

Christy nodded.

"Good thing," he said. "Nothing personal, but my arms are about to give out."

He set her down gently. Instantly the room began to sway, and Mr. Grantland held out an arm to steady her. He pointed to the older woman.

"This is my sister, Ida. Her bark, you'll soon find, is worse than her bite."

"You may call me Miss Ida." The woman clucked her tongue at the puddle forming on the floor. "Look at this mess! She brought half the creek in with her."

"Now, Ida," Mr. Grantland chided. "Miss Huddleston has had a rough day."

"That she has," Mr. Pentland agreed. "Walked all the way here, she did. Then helped the Doc with his surgery, and plumb fell off a bridge to boot."

Miss Ida seemed to soften a little. "Let's get you upstairs and into some dry clothes," she said, leading Christy toward the stairway.

Christy turned. She gave a weak smile to Mr. Pentland and Mr. Grantland. "Thank you," she said. "Thank you both for everything."

Mr. Pentland gave a courtly nod. Mr. Grantland grinned. "Not at all," he said. "It isn't every day I get to save a damsel in distress."

His sister rolled her eyes. "Damsel in distress, indeed!"

She took Christy's suitcase and helped her up the wooden stairs, all the while grimacing at the trail of muddy water Christy was leaving in her wake.

At the top of the stairs, Miss Ida gestured to a simple room. It was not luxurious, to say the least—a washstand with a white china pitcher and bowl, an old dresser with a cracked mirror above it, two straight chairs, the plainest kind of white curtains, and two cotton rag rugs on the bare floor.

"First things first," Miss Ida said. "We need to get you into some dry clothes." She handed Christy some towels.

"I have some things . . ." Christy paused, ". . . in my suitcase." She was tired, so tired. Had she ever been this exhausted? The very insides of her bones ached. Never had a bed looked so inviting.

Miss Ida unlatched the suitcase. She pulled out Christy's diary and set it aside. Carefully she removed a nightgown. "Here, now," she said. "You get yourself good and dry; then put on this nightgown. Whatever you do, don't sit on that bed in those soaking clothes."

Too tired to respond, Christy did as she was told. By the time Miss Ida returned, Christy had managed to put on her nightgown and run a comb through her tangled, wet hair.

Miss Ida frowned at the pile of wet clothes in the corner. "I'll take care of those tomorrow," Christy promised, feeling guilty at the awful impression she must be making. She glanced longingly at the bed—the soft, warm, and *very dry* bed.

With a grimace, Miss Ida picked up Christy's wet clothes. "*I'll* take care of them," she said in a long-suffering tone.

"Thank you, Miss Ida. I'm so sorry to be such trouble. I guess I'm not making a very good impression. . . . " Christy's voice faded off.

"Oh, you seemed to have made quite an impression on my brother," Miss Ida said flatly.

Christy attempted a smile, but Miss Ida did not return it. "I suppose you'll be wanting something to eat?" Miss Ida asked.

"The truth is, I'm too tired to eat."

"Well, then. You can get yourself settled in tomorrow. Miss Alice will be wanting to meet you."

"I'm looking forward to it. And I can't wait to see the school."

For a moment, Miss Ida's expression warmed. "The building's almost complete. David did most of it himself. It's a sight to behold."

"I hope I do it justice," Christy said.

"I do, too," Miss Ida replied. The tone in her voice told Christy that she had her doubts.

At last the door closed and Christy was alone in her little room. Her whole body was sore. She could tell she was going to have a nasty bruise on her hip from her fall.

She retrieved her diary and pen. She wanted to keep track of her adventure as it unfolded, and so much had happened today. As exhausted as she was, she had to get it all down while it was still fresh in her mind.

Christy climbed into bed. The fresh sheets felt wonderful. She propped herself up against her pillow, with the diary on her knees.

Where should I begin? she wrote.

A few words, that's all. Just a few words. . . . Slowly her eyelids began to droop. Tired, she was so very tired. . . .

Christy set down her pen and lay her head against the pillow, her eyes already closed. As she pulled the sheets up to her chin, her hand grazed her neck.

It was only then that she realized her locket was gone. It had come off, no doubt, during her tumble into the creek. *I'll go back*, she told herself. *Maybe, by some miracle, I'll find it.*

But as she fell into a deep, dreamless sleep, in her heart she knew the truth—that the locket had been lost in the raging mountain creek. But she also knew that she must not dwell on the loss of her precious family keepsake. Instead, she must put her old life behind her and concentrate on beginning a new life in this strange place.

❧ Eight ❧

Christy slept late the next morning. When she awoke, her body was stiff and sore. Just as she'd expected, there was a large, ugly bruise on her hip.

The events of the previous day seemed like a dream. But if they were all a dream, what was she doing in this strange little room? The long, exhausting walk; the Spencers' cabin; Mr. Allen's surgery; her terrifying fall off the bridge . . . had it all happened in the space of one short day? Christy reached for the place at her throat where her locket should have been. She couldn't believe she'd lost it. What would she tell her father?

She hobbled stiffly over to one of the windows. Nothing had prepared her for what met her eyes. Mountain ranges were folded one behind the other. Some were snow-covered.

Others showed patches of emerald or deep green, and then the blues began. On the smoky blue of the far summits, fluffy white clouds rested like wisps of cotton.

She counted the mountain ranges. Eleven of them, rising up and up toward the vault of the sky.

Only yesterday at the Spencer cabin, watching a man undergo surgery because of her, Christy had wondered if accepting this teaching job had been a dreadful mistake. Now, staring at this peaceful view, she was not quite so sure what to think. Had Mr. Allen survived the night? She still did not know. But meanwhile, in the face of tragedy, these mountains were whispering a different message to her. A message that seemed to say, *Stay. This is your view. This will be your source of peace and strength.*

Someone knocked on her door. It was Miss Ida. For the first time, Christy got a good look at her. She was a plain woman with thin, graying hair. It was drawn into a tight bun, so meager that her scalp showed through in several places. Her nose was too large for her narrow face. Already Christy could tell she was a nervous person. When she smiled, it seemed to be an afterthought, as if her brain had ordered, "Now, smile," but her feelings hadn't joined in.

"You slept well, I hope?" Miss Ida asked.

"Just fine."

"I've cleaned up your clothes. They're downstairs, drying."

"Thank you so much," Christy said gratefully. "Oh, Miss Ida, tell me—I've got to know. Mr. Allen, how is he? Is he—" She couldn't quite say it.

"Alive? Oh, yes. Dr. MacNeill spent the night there. Miss Alice Henderson, too. She went right to the Spencers' soon as she heard about the operation. She's catching a wink of sleep now."

"Then Mr. Allen's out of danger?"

"Not yet, I take it, or the doctor wouldn't still be there. Now about breakfast—everybody else has eaten. When you get changed, come on down to the dining room. I'll see you get something."

Christy wondered who "everybody" was. How many lived in this house?

"Miss Alice would like to see you today," Miss Ida said. She crossed the room to the window and pointed. "See that smoke? That's her cabin. Just there, beyond the trees."

After Miss Ida left, Christy dressed quickly and rushed downstairs. She felt as if she hadn't eaten in days. The dining room turned out to be a simple square room at the back of the house. A round, golden oak table sat in the center.

Miss Ida provided a wonderful breakfast— hot oatmeal followed by buckwheat cakes and maple syrup. "David's at the Low Gap School near here," Miss Ida said as she watched Christy eat. "He said to tell you he was sorry not to be here when you woke up."

"I'm sorry I overslept. Does Mr. Grantland teach at that school?"

"Oh no, that school is closed. There were some old school desks there. They said we could use them. Supplies, you'll soon see, are always a problem here." She pointed out the window to an unfinished building about a thousand yards away. It was rectangular, with a half-finished belltower. "David can build anything he sets his hand to," she said proudly. "He's working on the steeple now."

"Then will that be the church as well as the school?"

"That's right," Miss Ida said, with a tone in her voice that made Christy uncomfortable. "We haven't the lumber and funds here to put up two buildings when one would do. This will be used for school on weekdays, and church on Sundays."

"They've never had a school here before?"

Miss Ida watched, curling her lip just slightly as Christy helped herself to a second round of buckwheat cakes. "You've quite an appetite, haven't you?" she said. "But you asked about the school. No, this will be the first term."

"Does Mr. Grantland live here, in the mission house?"

Miss Ida shook her head. "He has a bunk-house, down by the creek. That's why it's lucky you fell in there. He and Miss Alice take their meals here in the house, though." She smiled proudly. "David begged me to come and keep house for him. He says maybe we can find a mountain woman to train as a housekeeper. But I have doubts myself that anybody else can cook to suit him."

Just then the side door banged and suddenly Mr. Grantland stood in the kitchen doorway. A young girl with snarled red hair peered curiously from behind him. "Miss Huddleston," he said with a smile, "I must say you're looking much better—not to mention drier—this morning."

"I'm not sure I thanked you properly yesterday," Christy said.

"For—"

"For everything. For carrying me here, for . . ." she hesitated as the words sunk in, "for saving my life."

Mr. Grantland laughed. His big, booming voice filled the room. "All in a day's work. Oh—" he turned and beckoned to the red-haired girl, "allow me to introduce Ruby Mae Morrison. She's staying here at the mission house with us for a while."

The girl stepped forward. "Howdy," she said eagerly. Her eyes took in every inch of Christy. She was a teenager, maybe thirteen or so,

Christy guessed, with abundant red hair that looked as if it had not been combed in a long while. Her plain, thin cotton dress was torn at the hem. She was barefoot, just as the Spencer children had been.

"Nice to meet you, Ruby Mae," Christy said. She pointed to some leftover buckwheat cakes. "Would you two like to join me?"

"They both had breakfast," Miss Ida reminded Christy primly. "*Hours* ago."

"Reckon I'm hungry again, though," Ruby Mae said, pulling up a chair.

Miss Ida groaned. "I suppose, if Miss Huddleston is done, you may as well finish up what's left. But, please, Ruby Mae, go wash up in the basin in the kitchen."

"Wash up, wash up, wash up," Ruby Mae muttered, rolling her eyes heavenward as she reluctantly headed for the kitchen. "If'n I wash up much more, I'll wash my skin clean off!"

Mr. Grantland laughed as she disappeared into the kitchen. "She's a character, that one," he said.

"She's trouble, is what he means," Miss Ida said, scraping crumbs on the table into her palm. "She'll talk your ear off if you let her. And gossip! Where that girl gets her information, I'll never know."

"Ruby Mae is a one-woman newspaper," Mr. Grantland said.

"Why—" Christy lowered her voice, "Why is she staying here?"

His face went serious. "She and her step-father don't get along. After a particularly bad argument, he ordered her out of the cabin. She had nowhere else to go, so we took her in."

Ruby Mae returned, thrusting her hands in front of Miss Ida for inspection. "Ain't no more of those germy things a-growin' on *these* hands," she declared. She winked at Christy. "Not that I've ever seen one, mind you. But Doc MacNeill and Miss Ida and Miss Alice, they keep a-swearin' they're there." She pointed to Christy's plate. "You done with those?"

"Oh—yes. Here, please. I couldn't eat another bite." Christy passed her plate to Ruby Mae, who began to eat like she hadn't seen food in weeks.

"She's got the appetite of a grown man, that girl," Miss Ida said with evident distaste.

"That's all right," Christy said, smiling at Ruby Mae. "So do I."

Ruby Mae grinned back gratefully, her mouth stuffed with buckwheat cakes. "Maybuf latef I shoof yoouf aroumf."

"Allow me to translate," Mr. Grantland said. "I speak Ruby Mae. I believe she was offering to give you the royal tour of the mission."

Ruby Mae nodded enthusiastically.

"Which would probably be a fine idea," he continued, "since I, unfortunately, cannot do the honors myself. I've got another load of school desks to pick up."

"I'd like that, Ruby Mae," Christy said.

Ruby Mae glowed, obviously thrilled at being assigned such an important duty.

"I'm afraid it will be a rather brief tour," Mr. Grantland said. "There's not much to see, really."

"Oh, yes, there is," Christy replied. "When I looked out my window this morning, it practically took my breath away. The mountains, the sky . . . it's amazing."

"Yes," Mr. Grantland gazed at her thoughtfully. "I'm glad you can see that, too." His voice went soft. "Sometimes, with all the problems here in the Cove, it helps to see God's beauty in His creation." He smiled a little self-consciously. "Well, I must be off. Enjoy your tour. And enjoy your meeting with Miss Alice."

He gave a little wave and in a few long strides had disappeared out the door.

Ruby Mae leaned across the table. Her mouth was still full of buckwheat cakes.

"Swallow," Miss Ida chided.

Ruby Mae obeyed dutifully, but not without another roll of her lively brown eyes. "He's not married, you know," she confided to Christy in a loud whisper.

"You mean . . . Mr. Grantland?" Christy asked uncomfortably, noting Miss Ida's grimace.

"He don't even have a gal-friend, near as I can tell. And believe you me, I would know. I keep up on everybody's comings and goings."

"David has his mind on far more important

things than a *gal-friend*, Ruby Mae," Miss Ida snapped. "He's here to do the work of the Lord, not to fall in love."

"I reckon sometimes that's sort of the same thing, ain't it?" Ruby Mae asked thoughtfully.

Christy tried very hard to hide her smile. It was clear that Miss Ida was not amused.

—— —— ——

"And this here's the outhouse," Ruby Mae said with a grin. "Reckon you ain't seen nothing this fancy before."

Christy blinked. Actually, the outdoor toilet was more primitive than anything she'd ever seen. And drafty, too, in this January cold!

It had not occurred to her how simple the mission buildings would be. She gazed back at the white three-story, frame building with a screened porch on either side. The mission house where she'd slept last night was a palace compared to the Spencer cabin, of course. But still, there was no electricity, no telephone, no plumbing. The house, along with the church-schoolhouse, a lattice-covered springhouse, the double outhouse, Mr. Grantland's bunkhouse by the creek, and Miss Henderson's cabin were the only buildings at the mission.

"It's a fine outhouse," Christy managed to say, and Ruby Mae beamed with pride, as if she'd built it herself.

The girl had not stopped talking during Christy's tour of the mission. One question, one smile from Christy was all it took for Ruby Mae to break into a beaming grin so full of excitement that Christy wondered when the last time was that anyone had really paid attention to the girl. Would all her students be this needy, this dying for affection? As Ruby Mae's questions began to accumulate, so too did Christy's. She was anxious to talk to Miss Alice and get some answers.

"And now, for the finest part of my showin'," Ruby Mae announced. "The school!" She took Christy's hand and led her toward the simple church building. "I saved the best for very last."

Christy followed Ruby Mae up the wooden steps. As they entered the building, Ruby Mae fell silent for the first time.

The school room smelled of varnish and wood smoke. A small potbellied stove sat in one corner. A few battered school desks were scattered across the floor.

Slowly Christy walked to the teacher's desk near the stove.

This was hers. This was where she would soon be teaching. This was where her adventure really would begin.

"Fills ya up with excitement, don't it, just to come inside?" Ruby Mae asked in a hushed voice. It was the same voice you would use in a church, Christy thought—then she realized that this *was* a church, every Sunday.

"I can't tell you how much we-all have been lookin' forward to havin' a real school with a real, live teacher," Ruby Mae said sincerely.

Christy smiled. "I *hope* I turn out to be a real, live teacher."

"I don't rightly see your point," Ruby Mae said, her face puckered up in concentration.

"It's just—" Christy stared into the girl's bright eyes. "Well, I've never taught before, you see. I suppose I'm a little nervous."

"*You*, nervous? That's a good one!" Ruby Mae laughed loudly, slapping her leg, as if she'd never heard anything funnier. Slowly she realized that Christy was serious. Her face went instantly solemn. "Oh, Miz Huddleston, I declare. I weren't laughing *at* you. It's just that I figure it's us students who have the right to be all nervous-like. I mean, Lordamercy, *you're* the teacher!"

I'm the teacher. Christy tried out the words in her mind. She liked the sound of them.

Sure, it had been a long and dangerous journey here. Sure, things hadn't gone as she'd hoped so far. But what was she so worried about? Ruby Mae was right. Christy *was* the teacher.

Now that she was finally here, what else could possibly go wrong?

❧ Nine ❧

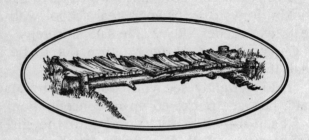

That afternoon, Christy knocked on the door of Miss Alice Henderson's cabin. The young teacher took a deep breath to calm herself. Already, the stories about Miss Alice had impressed Christy. She wanted to do her very best to impress Miss Alice, too.

The woman who answered the door had beautiful, clear features and deep gray eyes which looked both excited and tired at the same time. Her hair had once been blonde, but now was sprinkled with gray. She was wearing a straight blue woolen skirt and a clean, white linen blouse. Mr. Pentland had said there was something queenlike about her, and he was right.

"Do come in," she said, staring at Christy intently.

Stepping into Miss Henderson's cabin was

almost like going home to Asheville. There was warmth and color and shine here. Firelight gleamed on the old pine and cherry furniture and the polished brass and pewter. Windows along the back of the room brought the beautiful Cutter Gap scenery indoors. The winter landscape and the towering peaks filled the room like a gigantic mural.

Christy had not realized how homesick she was until she felt the relief pouring through her. Then there *was* some beauty and order here in the Cove! It wasn't all just plainness and poverty.

"Come, sit down, child," Miss Henderson urged. "Does my cabin surprise you?"

"I'm sorry. I didn't mean to stare. After that nightmare scene yesterday at the Spencers', I wasn't sure that I . . . that I belonged here. But this is so beautiful that I want to hug it— if you could hug a room. It's like—well, like coming home."

"That's the nicest compliment my cabin's ever had. Here, sit by the fire. Got down to ten below zero this morning."

"Miss Henderson," Christy asked, almost afraid to hear the answer, "how is Mr. Allen?"

"About seven this morning he opened his eyes and asked about his ailing hound-dog. I think he's going to be all right."

Christy felt relief wash over her like a warm breeze. Now she wouldn't have to live with the guilt of thinking she'd caused Mr. Allen's death.

Miss Henderson sat down across from Christy. "Now, tell me, Miss Huddleston," she said suddenly, "why did you come to Cutter Gap?"

Surely she must be joking, Christy thought. But one look at her face told Christy she was not. "Naturally, I thought Dr. Ferrand would have told you," Christy answered. "I came to teach school, of course."

"He didn't tell me much. And anyway, I want to hear *your* version. Why *are* you here?"

It was such a complicated question. Christy hesitated. Where should she begin?

"I was so moved at the church retreat when I heard about the mountain people," she began slowly. "I volunteered right away."

"Looking back," Miss Henderson asked, smoothing out a crease in her skirt, "do you think you were carried away by the emotion of the moment?"

"Somewhat, perhaps," Christy admitted. She wanted to be completely honest with this woman. Something about Miss Henderson *demanded* honesty.

"And Dr. Ferrand *is* eloquent," Miss Henderson pointed out.

"But I've had plenty of time to think it over," Christy added quickly. "If I'd wanted to back out, I could have."

"And why didn't you?"

"Because I knew you were desperate for teachers. I've had a year and a semester of college, enough to start teaching. And—" She paused. It was so hard to explain what was in her heart. "I'd like my life to count for something."

Miss Henderson fell silent. It was different from the embarrassing lapses in conversation Christy had felt, talking to a boy she liked or a person she didn't know. This was a silence full of meaning, a comfortable silence.

Christy longed to tell Miss Henderson about the feeling she'd had that there was some special mission waiting for her. Maybe that feeling just came from reading too much poetry—or because she was young. But Christy didn't think so. She wanted her life to be full. She wanted to laugh and love. She wanted to help others. Those were the hopes that had sent her on this wild adventure into the mountains.

But she couldn't explain those things, not yet. So she just sat silently, staring at her hands.

"You'll need some information about your new job," Miss Henderson said, suddenly changing the subject. "School opens on Monday next. Your coming gives us an official staff of three—David, you, and me, with Dr. Ferrand in overall charge.

"By the way, those at the mission call me 'Miss Alice.' David, you've already met. He just graduated from the seminary. He's from Pennsylvania, like me."

"How long have you been here, Miss Alice?"

"I first came to the Great Smokies almost nine years ago. I started a couple of schools in the area, then I saw Cutter Gap and loved it. I felt this was my spot." She gazed around the room. "I wanted this cabin to be a sort of sanctuary, a quiet spot for me and for other people, where they could talk out some of their problems when they want to."

"You mean the mountaineers?"

"They prefer to be called 'mountain people' or 'highlanders.' And believe me, there's plenty of problems for them to talk out. These people were brought up on a religion of fear. I believe one of our tasks here is to show folks a God who wants to give them joy. How they need joy!"

Her eyes took on a soft, remembering look. "I am a Quaker, you may know. My father was a strict member of the Society of Friends. But he had one favorite saying as I grew up. 'Before God,' he would say to me, 'I've just one duty as a father. That is to see that thee has a happy childhood tucked under thy jacket.'"

"I like that," Christy said, grinning at the image. "And did you have a happy childhood?"

"The happiest imaginable." Her voice trailed off. "I would like a little of that for these children. They have such hard lives."

"I'm afraid the hardness is all I've seen so far."

Miss Alice nodded with understanding. "At first I couldn't see anything but the dirt and the poverty either. But as I got to know the people better, flashes of something else began to come through. It's like looking through a peephole into the past. The old ballads, the words from another century. You'll see. These are tough people, proud and self-reliant, with an intense love of freedom. They've got iron wills that could bring major achievements." She sighed. "Of course, now their wills are used mainly to keep feuds alive."

Christy shifted uneasily, remembering the warnings of the train conductor and Mrs. Tatum. "You mean real shooting feuds?"

"Real shooting and killing feuds." For the first time, Miss Alice's face was grim.

"What do you and Mr. Grantland do about it?"

"Well, the first thing I did was buy a gun and learn to shoot."

Christy's mouth dropped open in surprise. "You did! But I thought the Quakers—"

"Believe in non-violence. You're right. I've had my dear ancestors spinning in their graves ever since. Now that I've seen violence close up, I believe in non-violence more than ever. But I had to meet these men on their own ground. So now I'm a better shot than a lot of them, and they all know it and respect it. I tell them, 'I like your fierce pride and your loyalty to your family. That's why I long to keep you from doing anything that will shame your sons and your sons' sons.'"

The room was very quiet, as Christy considered the Quaker lady's words. *I can learn much from this woman*, Christy thought, *if only she will teach me.*

When at last Christy rose to go, Miss Alice held out her hand. "Christy Huddleston," she said, "I think you will do."

The warmth of her voice brought unexpected tears to Christy's eyes. She hoped Miss Alice was right.

～ ～ ～

That night, Christy sat in her bed, her diary propped on her knees. During dinner, she'd discussed lesson plans with Mr. Grantland and Miss Alice. They'd seemed a little amused at her ambitious ideas.

"Don't bite off more than you can chew," Mr. Grantland had warned. "We're talking about a lot of students, a lot of ages. You'll be lucky to get them all to sit still for an hour."

Christy chewed on the top of her pen, considering. At the top of a fresh page, she wrote:

Goals for School Year:
(1) Establish basic reading and
    arithmetic skills

(2) Penmanship exercises
(3) Calculus?
(4) French lessons?
(5) Latin?
(6) Music lessons?
(7) Hygiene and etiquette?

She scanned her list. Well, maybe etiquette was too much. It didn't much matter if you knew which fork to use if you didn't own any forks. Still, she had to set standards, didn't she? She had to aim high.

And what was the goal that Miss Alice had mentioned? *To show folks a God who wants to give them joy.*

Now, *that* was a tall order. How could she, Christy, begin to show these poor people what joy meant?

She thought about the question Miss Alice had asked her today. Again she began to write:

> *Miss Alice asked me why I've come here to Cutter Gap. It's a good question. It made me think back to my life in Asheville, full of parties and pretty things. Of course, there was nothing wrong with that life—in fact, now I see how very blessed I have been. But I can't help wondering what it all meant. Where was it leading?*
>
> *There must be more to life than that. Or is there—for a woman?*

What was I born for, after all? I have to know. If I'd stayed at home, going the round of the same parties, I don't think I ever would have known. Mother and Father didn't understand why I was so anxious to come here. But I couldn't wait forever.

Come Monday, I won't have to wait any longer.

❧ Ten ❧

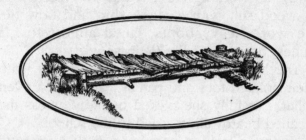

You okay?" Mr. Grantland inquired on Monday morning. "You look a little green around the gills."

Christy gave him a weak smile. "Butterflies," she said.

"I'm not sure I follow—"

"My stomach. It's full of butterflies. So full it's amazing I haven't fluttered away." She gazed at him hopefully. "Was it like this for you, the first time you preached a sermon, Mr. Grantland?"

"Don't you think it's time you started calling me David?" he asked.

"David," she amended.

"And the answer is yes. Matter of fact, I still get the shakes every Sunday. Feel better?"

"Not much."

He laughed, then extended his arm. They

started down the steps of the mission house. For this first day of school, David had put away his working clothes and was dressed in a tweed suit with a white shirt and bow tie. He wore heavy boots, laced almost to his knees, because of the deep snow.

The boots made Christy's dainty shoes, with their pointed toes and patent leather, look even sillier. Carefully she picked her way across the cleaned boardwalk that led to the school.

"Is this a fashion parade on Fifth Avenue in New York?" David teased. "Those are silly, silly shoes. Ice-pick toes!"

"I know," Christy admitted. She'd wanted to look just right for her first day, but suddenly she saw herself through the eyes of the mountain children. She would look silly and overdressed to them. "Is it too late to change?"

"Yes," he said, shaking his head.

Her right shoe began to skid on the boardwalk. "Hold on!" David called, reaching out his arm to support her. "We don't want you slipping again!"

She could feel the warmth of his hand even through her coat. She wondered if her hair still looked all right and if he liked the way she'd worn it.

But suddenly she had more important things to worry about.

The schoolyard was swarming with children waiting for the first glimpse of their new teacher. Their high-pitched voices rang in the clear air. Most were skinny, too pale, and none were dressed warmly enough for January.

Christy hesitated, watching them run in and out of the school building. So many students! And so lively! What if she couldn't handle them all?

"These children are really excited," David said. "You'd be surprised what a big event the opening of this school is in these people's lives."

As they noticed Christy and David approaching, the children stopped to stare. A little boy detached himself from the group and came running up to Christy. He had carrot-red hair and blue eyes.

"Teacher," he said with a shy eagerness, "I've come to see you and to swap howdies. I memorized your name. It shore is a funny name. I never heard a name like it afore."

"Miss Huddleston," David said solemnly, "this is Little Burl Allen, one of Bob Allen's sons."

So this was one of the children who would have been fatherless if Dr. MacNeill had not operated. All over again Christy felt grateful for the good news she'd heard about Mr. Allen.

She reached down for the little boy's hand. It was cold. "I'm delighted to swap howdies with you, Little Burl." He was so little—and those icy feet! She longed to pick him up and get him warm.

They headed up the steps to the school. As they entered, they were met by the smell of wet wool and cedar pencils. Already there were puddles of water on the floor from the melted snow the children had tracked in. Most of the children filed up to the teacher's desk to get a better look at Christy. Many of the girls were too shy to say anything, but the boys whispered furiously to each other. Christy overheard snatches:

"Got uncommon pretty eyes, ain't she?"

"You're already stuck on the teacher!"

"Reckon she'll have us a-studyin' like dogs?"

"Naw. She's too little to tan any britches!"

It took almost fifteen minutes before David could drag the children away from Christy's desk and quiet them down. To her surprise, the girls seated themselves on one side of the room and the boys on the other.

"Why are they separated that way?" Christy whispered to David as he shooed a straggler to his seat.

"Tradition," David said. "That's how their people have done it for centuries. Same way at church on Sunday."

Christy stood beside the battered teacher's desk on its raised platform and surveyed her class. Several of the pupils actually seemed to be as old as she was—including the three boys who had been the last ones to slink into the schoolroom. She noticed David eyeing them warily and wondered if they might be troublemakers.

On the other hand, some of the children were tiny, not more than five years old. They wore a strange assortment of clothes—coats several sizes too big, with sleeves turned up. Many of the youngsters looked very tired, with the serious, worn faces of old men and women.

"Ladies and gentlemen," David began, sending the class into a chorus of giggles, "I am indeed honored today to introduce to you our new schoolteacher, Miss Huddleston."

While he spoke, Christy tried to count the number of children in the room. She counted the number of desks in each row—nine—and the number of rows—eight. Seventy-two, with five desks empty! It was unbelievable! How could one teacher handle sixty-seven squirming children? All at once her careful lesson plans seemed crazy. No wonder David and Miss Alice had warned her about being too ambitious!

The introduction was over. Christy moved to the front of the desk. "Thank you," she began. "I—I'm glad to be here. I know that you have all sorts of things to do, Mr. Grantland, so we won't ask you to stay." She couldn't bear the idea of his watching her first fumbling attempt at teaching. Christy gave him a bright, confident smile, hoping that he would take the hint.

A titter began at the front of the room and swept backward. What had she said that was so funny?

She looked at David and saw amusement in his eyes. Had she made a mistake already?

"Don't worry," he said softly. "It's nothing. Your way of using English just sounds as funny to the children as their way of speaking sounds odd to you. You'll get used to one another."

Christy nodded with relief. "Sure you don't want me to stay?" David asked. The look in his eyes told her he thought it would be a good idea to let him. For a moment, staring at the big boys in the back of the room, she wavered.

"Lundy Taylor," David commented, keeping his voice low. He nodded toward a boy as tall as a grown man. He had a sullen expression, as if he were looking for a fight. "He's never been to school before with the Allen children."

"I don't understand—"

"There's a feud between the two families," David said. "As old as these hills."

Christy thought for a moment. The boys might cause trouble, and it would be nice to have David nearby for help. On the other hand, last night at dinner, Miss Alice had explained that in the mountains, women were still not accepted as equal. It was important, Christy knew, that she deal with this situation herself and make it clear that she was in charge.

"Thank you, David," Christy said, trying to sound confident. "I'll take it from here."

David nodded. He seemed doubtful, but she

could see a glimmer of respect in his eyes. Without another word, he left.

Christy took a deep breath. So now she was on her own. All at once the children seemed like giants. She leaned against the edge of the desk for support. A little boy in the front row whispered behind his hand, "She's scared."

"How can ya tell?" Little Burl asked.

"Look at her shakin'."

He was right. Her legs were trembling violently. Christy breathed deep and thought, *Well, it would be best to start at the beginning.* Her first task was to get an attendance roll on paper. She needed to know her students' names and have some information on how much schooling they'd had.

Christy beckoned to Ruby Mae, a familiar face. She knew Ruby Mae could write some. "Could you and two other girls help me take a roll?"

"Well, yes'm, I reckon so," Ruby Mae said thoughtfully. "What's *take a roll*?"

"Write down each pupil's name, age, address, and so on. I'll tell you what to do." She pointed to a pretty girl who looked about twelve or thirteen. "Who's that blonde girl, there? Red bow in her hair?"

"That's Bessie Coburn, my best friend. She's had schoolin' afore."

"She'll do fine. And over there—" Christy spied Clara Spencer, Fairlight's oldest daughter. "How about you, Clara? Would you like to help?"

Clara glowed and jumped from her seat.

"This is a special job, an important one," Christy explained as Ruby Mae puffed with pride. "We want to write down the full name of each pupil." Christy handed each girl a ruled tablet and a pencil. "Age . . . beneath that, parents' names . . . home address . . . and schooling the child might have had."

Bessie shook her head. "I vow and declare, Teacher. That home address—I'd be much obliged if you'd tell us what you're meanin' by it."

"Where they live. So I can send parents reports and notices and so on. We have to know that."

"Can't guess what she's gettin' at," Ruby Mae said to Clara, who seemed puzzled, too.

"Tell you what. Let's each take a row," Christy said. "You watch me with the first name, and then you'll understand perfectly."

All the pupils in Christy's row were boys. The first one looked to be about a second-grader. He was blond, with eyes that looked directly at her as he spoke. He had the firmest mouth she had ever seen on a youngster. "Your name?" Christy asked, her pen poised, ready to write.

"Front name or back name?"

"Well . . . er—both."

"Front name is Sam Houston."

There was a long pause. "A fine name," Christy prodded. "A Tennessee hero. He picked up where Davy Crockett left off, didn't he?" She paused. "Well now, your—what did you call it— back name?"

"Holcombe."

"Fine. And your father's full name?" Christy asked, writing away.

"He's John Swanson Holcombe."

"And your mother's name?"

"She's just Mama."

"But she has a name. What's her name?"

"Women folks call her 'Lizzie.'"

"But her *real* name?" Christy pressed.

The small brow wrinkled. "Let me study on it now. Oh, surely. Now I know. Elizabeth Teague Holcombe," the boy announced triumphantly.

Christy glanced over at her three helpers. Their faces seemed to say *You see, not quite as easy as you thought.*

Christy questioned Sam Houston Holcombe. He was nine years old. He had never before been to school. "Last question, Sam," Christy said.

"Generally go by Sam Houston, Teacher."

"Of course. I beg your pardon. And now your address. Tell me where you live."

"Well—" Again, the puzzled look appeared on the small face. "First you cross Cutter Branch. Then you cut across Lonesome Pine Ridge and down. The Gap's the best way. At the third fork in the trail, you scoot under the fence and head for Pigeonroost Hollow. Then you spy our cabin and pull into our place, 'bout two miles or so from the Spencers'."

Christy scribbled something down quickly, aware of the three girls watching her. Obviously she was going to have to come up with some new system in a hurry for addresses in Cutter Gap!

Slowly she worked her way down the row. Her third student was a boy who claimed his name was Zacharias Jehoshaphat Holt. As soon as the name was out of his mouth, the room burst into snickers.

The boy immediately behind him said softly, "Plumb crazy. That ain't your name at all."

Christy smiled. She recognized the Tom Sawyer look-alike as Creed Allen, one of the boys she'd met at the Spencers' cabin that awful day.

"This isn't the time for fooling," Christy said with just a hint of sternness. "We're trying to get the roll down. Now tell me your real name."

"Zacharias Jehoshaphat—" With that, the boy's right ear jerked violently.

The children laughed uproariously, some of them doubling over. Creed, still straight-faced, volunteered, "Teacher, that's not his name. He's packin' lies. You can tell. Just look at his ear."

Sure enough, Zacharias' ear jerked again. "Certainly, I see his ear," Christy said. "But what's that got to do with not telling the truth?"

"Oh, ma'am! All those Holts, when they tell a whopper, their ears twitch—"

Christy ignored him. She turned again to the boy in front. "Tell me your name," she tried again.

"Zacharias—" He snickered, then swallowed. "Jehoshaphat—"

Once again, the ear wiggled. But this time Christy saw it—the boy had a string over his ear!

She reached over to remove the cord. But Creed jerked it away from her and stuffed the string in his desk.

That did it! Christy knew she had to control the class, or this sort of prank would get out of hand.

She marched to Creed's desk and reached in. Her fingers touched a mass of wriggling fur. She squealed and stepped backwards, and a small animal as frightened as she was climbed onto the desk, screeching in protest.

A ring-tailed raccoon sat there, looking at Christy from behind his funny mask of a face. He began scolding her, as if he were the teacher and Christy were the naughty pupil.

Naturally, the schoolroom was in chaos— the girls giggling, the boys holding their middles and laughing so hard that one of them got the hiccups.

"Now," Christy said, "let's begin all over." She was trying her best to be patient, but who had ever heard of having this much trouble getting a few names on paper?

"Creed there put me up to it," said the boy

who claimed his name was Zacharias. "Said if I'd do it, he'd let me sleep with his coon for one night."

Christy turned to Creed. "This is your raccoon, Creed?"

"Yes'm. Pet coon. Scalawag."

"Might be a good name for you, too," Christy commented. She turned to the boy in front of Creed. "All right now, let's have your real name."

"Front name is Zacharias, for a fact, Teacher. You can just call me Zach. That 'Jehoshaphat' now, that was made up. Back name is Holt. Six of us Holts in school."

At last, she was making progress. With some effort, Christy obtained the rest of the information she needed. That brought her back to Creed, whose eyes glittered with—was it intelligence or mischief? Perhaps both. Quickly she decided that she'd better try to make friends this first morning.

"How old is Scalawag, Creed?"

"Got him from a kit last summer."

"What's a kit?"

"Like a nest. He's most grown now. Sleeps with me." Seeing the expression on Christy's face, he added, "Oh, he's clean all right. Coons wash every natural blessed thing before they eat. They're the best pets in the world. Teacher, come spring, maybe we could spy out a kit and get one for you."

"Uh, thanks, Creed. Tell you what. Let me think about that offer. Now, about Scalawag and school—"

"Oh, Scalawag won't cause no trouble. Cross my heart and hope to die."

What could she say without caving in this friendship before it got started? Suddenly Christy had an inspiration. "It's like this, Creed." She lowered her voice. "This is just between you and me. Promise you won't tell?"

"Cross my heart."

"Scalawag is such a 'specially fine coon—I can see that already—you know, so good-looking and such a little comic actor, that the children will want to watch him instead of doing their lessons." She grinned.

"How about you and I make a pact? You leave Scalawag home after this. Then I'll let you bring him to the last social, the big recitation just before school closes. We'll fix it so that Scalawag will be part of the entertainment!"

"Honest, Teacher?" Creed's face was shining. "That's a sealed bargain, fair and square. Why, pretty much everybody in the Cove will see Scalawag then. Put it there, Teacher!" He stuck out a grubby hand.

Well, then. She'd handled that little crisis, at least. Christy gazed around her. Sixty-seven eager faces were waiting for her next move.

It was going to be a very long day.

❧ Eleven ❧

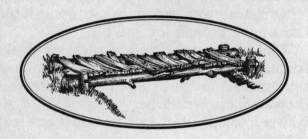

As the day wore on, Christy had a growing uneasiness about the big boy in the back row, the one David had pointed out named Lundy Taylor. She tried to tell herself that David had been overreacting, but it was true that the Taylor boy was uncooperative. He never joined in the singing, never took part in anything. Resentment of some sort smoldered in him. Already he seemed to dislike Christy.

There were so many other problems, too. The fire in the stove—it was much too hot close to it, much too cold in the rest of the room. The dripping noses, and the complete lack of handkerchiefs. The dirty, often smelly clothes, and the need for warmer ones. The mountain dialect was often impossible for Christy to understand. The fact that children who wanted a drink went back and forth to the cedar water bucket in the back of the room, everyone drinking from the same gourd—a good way to start epidemics.

And then there was the utter lack of books. How was she supposed to teach sixty-seven students without any materials?

During the noon recess, which the children called "the dinner spell," Christy sat on the steps, watching the children and wondering how she was going to handle them all. She was surprised when Little Burl came up and sat down beside her like an old friend. He was eating his lunch, a biscuit split in two with a thin slice of pork between the halves.

"I'd be proud to share, Teacher," he said.

"Thank you, Little Burl," Christy said, "but I've already eaten." It wasn't exactly true. Actually, she was simply too anxious to eat.

Just then a pair of black-capped chickadees fluttered to the tree nearest the schoolhouse entrance. Little Burl hesitated, then tossed part of his biscuit to the birds, who swooped down, devouring every last crumb.

"That was nice of you, Little Burl," Christy said, knowing that the boy probably didn't get enough to eat as it was.

"They're pretty little birds, aren't they?"

"Eat upside down sometimes, chickadees do," Little Burl said. He shook his head. "Crazy birds."

"Isn't it great how many different kinds of birds there are, each one so special!" Christy exclaimed. "God must have cared about them, or He wouldn't have made them so beautiful."

Little Burl thought about this, nodding as he finished his biscuit.

"He loves everything He's made—every bird, every animal, every flower, every man and woman, every single one of you," Christy said. "Loves *you* extra-specially."

Little Burl didn't answer. Suddenly quiet, he was staring off at something only he could see. *I'm trying too hard,* Christy thought. *Will I ever be able to reach these children?*

Just then the background hum of high-pitched voices was shattered by a screech of pain and then violent crying. Christy ran around the corner, her shoes slipping in the snow. Vella Holt, a tiny five-year-old with auburn pigtails, was crumpled up on the ground, sobbing. The other children had gathered in a circle around her.

"Has a pump knot on her head," a voice volunteered as Christy took the child in her arms.

The little girl did have a large bump. It was going to be a nasty bruise. What was worse, the blow had been dangerously close to her temple.

"What happened?" Christy asked.

No one answered. Christy looked up. The circle of faces looked too grave, too careful. "Someone has to tell me," Christy persisted. "Did Vella fall down?"

"No'm," Ruby Mae said softly. "She got hit."

"How? With what?"

Someone thrust a homemade ball into Christy's hands. It was so much heavier than she expected that she almost dropped it. It seemed to be made of strips of old cloth wound round and round and then bound with thread. But when she pushed a thumb through the cloth, she found a rock at the center.

"Vella got hit with this?" Christy cried. "No wonder she has a bump on her head! Who threw this?"

Again, the silence. Then, out of the corner of her eye, Christy caught a movement. She turned to see Lundy Taylor and another older boy, Smith O'Teale, slinking into the empty schoolhouse.

"Did Lundy or Smith throw this?"

The children did not say a word, but their eyes told Christy the truth. She felt chilled and frightened. Could either boy have done such a thing on purpose? As she comforted Vella and put cloths wrung out in fresh snow on her bump, Christy struggled with the problem. She decided to make the boys stay after school and get to the bottom of things then, rather than talk to them before all the other pupils.

The rest of the day did not go well. To begin with, Christy was running out of ideas. She'd had big plans for lessons, but now it was clear that much of what she'd planned was impossible, with this many mismatched students. She was glad David would be helping with the math and Bible classes in the afternoon.

What subjects had they not touched on today? Penmanship. Happy thought! Christy was proud of her handwriting. It was a nice script. She would enjoy putting some sentences on the blackboard to be copied.

As she headed for the cracked blackboard, she almost stepped on several marbles. Automatically, she stopped to pick them up. But at that moment a child hurled himself toward her in a flying tackle.

"Teacher, don't touch them!" It was Little Burl, hanging onto her arm, shrieking at her.

She was startled by his ferocity. "Why not? I can't leave them on the floor. Someone will step on them and go scooting."

The little boy looked at her, his face flushed and contorted. "Teacher, them marbles are hot. They'll burn you!"

"Hot?" What was he talking about?

Some of the pupils looked embarrassed. Obviously, there was something Little Burl did not know how to explain. In the back of the room, the laughter started again—Lundy Taylor and some of the older boys.

John Spencer, the fifteen-year-old son of Fairlight and Jeb, stepped forward. "Teacher, I'd thank you to let *me* pick up the marbles for you. Little Burl was afraid you'd burn your fingers. He's right. Them marbles are red hot."

"How'd they get so hot?"

"They was put in the stove, ma'am."

"You—did you—?"

"No, ma'am. Not me. Guess it was just foolery."

Calmly John took a rag from his pocket, gingerly picked up the marbles one by one and then left them on the rag on Christy's desk.

This was too much. A low-down prank—ingenious, but mean, almost as bad as the one on the playground. "Look, a prank's a prank," Christy said. "But this wasn't funny. There are tiny children in this room. What if some of them had stepped on red hot marbles with bare feet? They'd have gotten badly burned. You see, glass holds heat—"

"It sure does!" a self-assured masculine voice said from the doorway. "And your teacher's right."

As David strode toward the teacher's desk, Christy realized how drained she was. The marble trick had been one problem too many.

"Recess time for you, Teacher," David said.

Christy smiled gratefully. She hated to admit it, but she was as relieved as any child would be at the end of the school day.

She couldn't wait to leave.

The creek was running even faster than it had been the day she'd fallen in. It had warmed up slightly over the week, enough to melt some of the jagged ice that rose like frozen, miniature mountains from the stream.

The log bridge swayed like a baby's cradle, back and forth, back and forth, in the steady wind. Here, from the bank of the creek, the scene wasn't nearly as frightening—just a few logs over a stream that glistened in the winter light. It hardly seemed like a likely place to come face to face with death.

But then, maybe that's how many things were. Up close, things that seemed simple and straightforward could become complicated and frightening.

Coming to Cutter Gap was like that. She'd known it would be hard, teaching poor children in the mountains. But not *this* kind of hard. She hadn't bargained for mean students, nearly as old as she was. She hadn't counted on sixty-seven barefoot pupils, most of whom had never seen a book in their lives. She hadn't planned for the difficulties she would have in communicating.

She remembered, with a shudder, the "pump knot" on little Vella's head and the hot marbles on her classroom floor. She certainly hadn't bargained for that kind of meanness.

Christy brushed the snow off a boulder and sat down. She had her diary with her. She'd retrieved it from the mission house before coming here this afternoon. She opened to her list of goals and laughed out loud. Teaching French? Etiquette lessons? What had she been thinking?

She heard footsteps and turned, her heart pounding.

"I'd have thought you'd want to stay as far away as possible from this bridge," David said, laughing as he approached.

"You know what they say—when you fall off, you need to get right back up on the horse."

David frowned. "You didn't cross—"

"No, I'm afraid it may be spring before I cross that bridge again. I think I should let that particular horse thaw out a bit." She moved over, making room on the boulder. "Were you looking for me? I didn't forget a meeting, did I?"

"No. I just happened to notice you when I came out of my bunkhouse to chop some wood. Thought you might need a little moral support."

"Why's that?" Christy asked lightly. Had she done such a bad job that he'd already heard stories from the children?

"First days are always hard. And this is no easy job." David tossed a rock out into the stream. It landed with a musical splash, like a tiny fish.

"Somehow I pictured—" Christy hesitated. There was no point in telling him. He'd just laugh.

"Pictured what?" David asked. When she didn't answer, he said, "Let me guess. You thought it would be easy. That the children, all of them, would welcome you with open arms. That they would be poor, but it would be a nice, clean, easy poor, not one that came with ignorance and filth and smells and superstitions and feuds."

Christy met his eyes. They sparkled with humor, but there was something deeper there, too. "How did you know?"

"You forget. I haven't been here that long myself. I came to Cutter Gap with lots of high hopes about bringing the Word of God to these people, about changing their lives overnight." He laughed. "I suppose I expected them to be grateful. Instead, they've been resentful and slow to accept me. That's when Miss Alice helped me out."

"She did?"

"She told me I couldn't change the world overnight. That this place belonged to the mountain people and that I was the stranger. That it was up to me to understand them, not the other way around."

"And do you?" Christy asked hopefully.

"Nope." David shook his head. "But I'm learning."

"Did you—" Christy gazed up at the bridge, which was shimmering colorfully in the sunlight like an earthbound rainbow. "Did you ever think about going home, giving up?"

"Sure. I think about it every day." David said it lightly, but Christy thought she heard uncertainty there, too. "Sometimes I wonder if I can ever really be a part of this place, the way Miss Alice is. The way Doctor MacNeill is."

"He told me you were still learning," Christy said.

David rolled his eyes. "I suppose he's right," he said. "Although I might point out that the Doc's more than a little set in his ways." He shrugged. "Anyway. Take your time, Christy Huddleston. It will get easier."

He stood and touched her lightly on the shoulder. She was grateful for the warm smile that seemed to come from somewhere deep inside him. "Oh, by the way. I heard about the incident with Vella."

"I'd planned to talk to Lundy about it—"

"I see you've quickly figured out where the trouble's likely to start. I tried talking to Lundy and Smith myself this afternoon. Couldn't get anything out of them, so I guess we'll just have to keep an eye on things." His face went grave. "I don't want to worry you, especially when you're feeling nervous enough, but Lundy and his friends are bad news. This won't be the only time you'll have to confront them, and next time, it may be worse. If that happens, I want you to come to me, understand?"

Christy nodded. But as she watched David trudge back up the hill, she remembered some advice Miss Alice had given her about taking charge of the classroom. Christy knew she couldn't run to David every time there was trouble.

She gathered up her diary and started to leave. But after a few steps, she turned around. Slowly, methodically, she began to search the bank of the creek, hoping she might find the locket her father had given her.

She knew it was crazy. The necklace must have caught on something during her fall, or broken when she was underwater. It was probably miles down the stream by now, lost forever. Lost forever like her old life. And in its place was the new life she had chosen, a hard, demanding, terrifying, complicated, lonely life in Cutter Gap.

It's an adventure, she told herself. This was what she'd wanted, what she'd dreamed of. She was doing God's work.

But what if I can't do it well enough? a doubting part of her heart asked.

She gazed up at the bridge. She remembered wondering if Bob Allen's accident and her fall off the bridge had been signals that coming here was a mistake. It would be nice to have a sign that she was on the right track, but so far, God had not delivered one.

Christy trudged back and forth along the creek's bank until the sun began to melt behind the farthest blue-black ridge. In her heart, she'd known all along that the locket was lost. So why was it she couldn't seem to stop crying?

❧ Twelve ❧

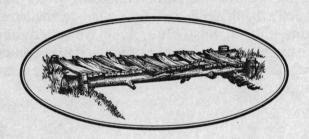

Y ou're not eating a thing," Miss Ida scolded the next morning.

"I'm sorry," Christy apologized, staring at her eggs unhappily. "I haven't got much of an appetite this morning."

"Had plenty of one every other morning," Miss Ida grumbled, pulling Christy's plate away.

Christy got up from the table. "I thought I'd go over to the school a bit early this morning, to get things ready." *Like myself*, she added silently.

"May I have a word with you, Christy?" Miss Alice asked.

"Of course. If it's about my lesson plans, I know they still need some work—"

"No, no," Miss Alice said, laughing. She gestured to the porch. They put on their wraps and headed outside. Their breath hung in the air. The sun was just rising, casting a pink glow over the school.

"Have you ever watched a baby learning to walk, Christy?" Miss Alice asked. "He totters, arms stretched out to balance himself. He wobbles, and falls, perhaps bumps his nose. Then he puts the palms of his little hands flat on the floor, hikes his rear end up, looks around to see if anybody is watching him. If nobody is, usually he doesn't bother to cry, just balances himself—and tries again."

"I don't understand—"

"That baby can teach us. You can't expect immediate perfection in your schoolroom. It's a *walk*, and a walk isn't static but ever-changing. We Quakers say that all discouragement is from an evil source and can only end in more evil. Feeling sorry for yourself is worse than falling on your face in the first place."

Christy felt unexpected tears sting her eyes. "I came here to do God's work," she whispered. "But what if I can't? What if I'm no good at it?"

Miss Alice draped an arm around her shoulders. "So you fall, like that baby. Maybe you even bump your nose. So you're human. Thank God for your humanness!"

Christy took a deep, steadying breath. "I'll try, Miss Alice," she said.

"That's all you can do, child. 'Give, and it

shall be given unto you,'" Miss Alice said softly. "You'll see."

Christy squeezed Miss Alice's hand. As she headed off across the boardwalk toward school, she could feel the woman's gaze upon her, warmer than the dawn sunlight peeking over the mountains.

The schoolroom was cold, even though David had already started a roaring fire in the potbellied stove. Christy walked back and forth across the empty room, straightening desks, cleaning off the blackboard, fussing and fidgeting. Her heart hammered in her chest. Her hands were shaking like leaves in a breeze.

"Give, and it shall be given unto you," Miss Alice had said. But what if she didn't have enough to give?

She heard the thump of little steps and turned to see Little Burl in the doorway. He was wearing a coat two sizes too big for him. One elbow had been patched a dozen times, it seemed. The sleeves were rolled up, yet still his little hands were hidden. His feet, again, were bare. His nose was running.

"Teacher," he said, "I came early."

"You certainly did," Christy said, trying to force lightness into her voice.

"I was a-thinkin' all last night."

Christy sat down in her chair and motioned for Little Burl to join her. He climbed up in her lap. "What were you thinking about, Little Burl?"

"About what you said. About the birds and all."

"The birds?" Christy flashed through yesterday's lessons. Had she mentioned birds? No. Raccoons, yes, but no birds. Well, there you had it. She really *wasn't* reaching these kids.

"I don't remember about the birds," Christy said gently. "We talked about Creed's raccoon, I remember that—"

"The birds, outside," Little Burl insisted loudly. "The chickadees!"

"Oh, you mean at lunch! The birds you fed. Of course."

Little Burl's funny little face held a look of intense concentration. "Teacher, you said that God loves everybody, right?"

"That's right," Christy said.

"Well, then, ain't it true that if God loves everybody, then we'uns got to love everybody, too?"

Christy looked at the little boy in astonishment. "Yes, Little Burl," she encouraged, "it *is* true." Forever and forever and forever, she added silently.

He broke into a smile, relieved. "Thought so."

Christy watched as he scampered back out the door. One comment, an offhand remark during noon recess, had set this little boy to thinking.

Something she'd said *had* mattered. Something she'd said had made a difference.

Perhaps God's work started in small ways.

She'd wanted a sign. Maybe this, after all, was the one she'd been waiting for.

Christy went to the door. The children began to appear as the day broke. In twos, in clumps, dancing, skipping, running, their faces filled with hope and joy. And sometimes, yes, filled with darker things—loneliness, hunger, fear, even anger.

She was surprised when she saw Fairlight Spencer walking toward the school, her children by her side. She was carrying a little leather pouch in one hand. The other held the toddler named Little Guy.

"Fairlight!" Christy exclaimed. Strangely, when Fairlight returned her smile, Christy felt like she was seeing an old, very dear friend.

"I tell you, these children hardly slept a wink last night, they were so excited about school," Fairlight said. She handed the leather pouch to Christy with a shy smile. "John found this a couple days back, over yonder by the bank of the creek."

Christy opened the pouch and reached inside. At the bottom, she felt the cool smoothness of metal.

"My locket?" she whispered.

Slowly she removed the necklace. The chain was gone. In its place was a thin braid of the softest yarns, in blues and greens and blacks and violets.

"I spun and dyed the yarn myself. I know it ain't the same. I sent John and Clara back to look for the chain, but it must have fallen in the creek when you fell in."

Christy grinned. "You heard about that?"

"Word travels fast around these here parts."

"So I hear."

Fairlight peered at Christy, her face lined with worry. "The braidin' is all wrong, I know—"

"It's beautiful," Christy insisted. "More beautiful than before. All the colors of the mountains." Her eyes overflowed with tears. "Thank you, Fairlight. It means more to me than you can know."

Gently Christy opened the locket. The pictures were damp, but unharmed. Her loving family gazed back at her. Christy closed the cover and slipped the braid over her head. She felt the silver heart, close to her own heart again. It was part of her old life, and now, with Fairlight's gift, part of her new one as well.

"Let's start those reading lessons soon, all right?" Christy said.

"I can't hardly wait," Fairlight said eagerly.

Christy nodded. "Neither can I," she said with sudden feeling.

She took a deep breath. The morning sun was full now, a glorious red-gold, filtering down through these mountains that were her home. She felt a tiny, cold hand take hold of hers.

"Ready?" Little Burl asked.

Christy smiled down at the little boy. "Did you ever see a baby learn to walk, Little Burl?" she asked, and then, at last, she knew the adventure she had longed for was about to begin.

Silent
Superstitions

The Characters

CHRISTY RUDD HUDDLESTON, a nineteen-year-old girl.

CHRISTY'S STUDENTS:
> ROB ALLEN, age fourteen.
> CREED ALLEN, age nine.
> BESSIE COBURN, age twelve.
> WRAIGHT HOLT, age seventeen.
> ZACHARIAS HOLT, age nine.
> BECKY HOLT, age seven.
> VELLA HOLT, age five.
> ISAAK MCHONE, age twelve.
> SMITH O'TEALE, age fifteen.
> ORTER BALL O'TEALE, age eleven.
> MOUNTIE O'TEALE, age ten.
> GEORGE O'TEALE, age nine.
> MARY O'TEALE, age eight.
> THOMAS O'TEALE, age six.
> RUBY MAE MORRISON, age thirteen.
> JOHN SPENCER, age fifteen.
> CLARA SPENCER, age twelve.
> ZADY SPENCER, age ten.
> LUNDY TAYLOR, age seventeen.

ALICE HENDERSON, a Quaker mission worker from Ardmore, Pennsylvania.

GRANNY O'TEALE, great-grandmother of the O'Teale children.

SWANNIE O'TEALE, a mountain woman.

NATHAN O'TEALE, her husband.
(Parents of Christy's students Smith, Orter Ball, Mountie, George, Mary, and Thomas.)

WILMER O'TEALE, the retarded, epileptic O'Teale son.

DAVID GRANTLAND, the young minister.

IDA GRANTLAND, David's sister.

DR. NEIL MACNEILL, the physician of the Cove.

JEB SPENCER, a mountain man.

FAIRLIGHT SPENCER, his wife.
(Parents of Christy's students John, Clara, and Zady.)

❧ One ❧

She's a witch, I tell you! Ugly as a coot, with hardly no hair. She's got monstrous red eyes and fingernails like the claws of a hawk!"

Mary O'Teale paused to warm her hands by the pot-bellied stove in the one-room schoolhouse. Her listeners crowded closer. "Old Marthy's her name," she continued, lowering her voice to a whisper. "Late at night when the moon's as full as a pumpkin, she comes 'round, makin' mischief. If she takes a dislikin' to you, she'll sneak inside while you're a-dreamin' and put a curse on you."

As she listened from her desk, Christy Huddleston couldn't help smiling. Eight-year-old Mary definitely had a vivid imagination. Christy knew her students loved to tell each other "haunt tales." But she worried about the younger children. They were easily frightened, and she didn't want the stories getting out of hand.

"You're just talkin' to hear yerself talk, Mary," said Ruby Mae Morrison, a thirteen-year-old with vibrant red hair and a personality to match. "Ain't nobody ever seen Old Marthy."

Mary jutted her chin. "My great-granny has," she replied. She inched her right foot closer to the old stove. Like most of the children at the mission school, she did not own a pair of shoes. Even now, in January, Mary and her friends walked to school barefoot.

Ruby Mae twisted a strand of hair around her index finger. "You're sayin' Granny's seen a witch, up-close like?"

Mary nodded. "Granny saw Old Marthy make someone eat a witch ball."

"What's . . . what's that?" asked Ruby Mae.

"A witch ball's a bunch of pine needles, all wrapped 'round and 'round with a person's hair."

"What happens when you eat it?"

"At the strike of twelve," Mary whispered, "you turn into a big, hairy old bat. And there ain't no turnin' back, neither!"

Christy cleared her throat. "You know, it's almost time for school to start," she said, giving Mary a patient smile. "Maybe we've had enough of these silly stories for one day."

"But Teacher, they ain't silly," Mary said. "They're haunt tales."

"Girls," Christy asked gently, "are any of you afraid of these scary stories?"

No one answered.

"Well, let me ask you this. Are any of you afraid of the dark?"

Vella Holt, a tiny five-year-old with auburn pigtails, climbed onto Christy's lap. "Oh, yes'm!" Vella exclaimed. "It's scary to have to leave the firelight and walk into the shadows to bed. Most nights, I put the covers over my head."

"Children!" Ruby Mae scoffed.

Christy couldn't help grinning. Christy knew for a fact that Ruby Mae still liked to sleep with a tattered rag doll.

"It gives me prickles to peer at the dark," Vella whispered to Christy. "I'm always scared for fear I'll see a ghost."

"I'll let you in on a little secret," Christy said. "I was like that when I was a girl."

"You was?" Mary exclaimed.

"I'd lie there in my bed, shivering and shaking, thinking of all the stories I'd heard about ghosts and witches and whatnot."

"So how'd you get over it?" Ruby Mae asked.

"One day they sang a certain song at Sunday school. Seemed as if it was just for me. I'll sing it for you—

God will take care of you
Through every day, o'er all the way,
He will take care of you,
He will take care of you."

Mary nodded thoughtfully. "That's right nice. I like the sound of it."

"So whenever I was scared of the dark," Christy continued, stroking little Vella's hair, "I'd sing those four lines over and over to myself. And you know what, girls? After a while, the love of God was more real to me than any old ghost. Pretty soon all the ghosts went away. Ever since then, the dark has seemed friendly and cozy."

Mary reached over and gave her a shy hug. "Sing it again, Teacher, will you? Then I won't disremember it."

As Christy repeated the song, more of her students rushed into the schoolroom that also served as a church. She watched them as they entered—ragged, pale, probably hungry, almost always dirty. And as she sang, she was reminded once again of the beauty in those eager faces, and that the task set before her was a huge and difficult one.

When Christy had arrived here just a little over a week ago, she'd been full of high hopes about her new job as a teacher at the mission school in Cutter Gap, Tennessee. She'd never dreamed her class would contain sixty-seven students, ranging in age from five to seventeen. She'd never imagined that she'd be teaching in such primitive conditions, with just a handful of worn books and an assortment of borrowed, battered desks. A few of her students had basic arithmetic and reading skills, but most had never set foot in a schoolroom before.

Christy finished the song, but Mary and the others kept singing it over and over. Teaching school in Cutter Gap wasn't going to be an easy job. Christy had quickly discovered this during her first long week at the mission school. But as she listened to Mary and the others raise their voices in song, she had the feeling it might just turn out to be more rewarding than she'd ever hoped.

~ ~ ~

That noon, Mary and her older sister, Mountie, slowly climbed up the steep hill behind the school. The dinner spell—Teacher called it "noon recess"—was almost over. But Mary wanted to get a look at the new ice slide the big boys had made. After the last snowstorm, the boys had created a long, narrow trail by packing down the snow. They'd drenched it with buckets of water, then let the slide freeze. Everyone agreed it was the best sliding hill anyone had seen in a long time.

Mary clutched Mountie's hand when they reached the top of the slide. Several of the older boys were lined up, waiting to belly-flop down the icy chute. Some of them were using an old rag rug for a sled.

"Chicken."

Mary cringed when she heard the familiar voice. She turned to see Lundy Taylor approaching.

"We ain't chicken," Mary replied. She squeezed her big sister's hand a little tighter. "We just don't want to."

"Don't want to 'cause you're chicken," Lundy said with a sneer.

Mary watched as her big brother, Smith, sped down the steep icy path. He slowed to a stop at the edge of the schoolyard.

"Besides, Teacher said only the big boys could go," Mary said.

"So how's come you're up here?" Lundy demanded. "You and Mush-mouth?"

Mary stared up at the big boy looming above her. Lundy was seventeen and she was only eight, which was bad enough. It didn't help that he was the biggest bully in the state of Tennessee, maybe even in the world. It was too bad Lundy and her brother were friends. Still, she had to stand up for her big sister. People were always picking on Mountie because she couldn't talk like everyone else.

"Don't you go callin' Mountie names," Mary said. She put her arm around Mountie's thin shoulders. Mountie was two years older than Mary, but she needed a lot of protecting.

A bell clanged loudly. Mary looked down to see the new teacher on the porch, ringing the bell. She was so beautiful! After four days of school, Mary still couldn't get over it. Maybe it was because Teacher came from a big city. Or maybe it was her fancy clothes—shoes of real leather and a red sweater so soft you could melt for the feel of it.

But Mary was pretty sure there was something else that made Teacher so beautiful. It was her eyes, wide and blue as a June sky. Every time Mary looked into those eyes, she felt safe and warm, the way she felt all wrapped up in one of her Granny's quilts. Those were magic eyes. Pure magic.

The bell clanged again. "The dinner spell's over," Mary said.

Lundy held up a hand. "Not for Mush-mouth, it ain't."

Mary could hear trouble in his voice, but by the time she yanked on Mountie's arm, Lundy's strong hands had already clamped onto her sister's shoulders. Mountie's eyes were bright with fear.

"Let her go, Lundy!" Mary cried. "You're hurtin' her!"

"Whatever you say," Lundy said, shoving Mountie aside.

Mary grabbed Mountie and turned to leave, but suddenly Lundy's big foot was in the way. Mary felt a slight push on her back.

She tumbled forward, Mountie's hand slipping from her grasp. Mary landed hard on the ice-covered slide. It felt as if someone had punched her in the stomach. The ice was slick, and Mary could feel herself slowly gaining speed. She grabbed for a bush as it whizzed past, but she couldn't hang on.

Faster and faster, she was flying down the mountain, screaming hard, her voice lost in the cold wind.

Mary reached out her hand again, hoping for something to slow her fall. Her palm smacked hard against something, and then she was flipping in an endless somersault, 'round and 'round. The school and the trees and the sky went topsy-turvy. Somewhere, up high, she could hear Lundy's dark, loud laughter.

Then she hit, plowing head first into the trunk of a big oak. The world was very quiet. Lundy's laughter had vanished. Mary's arm burned like fire. And though she'd stopped tumbling, her head was still spinning. She could hear the shouts of other children; then everything went black and silent.

❧ TWO ❧

As Christy ran across the schoolyard with Mary in her arms, she said a silent prayer. *Please let Mary be all right. Please, God.*

Thank goodness Miss Alice was home today. Alice Henderson, who had helped found the school where Christy taught, lived in a small cabin near the main mission house.

"Miss Alice!" Christy called as she made her way up the cabin steps.

The door opened to reveal a lovely, regal-looking woman wearing a crisp, blue dress. "Christy!" Miss Alice exclaimed. "What on earth—"

"She went down that icy slide the boys made," Christy said breathlessly.

Miss Alice held open the door, and Christy carried Mary into the cozy warmth of the cabin. Several of the local women were gathered by the fire, sipping tea from china cups.

"Prayer meeting," Miss Alice explained.

"That's my Mary!" cried a wiry little woman. Her thinning gray hair hung in a long braid down her back. She wore a drab brown skirt and a faded calico blouse buttoned high on her neck. Her milky blue eyes were set deep in skin crisscrossed with fine wrinkles. And her lips were stained by tobacco juice.

The woman bustled over, leaning on a wooden walking stick for support. "Put her down," she said to Christy. "She ain't your kin."

"I'm fine, Granny," Mary mumbled, still dazed by her tumble down the hill. She had blacked out for a moment after hitting the tree. But she'd regained consciousness by the time Christy reached her.

"Christy, this is Mary's great-grandmother," Miss Alice explained. "Granny O'Teale, this is Christy Huddleston, our new teacher at the mission school."

Granny did not answer. She tried to tug Mary out of Christy's arms, but Mary hung onto Christy's neck, refusing to go.

"Put her down, I'm a-tellin' you," Granny commanded. "Lordamercy, what have you done to my little Mary?"

"Some of the children said she was tripped," Christy said. "Is that what happened, Mary?"

The little girl nodded, but refused to meet Christy's eyes.

"Who tripped you, sweetheart?" Miss Alice asked.

Mary buried her head on Christy's shoulder.

"Lundy Taylor," Christy muttered. "I've no doubt. He was up there with her."

"It might—" Mary began. "It might have been an accident. I can't rightly recollect how it happened. We'uns was all up there, and it was mighty slippery-like."

Christy exchanged a glance with Miss Alice. Mary was probably afraid to accuse Lundy. He terrified the younger children. Even Christy felt nervous around the hulking bully.

Miss Alice led Christy to her bedroom. Christy set the little girl down gently on Miss Alice's quilt-covered bed. Granny trailed behind, muttering something Christy couldn't quite make out.

"Why don't you two give me a minute to examine Mary and make sure she's all right?" Miss Alice said.

"I promise I'm fine, Miss Alice," Mary said quickly. "My arm's pretty banged-up, is all."

"Looky here," Granny said. "Any doctorin' needs doin', I aim to do it."

"I'd be proud to have your help, Granny," Miss Alice said. "Why don't you let me take a look at Mary first? Then you can take over."

"I need to get back to the other children," Christy said. She hated to leave, but Mary did appear to be all right. Her right arm was badly scraped. The beginnings of an ugly bruise were already visible. And there was a small knot where she'd bumped her head on the tree. But Mary was smiling calmly, apparently enjoying all the attention.

"I'll let you know how Mary's doing," Miss Alice said. "You go back to work."

Christy knelt beside the bed. "Mary, you take care of yourself, understand?"

Mary nodded. "Will you keep watch on Mountie for me? The others . . . they like to pick on her."

"Of course I will," Christy said. She took the little girl's tiny, cold hand in her own.

Suddenly another hand, withered and spotted with age, grabbed hold of Christy's. "Don't you go near my girl, you hear?" Granny cried.

"But I was just—"

"You're nothin' but trouble, and that's for sure and certain," Granny said, releasing her grip. "We don't need no brought-on teachers comin' from clear across state lines to learn our children all kinds of cityfied notions. Flatlanders don't belong around here. Who asked you, anyways?"

"Granny," Miss Alice said firmly, "Christy is a wonderful teacher. She only meant to—"

"If'n she's so all-fired wonderful, how come my little Mary's lyin' here all black and blue?"

"It was an accident," Christy said. "It was

recess, and I was watching the younger children playing in front of the school. I told them that only the biggest boys could slide down that hill—"

Granny pointed a long, yellowed fingernail at Christy. Granny's eyes had a wild brightness in them. "An accident, heh? And how about Bob Allen? Were he an accident, too?"

"Granny," Miss Alice soothed as she gently examined Mary's arm. "You know what happened. A tree fell on Bob Allen on his way to pick up Christy at the train station."

"And how come is *that*, I'm askin' you?"

"Probably because the branches were weighed down by snow. That was a very big storm we had, you remember."

Christy shuddered, remembering Mr. Allen's pale, nearly lifeless form. She'd felt so guilty, knowing he'd been hurt while trying to reach her. After Mr. Allen had been found, she'd helped the local doctor operate on him to relieve the bleeding inside his head. On her very first day in Cutter Gap, she'd ended up playing nurse in the most primitive conditions imaginable. It was truly a miracle that Mr. Allen had survived.

"Maybe it were the snow, and maybe not." Granny narrowed her eyes. "Maybe this girl brought a heap o' trouble with her. Maybe she nearly killed Bob Allen with her comin', and now my little Mary."

"I'm right as rain, Granny, really I am," Mary protested. She cast Christy an apologetic look.

"Bob Allen is fine, Granny," Miss Alice said. "And Mary's going to be, too, from what I can tell."

"She's trouble, I'm tellin' you," Granny said, her voice trembling. She pushed her way past Christy. For a tiny old woman, she was surprisingly strong. "I can tell from a mile off when a person's cursed. And you, my girl, have the touch of it on you. The signs are all there."

"Cursed?" Christy repeated, half angry, half amazed.

"More'n likely ain't even your fault," Granny said. "Folks get cursed for all kinda reasons. Old Marthy coulda done it."

"You don't actually believe that, do you?" Christy asked.

"Seen it happen with my own eyes a hundred times. But mind you this, once you're cursed, you pass it on to everyone you're near. You best be headin' on back to where you came from, before you do any more damage."

"Granny, I wish you'd give me a chance," Christy pleaded.

"Maybe you should be getting back to the other children," Miss Alice advised, sending Christy a look that clearly meant there was no point in arguing with Granny.

Christy sighed. "You take care, Mary," she

said. As she turned to leave, she met Granny's eyes. "Nice meeting you, Granny. Maybe sometime we can get together and talk some more."

The old woman glared back at her with such a frightful look that it was all Christy could do to keep from running from the cabin.

———

Later that afternoon, Mary returned to class. Christy was relieved to see that the little girl was all right, but the accident on the hill had left Christy feeling unsettled. First of all, she had to decide what to do about Lundy. No one would directly accuse him of anything, and Christy knew she couldn't punish the boy without proof. She finally decided that her only option was to keep a close watch on Lundy and his friends.

And then there was Granny O'Teale. Christy couldn't seem to forget the frightful look on the old woman's face. Of course, Christy didn't believe in curses. But it was hard to ignore the fact that, for whatever reason, Granny had decided that Christy did not belong here in Cutter Gap.

Christy tried to shake off her nagging thoughts. She had other things to worry about this afternoon, like completing her first official week of school.

"As you are all aware," Christy said, leaning

against her battered desk, "today marks the end of our first week of school." She was not surprised when a couple of the older boys—the troublemakers—began to whistle and clap.

"Thank you for that show of support, Smith and Wraight and Lundy," she said crisply. "Now, since it is Friday afternoon, I thought this might be a nice time, instead of working on our arithmetic, to hear from some of the older students. You'll remember that on Wednesday I assigned a theme on 'What I Want to Do When I Grow Up.' Clara, why don't you start us off?"

Clara Spencer blushed, clearly flattered at the chance to go first. She was the daughter of Fairlight Spencer, a kind and gentle woman Christy had met on her journey through the mountains to Cutter Gap.

Clara straightened her patched cotton dress and cleared her throat. "When I grow up," she began, "I want to have lots of shoes—two, maybe three pairs, even. And I want a fine house with enough pans to cook in and a rug on the floor to sink my toes in." She looked over at Christy. "That's all, Teacher."

"Well, that was a fine job, Clara," Christy said. "An effort to be proud of." She pointed to Rob Allen, one of the older boys. "How about you—"

A deep, snuffling noise, like a grunt coming

from deep within the earth, cut her off in mid-sentence. Christy put her hands on her hips. "Wraight Holt, was that you?"

Wraight glared at Christy. "Weren't me. I ain't no pig."

"Now, that there's a lie if'n I ever heard one," said Smith O'Teale, Mary and Mountie's big brother. "I've done seen you at the supper table, Wraight Holt, and it ain't a pretty sight to behold!"

Laughter filled the room. "All right," Christy said. "That's enough." By now, she'd learned that she had to be firm, even when she wasn't feeling sure of herself. "As I was saying, Rob, why don't—"

Again, the grunting noise interrupted Christy. "What *is* that awful noise?" she demanded.

Creed Allen, a nine-year-old boy with tousled hair and two missing front teeth, waved his hand frantically. "Teacher, I know what that there noise is. It's them hogs," Creed said. He tapped a bare foot on the wooden floor. "The ones underneath the school."

Christy sighed. In the Cove, as the area was often called, most hogs weren't penned. They wandered wherever they pleased, fattening themselves on beechnuts, acorns, and chestnuts. Some of them had even taken to sleeping under the schoolhouse, grunting with what had to be, Christy felt certain, the most repulsive sound in the world. It was hard enough, teaching sixty-seven children, without being interrupted by pigs.

"Are you sure it's the hogs?" Christy asked. "They aren't usually so . . . so *vocal.*"

"Well, the thing of it is," Creed said, "it's a-goin' to storm."

"What does that have to do with the hogs?"

"They grunt extra loud afore the wind picks up," Creed said.

"I'm sure that's just an old wives' tale, Creed."

"No'm," Clara broke in. "It's the truth, I promise you. They jerk their heads and grunt and carry on, sure as can be."

"I see," Christy said. These children were full of the strangest superstitions and mountain lore! She suspected that most of it was pure nonsense, but there was probably a grain of truth to some of the superstitions.

"Here, I'll show you," Creed volunteered, leaping out of his chair. He went to the center of the room, where a trap door had been cut into the floor. A rope was attached to the door.

"Creed, I don't think—" Christy began, but Creed had already pulled the door open to reveal the crawl space beneath the school floor. There, grunting and grumbling, were several hogs.

"See?" Creed said. "See how they jerk their heads? Weather's changin' for sure."

Christy walked over to the edge of the trap

door. "Yes, they certainly are noisy little fellows," she agreed. "Now, close that up, Creed."

"Want to pet one, Ma'am?" Creed asked. "They're all whiskery and funny-feeling."

Christy couldn't help making a face. "I'm not a big fan of hogs, to tell you the truth. Actually, I like dogs better."

"But hogs is the cleanest, smartest pets you ever did see, 'cept maybe for raccoons," Creed said.

"It's true," said Clara. "Our pet hog, Belinda, sleeps with me sometimes."

"Yes, I remember meeting Belinda when I visited your cabin, Clara," Christy said politely. "She was very, uh . . . very outgoing, for a hog."

"Course she snores somethin' terrible," Clara admitted. "I drew a picture of her. Want to see?" Clara fumbled in her desk until she located a small piece of paper. Christy leaned down to examine the picture. A carefully drawn hog grinned up at her.

"Very nice, Clara," Christy said. "You'd almost think Belinda was smiling."

"Oh, but she is, Miz Christy! She smiles all the time, 'specially after supper. Pa says that's just her indigestion, like when babies get gas and they smile all funny-like." She lowered her voice. "Truth to tell, Belinda does get some mighty bad gas. 'Course, I love her, anyway—"

Behind her, Christy heard giggling. She spun

around. Apparently, while she'd been talking to Clara, Creed had jumped through the trap door into the crawl space below the floor. The hogs looked quite happy to have some company.

"Creed, get out of there, this minute!" Christy cried.

"I just figured you might want to meet one of the hogs," Creed said. He positioned a crate near the edge of the hole and herded one of the hogs toward it.

"Creed, I really don't need to meet any of the hogs," Christy said. "Now, come out of there, right now—"

But instead of Creed, a fat, grunting hog lumbered up onto the crate and out of the hole.

"I call that 'un George, on account of he looks like my Uncle George over in Cataleechie," Creed announced from the hole.

The hog sniffed the air curiously. The children leapt from their seats and surrounded him, screeching with laughter.

"Go ahead and pet him, Miz Christy," Ruby Mae urged. "He's a nice enough hog, truly he is."

"I want that hog out of this classroom this instant," Christy said, but she couldn't help grinning as she said it. He looked so ridiculous, waddling around the classroom, snuffling and snorting like he owned the place. None of her teacher training had ever prepared her for this!

"Here's another one," Creed called. "I call this 'un Mabel, after my great-aunt, on account of he looks like my Great-aunt Mabel over in Big Gap. 'Cept for the tail, of course."

Mabel eyed Christy doubtfully. She did not seem very happy to have joined the class. Clara reached out to pat the hog, and Mabel decided to run for cover. Unfortunately, she made a bee-line for Christy. She didn't stop until she was hiding directly under Christy's long skirt.

"Help!" Christy cried. "Stop her!"

At the sound of Christy screaming, Mabel started to run again, pulling Christy's skirt—and Christy—along with her. Christy tumbled back onto the floor. Mabel peered out from under Christy's skirt and ran free, squealing in terror.

While Christy caught her breath, some of the children tried to round up Mabel. Unfortunately, Creed had released two more of the hogs in the meantime. Christy sat on the floor, watching with a mixture of amusement and horror as four hogs ran in crazy circles through the schoolroom. Students stood on desks and hid under desks, hoping to catch the animals. Screams and laughter filled the air.

Christy stood and brushed off her skirt. She had to get control of the situation, and fast.

First things first. She crossed the room and opened the door. "Mabel, George, and the rest of you hogs," she called, "school's over for you."

The hogs kept running wildly, ignoring Christy—and the door—entirely. They seemed to be in no hurry at all to leave.

"All right, now," Christy said with determination. "We've got to think like a team. I want all of you to get on the far side of the room. We're going to make a long line and herd these hogs right out of the door!"

"Can't herd hogs, Miz Christy," Creed informed her as he finally climbed out of the trap door. "You can herd sheep and such. And cows, maybe. But hogs, they ain't much for bein' herded."

"Well, these hogs don't have a choice," Christy said.

She pushed some of the desks to the side of the room, leaving the four hogs milling in the center. The children gathered in two long rows at the end of the room. Slowly they walked forward, arm and arm. Mabel ran straight into Clara Spencer's legs, then bounced off with an outraged squeal.

When the line of students was halfway across the room, George finally seemed to get the message. He scooted out the door with a last goodbye grunt. Soon two of his companions followed. Only Mabel remained. She didn't seem to want to go outside.

"Sorry, Mabel, you're being expelled," Christy said.

Mabel stopped. She stared at Christy and

blinked. With a defiant squeal, she made a mad dash for the coat rack. It toppled with a crash, landing right on top of Mabel.

For a moment, silence fell.

"Oh, Mabel, are you hurt?" Christy cried.

The hog scrabbled beneath the pile of old coats and worn sweaters. Suddenly she emerged. A green, well-patched sweater was draped over her shoulders, and somehow a battered felt hat had landed directly on her head.

She turned to look at Christy one last time, her snout high in the air, her hat at a jaunty angle. Then, with a queenly snort, she strode out into the yard.

Seconds later, David Grantland, the mission's young minister, appeared in the doorway.

"Am I crazy," he said, scratching his head, "or did I just see a hog wearing a hat and coat come out of here?"

"Actually," Christy said with a smile, "It was a sweater."

"Ah," David said. "That explains everything."

Christy nudged Clara. "I know this sounds crazy," she said, "but I could have sworn Mabel was smiling when she left."

When they finally retrieved the sweater and hat Mabel had borrowed, Christy managed to get the class to settle down. Once again, she turned to Rob Allen. "Rob, why don't you read us your theme? And this time, if any hogs interrupt, just ignore them."

Rob headed to the front of the class. He was a tall, slender fourteen-year-old who had already proved to be a gifted student. "Sometimes," Rob read, "I get to feeling lonesome. I want to tell my thoughts, my good thoughts on the inside, to somebody without being laughed at. It would pleasure me to know the right way to put things like that on paper for other people, too."

With a little nod at Christy, Rob returned to his seat. "Thank you, Rob," Christy said warmly. "I'm absolutely sure that someday you will make a fine writer."

The boy sent her a shy smile. Students like Rob gave Christy hope, but she knew it was just as important—maybe even more important—to encourage the difficult ones. Some, like Lundy, came to school with a chip on their shoulder and an angry word for anyone who got in their way. Others, like the strange, silent Mountie O'Teale, seemed completely unreachable.

Out in the yard, one of the hogs offered another ferocious grunt. The class erupted into laughter. Christy returned to the window. Outside, the wind blew stronger.

"It seems the hogs may be better predictors of the weather than I gave them credit for," she said with a laugh.

She noticed a group of women streaming out of Miss Alice's cabin. Apparently, the prayer meeting was breaking up. Christy watched as Granny O'Teale, leaning on her wooden stick, slowly made her way toward the school.

Just then, the wind gave a sudden piercing howl, like a frightened animal. It was followed by a noise that sounded like rapid, muffled clapping.

The children fell silent. Christy gazed toward the ceiling. "Does anyone know where that sound is coming from?" she asked. Before anyone could respond, she had her answer. A sleek, black bird soared through the air above the children.

"A raven!" Mary cried. The big bird swooped in a large circle, as if he were surveying the room. Several of the students ducked. A few covered their heads.

"Just what we need," Christy said as she sat down at her desk. "Another uninvited guest. How on earth did he get in here? And don't tell me Creed let him in through the trap door!"

"Through the steeple up top, I'll wager," Creed said in a trembling voice. "It ain't all the way finished yet. I reckon that bird just sneaked his way on in."

"Nasty birds, ravens is," Ruby Mae said, eyeing the bird warily. "Like nothin' better than to pick out the eye of a lamb or a fawn."

The awful image made Christy shiver. "You mean when they find a dead one?" she asked.

"Naw. It's the eyes of livin' animals they like."

Christy watched the bird swoop and circle once again. It slowed as it neared her, then landed gracefully on her desk.

"Well," she tried to joke, "it's always nice to have another student. Mr. Raven, have you met Mabel and George? Perhaps our new arrival would like to share what he wants to be when he grows up."

A glance at the class told her they did not appreciate her joke. All eyes were locked on the shiny, strutting bird. Creed's hands were clenched in tight balls. Vella looked as if she were on the verge of tears. Ruby Mae was biting her lip nervously.

"Come on, now," Christy chided. "It's just a raven." The bird cocked his head to one side, gazing at her with an eye like a black bead. Christy eased her chair back a few inches. She loved birds, but something about this one made her uneasy. He was too sure of himself, swaggering across her desk as if he were on some special mission.

Still, Christy was a "city-gal." It seemed odd that the raven was making these mountain children uncomfortable, too. After all, they'd grown up surrounded by wildlife. They certainly hadn't been afraid of the hogs.

"Creed," Christy said, "open the door, would you? Maybe our uninvited guest will take the hint."

Creed ran to open the door. A blast of cold air filled the room. "All right," Christy said to the bird, "it's been nice visiting with you, but it's time to go."

The raven did a little dance around her desk, pecking at the surface and bobbing its head. Suddenly he stopped cold.

Christy heard a gasp. Granny O'Teale stood in the doorway, a horrified expression on her face. The old woman pointed a trembling finger at the raven.

"Mountie, Mary, Thomas!" Granny cried. "Get out here, now! I want all the O'Teale children to come with me."

The raven locked a glassy eye on Christy. It let out three cries—*CAW! CAW! CAW!* Then, with a flourish of its wings, it whipped past Granny and sped out the door.

"*Now*, I tell you!" Granny yelled, beckoning with her arm. One by one, the O'Teale children began heading toward the door.

Christy stared past Granny at the darkening sky and dancing pines. "Why don't we call off school early today?" she said to the class. "I don't want you to get caught in bad weather, and I know that some of you have a long walk ahead. Class is dismissed. I hope to see many of you at church here Sunday morning. Assuming, that is, that the weather doesn't cause us any trouble."

She was surprised to see the relief in her

students' eyes. Other days this week their departure had been filled with joyous laughter, dancing and running, and goodbye hugs. But today, the students filed past Christy in a quiet, anxious procession. A few gave halting goodbyes. Creed and his friend, Zacharias Holt, paused just long enough to examine the top of Christy's desk, then dashed off through the door at high speed.

"Mary, I ain't a-goin' to tell you again," Granny cried, almost frantically.

"I'm comin', Granny," Mary called. "I'm just gettin' Mountie's coat on for her."

Christy watched as Mary and Mountie made their way through the maze of desks toward the door. As usual, Mountie's hair was snarled, her face smudged. She wore a dress two sizes too big for her, and over that, a ragged coat with patched elbows and no buttons. She walked past Christy without expression. Her eyes were flat and dull. In her first week of teaching, Christy had never once seen Mountie smile or laugh.

"Mountie," Christy said gently.

The little girl paused. She did not turn.

"Mountie," Christy said again, touching the little girl's shoulder, "I just wanted to tell you how very lucky I feel to have you in my classroom. I hope we can be friends. I'd really like that."

Then Christy lifted her hand from Mountie's

shoulder, and the girl moved on. Her face showed no sign she'd registered Christy's words. How could a little girl so young and innocent seem so dead inside?

"Take care of that arm, Mary," Christy called as the two girls joined Granny.

Granny shook a finger at Christy. "Stay away from my girls, you hear? I'm a-warnin' you. I seen all I need to see. You're bad luck, you are."

With that, Granny yanked the two girls away. Christy watched Mountie's small bare feet padding across the snow. Big, feathery flakes were starting to fall.

"What is that old woman so afraid of?" Christy whispered. "I just want to help."

As if in answer, one of the hogs under the school let out a very uncivilized grunt.

"Another vote of support," Christy said. She smiled, but as she watched Mountie clasp Mary's hand and slowly disappear into the dark woods, her smile vanished.

High up in a swaying pine, the shiny, black raven stared down at Christy with a haunting glare.

❧ Three ❧

"And that's the end of it," Granny said firmly as she led Mary and Mountie into the O'Teales' tiny cabin.

The girls' mother, Swannie O'Teale, was poking at the fire. "End of what?" she asked. She held out her arms, and Mary and Mountie ran over to give her a hug.

Granny dropped into her rocker. The door swung open and Smith, Orter Ball, George, and Thomas dashed inside. Smith was carrying a snowball.

"Out with that," Swannie O'Teale said wearily.

Six-year-old Thomas ran to Granny's side. "Did ya tell Ma?" he asked excitedly.

"Tell me what?" Mrs. O'Teale asked.

"About the raven," Thomas said.

Smith tossed the snowball out the door. "Today a raven, big as you've ever seen, came a-flyin' straight into the school," Smith said, his voice low and spooky.

"Big as an eagle, it was," Orter Ball added.

George nodded. "Swooped around that room and went straight for that teacher like a huntin' dog sniffin' out a coon."

Mrs. O'Teale pulled Mountie into her lap. "Ravens is evil birds. Where'd it come from, do you 'spect?"

"Came out of nowheres," Smith said. He made a low moaning noise, like the wind outside. "Just like a witch-bird."

"Stop it, Smith, you're a-scarin' me," George whined.

"I 'spect it came in through the steeple up top," Mary said. "The preacher ain't finished it all up yet. I'll bet there's holes up there. Raven probably came in to get warm." She smiled at Granny. "Or like Teacher said, maybe he wanted some book learnin'."

Granny shook a finger at her. "This ain't nothin' for you to go makin' light of, girl. A raven's a bad omen. Outside a house is bad enough, but inside, like this 'un . . ." She shook her head. The fire danced in her eyes. "This flatlander's bringin' a heap of badness with her, I'll wager."

"Tell me the rest," Mrs. O'Teale urged. "What happened to the raven?"

"He done flew straight to that teacher's desk like he knowed right where he was a-goin',"

Smith said. "And then he locked a beady eye on her and let out three loud calls for all the world to hear."

"*CAW! CAW! CAW!*" Orter Ball and George piped up.

"And then Creed Allen opened up the door, and that bird flew out like he'd done what he set out to do," Smith finished.

A hush fell over the cabin. Outside, a branch cracked and tumbled, bouncing off the roof. The wind moaned and whistled. Mountie reached for Mary's hand and squeezed it.

"That mission school is the work of the devil!" Granny hissed. Her eyes were wide and filled with fear.

"Might be you're right, Granny," Mrs. O'Teale said, nodding.

"I told you no good would come of sending the children to those people. They ain't like us. And now you have the proof of it, plain as day. Tell her about your arm, Mary."

"Ain't nothin', Mama," Mary said quickly, but it was too late. Her mother had already noticed the ugly mark.

"Mary! Did that teacher—"

"No, Mama, no! Lundy Taylor done tripped me, is all. I fell down the slidin' hill and hit a tree."

"It's another sign," Granny said, her voice quavering. "That, and the tree a-fallin' on Bob Allen, and probably this storm to boot."

"Granny, it's January," Mary argued. "We have storms like this all the—"

"Don't go sassin' me," Granny said. "That raven went straight for that city-gal. And that's a sign she's cursed, sure as I'm a-sittin' here."

"I say she's a witch," Smith said.

"Smith don't like her cuz she told him not to talk out of turn," Mary said. "Teacher's not really bad, Mama, I promise you. She's got this way of talkin', so pretty it well-nigh sounds like music. And a red sweater so soft you'd a-swear it were made of sunrise clouds. And her eyes! There be something magic about them—"

"Black magic," Granny cried. "Already she's got you under her spell, girl." Granny got up from her rocker and went to Swannie O'Teale's side. "You mustn't send these children back to that mission school," Granny said. "No good will come of it. Wherever that teacher-gal goes, troubles will follow like the moon follows the sun. I'm a-warnin' you."

"But we wanted the children to have some book learnin'," Mrs. O'Teale said slowly. "I was hopin' they could learn Latin, all proper-like . . ."

"Look what happened to Bob and to Mary," Granny argued. "Could be worse, much worse, next time."

"I s'pose yer right."

"But Mama—" Mary cried. Her heart sank. She could already tell that her mother was going to give in to Granny's demand.

"No point argufyin' with Granny," said Mrs. O'Teale. She hesitated. "Course, I would like to get to church on Sundays still. Do you think that would be safe, Granny? After all, she were at church last Sunday and nothin' bad happened."

Granny stroked her chin. "Coulda been lucky that time. I'd advise against goin' back."

"On the Lord's day," Mrs. O'Teale said, "with the whole of the Cove there to ward off her curse? And no teachin' a-goin' on, just proper preachin'?"

"Well, I s'pose that might be safe," Granny gave in reluctantly. "If'n I brew us up some powerful herbs to ward off that gal's curse, we might just could go. I'd have to think on it a spell. A little garlic, a pinch o' dill to ward off the evil. A clover leaf, if'n I can find some dried. . . . If I put together a proper recipe, I 'spect we could go to church."

"Too bad for that," muttered Smith.

"Mind you, now," Granny warned, "you can't be a-lettin' her in on why you're wearin' my recipe. Gal with a curse on her that strong, she'll be able to work against all my medicine. So you'uns keep your mouth hushed when you're over to the church."

"So we don't have to go to that mission school no more?" Smith asked.

"Looks like not," said Mrs. O'Teale.

"Good thing," Smith said. "She was way too bossy for a gal-woman, if'n you ask me."

"Please, Mama—" Mary began.

"Hush now," Granny interrupted. "I need to figure on what herbs and such will ward off a curse that strong."

"Could you make it somethin' that don't smell too bad, Granny?" Orter Ball asked. "'Member that time we was afraid of catchin' sick and you done made us rub that lard mess on ourselves? Stank to high heaven, it did."

"You stop your fussin' and be thankful you got a granny who knows such things," Granny replied. She cast a warning look at Mary. "And not another word about that teacher-gal, you hear?"

Mary lay in her bed that night, listening to the wind howl and carry on. Creed Allen had been right when he'd told Teacher it was going to storm. Tree limbs heavy with snow cracked like lightning. The icy wind found every chance it could to sneak through holes and cracks.

Mary shivered beneath her thin blanket. Mountie lay beside her on a straw mattress on the floor. Three of their older brothers slept in the loft, a hole cut in the ceiling that led to a small space they reached by ladder. Their mama and papa slept in the far corner of the room.

Thomas, the youngest, slept near them. The oldest brother, Wilmer, who had fits, slept in a sort of half-bed, half-pen, in the corner. Granny, on account of her age, had the only bed off the floor, and it was just a straw mattress on some crates to keep her away from the cold floor.

It was not much of a cabin, Mary knew. Most of her friends at school had nicer ones. Cleaner, anyway. Once, when she'd gone to the Spencers' cabin to play with Zady, she'd seen a bunch of flowers in a bowl, just sitting right there on the eating table for no reason except to look pretty. Miz Spencer was like that, always laughing and singing and picking flowers.

Mary's mother never sang. She had saggy shoulders, as if she were carrying some awful load of rocks she could never put down. Sometimes Mary wondered why that was. It could be that Wilmer, who'd been simple-minded ever since he was born, made their mother extra tired. He was a heap of trouble and pain, drooling and muttering and running away when no one was looking.

Even though Wilmer barely knew who Mary was, she loved him just like she loved all her brothers. She even loved Smith, although he had a bit of a mean streak running through him. But Mary saved most of her love for Mountie, because her sister seemed to need it more than any of the others. Their mama and papa were too busy to pay much attention to the silent little girl, and Mary had always been the one to watch out for her. Granny loved Mountie as much as Mary did, but she had a hard time showing it.

Mary rubbed the bruise on her arm. Already it was the color of a ripe blueberry. Granny said it was Teacher's fault, but Mary didn't see how that could be. Lundy Taylor was always causing trouble. You couldn't expect Teacher to fix the whole world on her first week, now, could you?

But she hadn't said that to Granny. She loved her great-grandmother, but she was afraid of her, too. Granny had a hot temper, and a way of looking at the world that other folks didn't have. Some even said she had second sight and could see clear into the future. And it was true enough that Granny could see signs and portents where no one else could.

The wind let loose a powerful shriek. In the corner near the fire, Granny snored away. Mary thought again of the strange raven who had flown to Teacher's desk that afternoon. Remembering the bird's evil black eyes, Mary shuddered.

She nudged Mountie, who rolled over and smiled. "Mountie," Mary whispered, "do ya s'pose that raven comin' to Teacher's desk meant anything bad? Bad, the way Granny says, I mean?"

Mountie gazed at Mary thoughtfully. She hardly ever spoke. Once or twice Mary had heard her say a clear word, but mostly Mountie just communicated in grunts and nods. Still, Mary knew her sister understood everything. She could see it in Mountie's eyes.

"Some folks say ravens near a house is a bad omen," Mary continued. "So what do you s'pose a raven comin' right into school like that could mean? What if Granny's right, and it's a powerful bad sign?"

A head dropped down from the ceiling. It was Smith. "Can't you quit your jabberin'?" he demanded loudly. "Good thing cat's got Mountie's tongue for good, or I'd have to listen to two gal- folk carryin' on like a couple of crows. You ask me, that Teacher's trouble, and Granny's right about her."

"You just don't like her 'cause she makes you and Lundy Taylor mind," Mary said.

"You think that raven was some kind of accident?" Smith said.

"Could be."

"Naw. It was a sign for sure."

"Smith?" Mary whispered. "S'pose I wore Granny's herbs and kept a-goin' to school? You think Granny'd let me?"

"Ask her, why don't you?" Smith wadded up a piece of straw and tossed it at Granny's bed. The old woman stirred slightly, grunting. "Granny!" Smith said in a loud whisper.

"No, Smith!" Mary hissed. "Don't go wakin' her. You know how ornery she gets."

Granny's eyes fluttered open. "What in tarnation is your trouble, boy? Can't you see I'm a-tryin' to sleep? Not that it's easy, mind you, with that storm wallopin' the walls."

"Go ahead," Smith urged Mary. "Ask Granny."

Orter Ball and George stuck down their heads. "*CAW! CAW! CAW!*" they cried in unison.

"Next bird I hear, I'm a-shootin' for," warned Mr. O'Teale.

Granny yawned. "Ask me what, child?"

"S'posin' I wore your herb recipe and kept on a-goin' to school?" Mary asked softly. "Me and Mountie, we could sit way in the back, where nothin' bad could get to us—"

"A curse like that don't care what row you're a-sittin' in, girl," Granny said.

Mary gazed at her great-grandmother. Her eyes blazed with life. It was almost as if she were enjoying what was happening to Teacher, the way some people like to watch a storm unwind.

"Night, Granny," Mary said. With a sigh, she leaned back. "I guess that's all the book learnin' for you and me for a while, Mountie," she whispered.

Mountie didn't react. But much later, when everyone else was asleep, Mary wasn't surprised when, over the moaning of the endless wind, she heard her sister softly crying.

✒ Four ✒

I just don't understand it," Christy said at dinner Saturday night.

"Give them time, Christy," Miss Alice advised as she reached for a biscuit. "Rule number one here in the Cove—everything takes time."

"Sometimes centuries," joked David Grantland.

All the workers at the mission gathered in the main house for dinner each evening. Although Christy had only been there a few days, she was already beginning to feel at home. Miss Alice, of course, made that easy, and so did David, who had only been there a short time himself. David's sister, Ida, was more difficult—a crotchety, no-nonsense sort. And then there was Ruby Mae Morrison, who was staying at the mission temporarily because she was not getting along with her family. Ruby Mae seemed to have appointed herself as

Christy's official shadow. She followed Christy everywhere.

"But why would Granny O'Teale react that way to me?" Christy asked for what seemed like the millionth time. "I understand that she was upset about her great-granddaughter. And maybe she was right. I do need to find a better way to keep an eye on the children at all times."

"Sixty-seven children, Christy," David said. "Nobody can keep track of all of them every minute. Trust me, I know." David helped out with Bible and arithmetic classes in the afternoon.

"I wouldn't worry too much about Granny, Christy. Her reaction isn't unusual," Miss Alice said. "These mountain people are proud of their heritage, and stubborn, too. It's going to take them a while, maybe even a long while, to accept you. It's taken me years to be accepted."

"But she sounded so . . . so angry," Christy said. "As if she blamed me for Bob Allen's accident. She said she saw signs that I was cursed."

Ruby Mae dropped her fork. "Granny knows all about signs and such," she said nervously.

"Come on, Ruby Mae," David scoffed.

"No, I swear, it's true," Ruby Mae cried, pushing her long red hair out of her eyes.

"Give me one example," David challenged.

"How about the time Granny O'Teale was charming a wart off her finger, when along comes Mr. McHone. He laughs at her, and

Granny warns him, says, 'you'll be sorry for laughin'.' And sure enough, the next day, Mr. McHone's got a hundred warts growing on his finger in the exact same spot!" Ruby Mae shook her head. "She's powerful, Granny is. And smart, to boot."

"Powerful silly, is more like it," David said. "I—"

He was interrupted by a loud knock at the front door. Miss Ida went to answer it.

"Doctor MacNeill," she said, "come on in out of that cold. Would you like a bite to eat?"

The doctor, a big, handsome man with unkempt red hair and deep lines around his eyes, came inside. "Thanks, Miss Ida," he said, "but I've eaten already. I'm on my way home and just thought I'd do myself a favor and thaw out a bit, if you don't mind." He took off his gloves. "Strangest weather I've seen in a long while. Snow yesterday, hail today—" His eyes fell on Christy. "Well, if it isn't Florence Nightingale," he said, breaking into a broad grin. "Did Miss Huddleston tell you how she helped with Bob Allen's surgery?" he asked the rest of the group. "She turned the nicest shade of green you've ever seen." He winked at Christy.

She felt a blush rise in her cheeks. The doctor placed a hand on her shoulder. "Actually, she was a godsend," he said. "Don't know what I would have done without her."

"Granny O'Teale seems to think I'm the cause of Bob's accident," Christy said.

The doctor laughed as he pulled up a chair near Christy. "Don't take it to heart."

"That's what everyone keeps telling me," Christy muttered.

"So how goes the first official week as teacher?" the doctor asked.

Christy shrugged. "It's hard for me to say. There are so many children, and we need so many supplies. . . . I guess I'll find a way to handle it all."

"She's doing great," David said. "We're very proud of her."

Miss Ida cleared her throat loudly. "Well, I think I'll be getting these dirty dishes to the kitchen."

"Let me help, Miss Ida," Christy said, pushing back her chair.

"Oh, no, that's not necessary," Miss Ida said. She cast a glance from the doctor to her brother. "You've obviously got your hands full. Ruby Mae can help."

Ruby Mae grabbed a dish and followed Miss Ida. "Do you think Miz Christy's got two suitors already?" she asked loudly.

Christy covered her eyes. She needed to have a talk with Ruby Mae about learning to whisper. "Ruby Mae's very, uh . . . imaginative," she said.

"Quite a talker, that one," Miss Alice agreed, smiling at Christy's discomfort.

"Doctor MacNeill, I was wondering about

something—some*one*, actually," Christy said, anxious to change the subject. "Is there anything that can be done for Mountie O'Teale? She barely speaks, and when she does, it's so garbled she sounds like a frightened animal. It breaks my heart."

The doctor shook his head. "Swannie tells me she's been like that for years."

"Swannie?"

"Mountie's mother," Doctor MacNeill explained. "My guess is it's more emotional than physical, but I can't even be sure of that. As far as I know, Mountie won't communicate with anyone."

"She's been that way as long as I've been at the mission," Miss Alice said.

Ruby Mae returned for more dishes. "Maybe she's got a spell on her," she suggested.

"Ruby Mae!" Christy exclaimed.

"It happens!" Ruby Mae insisted. "I heard tell of a boy over in Cataleechie. He had a spell on him so's all he could do was mew like a kitten. Lasted two whole months. Even when that spell was took off him, he never did drink milk normal after that. Always had to lap it out of a bowl."

Christy smiled sadly. "I almost wish that there was such a thing as spells and that that was the cause of Mountie's problem, Ruby Mae," she said. "Then we could just look for a way to break the spell."

When the doctor, David, and Miss Alice had left for the evening, Christy went up to her room. Miss Alice had her own cabin, and David lived in a nearby bunkhouse. That left Christy, Miss Ida, and Ruby Mae in the main house, a white three-story frame building with a screened porch on each side. Compared to Christy's home back in Asheville, North Carolina, it was very plain. It had no telephone, no electricity, and only the barest of furnishings. She often missed the polished mahogany dining room table back home, the thick Oriental rugs, the lace curtains—not to mention the indoor plumbing.

Still, Christy was growing accustomed to her simple room at the mission. It was a stark contrast to the frills and pastels of her old bedroom—just a washstand with a white china pitcher and bowl, an old bed and a dresser with a cracked mirror, a couple of straight chairs, and two cotton rag rugs on the cold bare floor.

But this room offered something her old room could not—a view so breathtaking that each time she looked out her window at the haze-covered peaks of the Great Smoky Mountains, she felt a little closer to God. Mountain ranges folded one into the other, touching the clouds, a sight so peaceful and calming that already Christy had begun to think of it as *her* view, a source of hope and strength. Even tonight, with the wind whipping fiercely and the moon and stars hidden, she could see those peaks in her imagination with perfect clarity.

Christy reached into the top drawer of her dresser. Underneath a neatly folded, white blouse was her black leather-covered diary. She had brought it with her from Asheville, promising herself she would write down everything that happened to her at the mission—the good and the bad. This was, after all, the greatest adventure of her life, and she wanted to record every moment of it.

She'd had to argue long and hard to convince her parents that a nineteen-year-old girl should venture off to a remote mountain cove to teach. Christy had first heard about the mission and its desperate need for teachers at a church retreat last summer. Somehow, she had known in her heart that she was supposed to go teach in this mountain mission school. There was so much less here materially, but in many ways life in Cutter Gap was much richer than her old life in North Carolina, filled with tea parties and dress fittings and picnics.

Christy climbed onto her bed. Propping the diary on her knees, she uncapped her pen, tapping it thoughtfully against her chin. Where to begin? It had been two days since she'd written.

Saturday, January 20, 1912
My first week of school completed! Hooray!

I have put up with freezing temperatures, vicious bullies, and raccoons in desks, and still I've survived to tell the tale. Perhaps I will make a good teacher yet.

David and Miss Alice are encouraging but realistic. "You cannot change the world overnight," Miss Alice keeps saying.

I can't admit this yet, not to them, not to anyone. . . . It's even hard for me to write this down in my own private diary. But the truth is, I feel like such an outsider here. David seems to feel like an outsider, too. Even Miss Alice says it took her years to be accepted by the mountain people. But the littlest things make me feel I'll never really belong here.

I came to school my first day in my fancy leather shoes, only to see practically all the children barefoot in the January snow. When I talk, they still giggle and whisper. (David says this is because my "city accent" is as strange to their ears as their way of talking is to me.) And when someone like Ruby Mae Morrison (my very own personal shadow, it seems!) talks constantly about the strangest things, I sometimes wonder if we aren't from different worlds.

Ruby Mae's non-stop chattering has me seriously considering making cotton plugs for my ears. Miss Alice has a Quaker saying she often uses—"Such-and-such a person is meant to be my bundle." Well, like it or not, Ruby Mae is clearly going to be _my_ bundle.

175

Sometimes, I think I am beginning to make progress. Yesterday, Mary O'Teale and Ruby Mae and some others were telling each other "haunt tales" about an old witch, and when I tried to reassure them not to be frightened of the dark, I think I actually managed to reach them. Of course, that was easy for me to understand—I had the same fears as a child. (When I remember the ghost stories George and I used to tell each other, I still get the shivers!)

But later, when Lundy Taylor (another big problem) tripped little Mary and sent her falling down the icy mountain slide the boys had made, Mary's great-grandmother blamed me. It wasn't just that Mary had been hurt, it was something more—some deep fear and resentment for anyone not from the Cove. Try as I might, I'm certain that in a million years, Granny O'Teale will never like me.

Time. Maybe that's all it will take. I'll make friends with these people, I'll come to understand them, and maybe as I do, I'll come to understand my purpose in the world.

A loud knock at her door interrupted Christy. She slipped the diary under her pillow and capped her pen. "Yes?"

"It's me, Ruby Mae."

Christy sighed. "Just a second, Ruby Mae."

When Christy opened the door, Ruby Mae burst into the room as if it were her own. "I was thinkin' you might like some company."

"Actually, I was about to get ready for bed."

Ruby Mae examined her reflection in Christy's cracked mirror. "I think the preacher and the doctor, they both got a hankerin' for you, Miz Christy."

Christy laughed. "Ruby Mae Morrison," she said, "what am I going to do with you?"

"You never know," Ruby Mae said with a grin. She ran a hand through her snarled, shoulder-length red hair. Halfway down, she winced.

"How long has it been since you combed your hair, Ruby Mae?" Christy asked. "Or shouldn't I ask?"

"Factually, I lost my comb. Disremember when. Onliest comb ever I had, too."

"There are some bad tangles," Christy said. "Come, sit here on my bed." She retrieved her own comb from her dresser.

Ruby Mae plopped down on the bed. "I'll try not to holler when you hit them mouse-nests," she vowed.

Christy started, gently pulling the comb down.

"Ohoo-weeee!" Ruby Mae cried.

"Sorry."

"Don't matter. What do you aim to do when you get it all combed out?"

"How about nice long braids? Like Miss Alice's?"

"Be tickled to death with braids. But you'll have to learn me how."

"Braiding's easy. I'll teach you."

Braiding hair was not the only thing she would have to teach Ruby Mae, Christy thought as she tried to unravel the snarls. Ruby Mae's sole idea of cleanliness was to wash her face and hands a few times a week—never a full bath. It was not pleasant to be near her. And it wasn't just Ruby Mae—it was all the children. After the hair combing, maybe Christy would suggest a bath to Ruby Mae in the portable tin tub, and then make her a gift of a can of scented talcum powder.

"I'm going to have to yank a little, Ruby Mae," Christy said when she reached a particularly stubborn snarl. She pulled as gently as she could, but Ruby Mae leapt back against Christy's pillow, howling.

"I'm really sorry, Ruby Mae," Christy apologized.

"What's this?" Ruby Mae asked, pulling at the corner of the diary Christy had pushed beneath her pillow.

"Oh, that? Nothing. It's private," Christy said quickly.

Ruby Mae frowned. "I just mean," Christy continued, "it's a place where I write down things."

"What sorts o' things?"

"Feelings, dreams, hopes. What happened today. People I meet, places I go. Diary things."

"Am I in there?"

Christy smiled. "The special thing about a diary is that it's private."

"What's private?"

"Secret. Things you keep to yourself."

Even as she tried to explain, Christy recalled her visit to the Spencers' cabin—seven people, living in two tiny rooms and a sleeping loft. How could she expect these children to understand privacy? It was a luxury they couldn't afford.

Christy divided Ruby Mae's hair into strands and began to braid. When Christy was done, Ruby Mae gazed at her reflection in amazement. "Lordamercy, Miz Christy, you done worked a miracle!" she cried. "I look as purty as a picture, if I do say so myself."

Christy smiled. "You do indeed."

She watched as Ruby scampered off, talcum powder in hand, on her way to take a full bath.

Christy closed the door and pulled out her diary.

A small victory, just now with Ruby Mae. No more snarls!

Is this why I came all this way? To braid a tangle of red hair? To pass out scented powder?

Maybe so. Miss Alice says that if we let God, He can use even our annoyances (take Ruby Mae, for example) to bring us unexpected blessings.

Today, braids. Tomorrow, the world!

❧ Five ❧

On Sunday morning, the driving snow had turned to driving rain. Clouds hung low, sifting and churning like a dark sea. Thunder rattled the windowpanes.

As Christy, Miss Ida, and Ruby Mae crossed the yard to the church, Miss Ida tried to share her umbrella. But as they made their way across the plank walk David had installed, everyone was splattered by the icy rain. The combination of snow and rain had turned the yard into a sea of mud.

"If it's this hard for us to get here," Christy said as they crossed, "I wonder how everyone else will make it."

"Oh, they'll make it," Miss Ida assured her. "Don't forget that church is the great social event here in the Cove. Remember how full the pews were last week?"

When Christy entered the room that had served as her school all week, she was surprised to see that it was nearly as full as it had been last Sunday. She settled into the pew nearest the pulpit. As she watched children enter with their families, she waved and smiled whenever she recognized a familiar face. Oddly, only a few of them waved back. She caught plenty of stolen glances in her direction, not to mention whispers and pointing. She was surprised when she called out hello to Creed Allen, only to be greeted by a stiff half-smile and an uncomfortable nod.

Christy was relieved when she felt a friendly tap on her shoulder. "Howdy, Miz Christy!" Fairlight Spencer said.

Christy smiled at the woman who'd befriended her on her journey to the mission. From the beginning, Christy had sensed that she and Fairlight could someday be good friends. Seeing Fairlight's warm smile today made Christy certain of it.

"Fairlight!" Christy exclaimed. "It's good to see a friendly face."

"Oh, they'll warm up to you. Just give 'em time. My children can't stop talkin' about school. It's Miz Christy this, and Miz Christy that. John tells me you might be a-findin' him a new arithmetic book."

"He's got a real head for math," Christy said. "John's going to be a joy to teach." She held up a finger. "And speaking of teaching, I promised you we'd get together for some reading lessons."

"Oh, but you're just gettin' settled in," Fairlight protested.

"Tell you what. Give me a couple more weeks to get settled, and then we'll get started."

"I'd be mighty pleased," Fairlight said.

She nodded toward the back pew. "I gotta get myself a seat before the preacher starts."

Christy watched Fairlight settle behind her with her husband, Jeb. As Christy waved to Jeb, she again noticed the whispers and stares her presence seemed to be causing.

"Am I crazy?" she whispered to Ruby Mae. "I feel like everyone is staring at me."

"No'm." Ruby Mae glanced over her shoulder. "They's starin', all right. I reckon it's 'cause you're new and all."

"But they weren't acting like this last week," Christy said.

"It is strange," Miss Ida said. "They're usually a more rambunctious crowd than this." She wiped a drop of rain off her forehead. "Perhaps it's this odd weather."

"Well, once the service gets going, they'll probably relax," Christy said uneasily.

"The way they carry on during David's services is undignified, if you ask me," Miss Ida said, shaking her head. "Singing and clapping and bouncing. David does the best he can."

Christy smiled. It was true that the services

here in Cutter Gap were nothing like what she was used to at her church back home. Before long, the first hymn was in full swing, and the atmosphere in the church did seem to change. The people sang joyously, tapping their toes and clapping their hands. No one seemed to be staring at Christy any longer.

Thunder rumbled like a bass drum as they launched into a second hymn:

> It's the old ship of Zion, as she comes,
> It's the old ship of Zion, the old ship of
>   Zion,
> It's the old ship of Zion, as she comes.
> She'll be loaded with bright angels,
>   when she comes,
> She'll be loaded with bright angels . . .

Suddenly Christy felt an uneasy sensation. She turned her head slightly and instantly realized why. Three pews back sat Granny O'Teale. She was not singing. Her milky eyes were riveted on Christy. She was wearing an old black shawl, and around her neck was a crude necklace, tied with a string. Mountie sat beside her.

Christy tried to send a smile to the girl. Granny wrapped an arm around Mountie protectively.

Christy turned around, but as the hymn continued, she imagined Granny's gaze sizzling across the crowded room like lightning. Christy had seen something in those tired old eyes. If she didn't know better, she would have called it fear.

When at last it was time for David's sermon, Christy began to relax. It was silly to worry so much. Of course these people were staring at her. She was from someplace far away, and she was bringing new ideas to their children. Their curiosity was only natural. Perhaps they'd reacted to her this way last week, and she had just been too preoccupied to notice.

David was dressed in fine style, even though his congregation wore plain work clothes. He wore striped pants, a white shirt, and a dark tie. His black hair was carefully combed. He spoke in a deep, rich voice, measured and dignified.

"I plan to preach to you today on Mark 6, verses 30 through 46, the story of the Feeding of the Five Thousand. Although I must say that with this weather, maybe I ought to be talking about Noah and his ark—" The room filled with laughter.

"But before I begin, I want to introduce a welcomed addition to Cutter Gap, our new teacher at the mission school, Miss Christy Huddleston."

Christy felt a blush creep up her neck. David hadn't done this last week. Perhaps he'd understood how nervous she was about meeting so many new people. But making a point of introducing her today, with everyone acting so strangely, did not seem like a good idea, either—at least as far as Christy was concerned.

"Christy, why don't you stand and let the folks get a look at you?"

Christy sent David a pleading look, but he just grinned back mischievously. Reluctantly she stood, turning toward the suddenly hushed group.

"Look, Mama, it's Teacher!" Vella Holt cried out, waving.

Christy gave a nervous smile, then quickly dropped back down to the bench.

"I'm sure you'll all do your best to make Miss Huddleston feel welcome. She's a wonderful teacher and is going to be a real help to this cove—"

Just then, someone let out a scornful laugh. Christy had an uneasy feeling as she recognized the source.

She turned around to see Granny, grinning back defiantly.

Miss Ida laid a comforting hand on Christy's. "Don't pay them any mind," she whispered. "They just don't know any better."

Christy looked at the woman next to her in surprise. It was the first time Miss Ida had revealed such kindness. But before Christy could thank her, Miss Ida withdrew her hand and returned her attention to David.

"I'm certain," David continued, his voice

taking on a sterner note, "that you will all give Miss Huddleston a chance to prove what a wonderful teacher she is."

Jagged lightning lit up the sky, followed by an ear-splitting clap of thunder. Christy shifted uncomfortably in her seat. It was going to be a very, very long service.

— — —

"You can say I'm crazy all you want," Christy said to David as they finished up their pancakes at breakfast the next morning, "but I'm certain there was a lot of whispering and staring going on at church."

"Well," David sipped at his cup of coffee, "perhaps they were just entranced by your charms."

"Stop teasing," Christy said. "I'm serious, David. And you heard that snort of disapproval. It was Granny O'Teale, I've no doubt of it."

"Could have been one of the hogs," David pointed out. "Talk about your hog heaven. With all that mud, they were having a real party out there."

Christy laughed. "Well, I've got more important things to worry about today, like figuring out how to get more organized with the children's lessons. To begin with, I thought about dividing them into grades, instead of this boys-on-one-side-of-the-room, girls-on-the-other nonsense."

Ruby Mae looked up in alarm. "No'm, I can't sit by no boy!" she cried. "That ain't no courtin' school!"

"Of course it isn't," Christy said reasonably. "But it just makes sense to seat children of the same level together, whether they're boys or girls."

"Makes no sense a-tall!" Ruby Mae exclaimed.

David cast Christy a smile. "Seems you do have other things to worry about today," he said.

Miss Alice gazed out the window at the unceasing, icy rain. "Have you ever seen it rain so hard?" she asked. "I'll be surprised if all your students make it today, Christy."

"That might be just as well," Christy said, grinning. "I was feeling a little outnumbered last week!"

With a last sip of coffee, Christy gathered up her notebook and sweater and headed across the plank walk to the school house. Ruby Mae followed behind, carrying Miss Ida's umbrella. David had already lit a fire in the schoolroom stove, and the chill was gone from at least part of the room. Christy and Ruby Mae straightened school desks while they waited for the children to arrive.

By seven-fifty, Christy was beginning to worry.

Only about a third of her sixty-seven pupils had shown up. "Where is everybody?" she asked Creed Allen. "Do you think the weather's keeping them away?"

"Yes,'m," Creed said in an unusually soft, polite voice. "Could be the weather. Strangest thing I ever did see, snowing somethin' fierce, then rainin' like it ain't never goin to stop." He cocked an eye at Christy. "You ever seen such weather, Teacher?"

As Christy opened her mouth to answer, she noticed that all of her students were watching her expectantly. A strange quiet had fallen on the room. "Well, Creed," she said, "come to think of it, I can't say that I have." She leaned against her desk, smiling at her pupils. "I must say, this is the most well-behaved I've seen you since we started school. Is it just because there are fewer of you? Or is it the weather?" She paused. "Come on, somebody tell me. To what do I owe this wonderful behavior?"

Nobody answered. Creed studied his dirty thumbnail. Vella Holt twirled one of her pigtails nervously. Even Lundy Taylor, sitting sullenly in the back of the room, seemed subdued.

"Well," Christy said, "I guess I should just enjoy my good fortune." She reached for her attendance book. "Let's see. Who is missing today? I don't see any of the O'Teales or the McHones."

As Christy took the roll, she strolled up and down the rows of students, noting each empty desk. With every step, she sensed eyes following her, just the way she had in church. *This is odd*, she thought. The children hadn't acted this way last week. They'd been barely able to control their excitement. Why would they be treating her differently?

Stranger still was the odd aroma, bitter and pungent, that seemed to follow her as she walked. Smells were nothing new, of course. These were children who had never been exposed to the basics of hygiene. Already Christy had come to hate her too-sensitive nose. She had found some relief by carrying a handkerchief heavily soaked with perfume up her sleeve.

But this smell was something altogether different. It reminded Christy of the horrid-smelling medicine her mother had made her take as a child when she'd had the flu. It smelled of strange, bitter herbs, and even a touch of garlic.

Christy considered asking someone about the smell, then hesitated. After all, maybe one of the children had been given some kind of homemade medicine. She didn't want to embarrass anyone by drawing attention to the odor. Still, it was odd that no matter where she went in the room, the scent seemed to follow her.

The sky was darkening with each passing moment. Christy lit two kerosene lamps. As she set one on her desk, she said, "How about a song to chase away the gloom?" She knew the children loved to sing. Although they didn't know some standards like "America," they knew all kinds of ballads from their Scotch-Irish and German heritages.

"How about 'Sourwood Mountain'?" Christy suggested.

A few children nodded.

"When I asked you if you wanted to sing that last week, you were all practically jumping out of your seats!" Christy exclaimed. "What is wrong with—"

A deep growl of thunder interrupted her.

"Now, don't tell me a little thunder's bothering you," Christy chided. She touched Vella's shoulder and the little girl jumped. "I'm sorry, Vella, did I scare you?"

"No'm, I ain't scared," Vella said quickly. "I ain't scared of you 'cause I got my—"

"Hush up, big-mouth." Her sister, Becky, yanked on one of Vella's pigtails.

"What were you going to say, Vella?" Christy asked, kneeling down to the little girl's side.

"Nothin'. I ain't scared, that's all."

Christy frowned. She eyed Becky, but the older girl just stared straight ahead. Her hands were clasped together, as if she were praying.

"All right then," Christy said. "'Sourwood Mountain.' I'll start it up, but you know the words much better than I."

She went to the front of the room. The kerosene flame flickered, sending long shadows dancing up the walls.

"'I've got a gal in the Sourwood Mountain,'"

Christy sang. To her surprise, only a few half-hearted voices joined in.

Christy sighed, hands on her hips. "Is this the same class that was here last week?" she teased. "If I didn't know better, I'd say someone had put a spell on you."

Several of the students gasped. Creed's eyes went 'round. "Ain't no spell, Teacher," he blurted. "I promise we is us, just like always. Ain't no spell or nothin'!"

"All right, Creed, relax. It was just a joke—"

Just then, lightning as bright as the noon sun sent a blinding flash through the room. Christy heard something cracking, a sound like the slow splitting of wood. Rain pelted against the windows. Deafening thunder, like nothing she had ever heard, shook the sky, drowning out the cracking sound.

And then it happened. Christy heard it before she saw it—the eerie, musical sound of glass shattering as a tree limb lurched through one of the windows, reaching into the schoolroom like a huge hand.

Desks overturned, children screamed and ran, rain fell in torrents. Everywhere she looked, Christy saw mud and dirt and branches and glass and splinters of wood.

"It's just a branch," Christy called to the terrified children cowering near the door. "Lightning hit that old pine, is all. Is anyone cut? Anyone hurt at all?"

Some of the children were sobbing. A few hid behind desks. Christy ran from child to child, checking for glass cuts or scrapes. "Vella, are you all right?" she demanded.

The little girl could only manage a terrified sob.

"Creed?" Christy called.

"Yes'm," he answered in a squeak of a voice. "I ain't hurt none."

Christy climbed over the great wooden carcass in the middle of the room. The smell of pine needles and mud had replaced the strange odor that had filled the room only moments before.

"Well, it looks to me like we may just have to move school over to the mission house for the rest of the day," Christy said as she checked Ruby Mae for cuts. No one responded. The children just kept staring at Christy, dazed and sobbing, as if they were afraid to take their eyes off her for even a moment.

At last Christy felt certain that no one had been hurt. She was grateful to see that the children had been spared injury. But no matter how hard she tried, no matter what words she used, she could see the dark fear in their eyes as she tried to comfort them, and something told her it was not the storm that they feared.

❧ Six ❧

That lightning was a sign, I'm a-tellin' you, Swannie," Granny said Friday morning as she settled into her rocking chair on the O'Teales' front porch. "It's a good thing we ain't lettin' the young'uns near that city-gal." She reached out her hand and pulled Mountie into her lap, rocking quietly as she stroked the girl's hair.

Mary stood in the yard, listening to her great-grandmother talk. She tossed corn kernels to the chickens, who strutted about the yard as if they owned it. Ever since Granny had heard about the lightning strike at the mission school on Monday, she hadn't stopped talking about it.

It hadn't taken her long to hear, either. News had a way of traveling fast in Cutter Gap. Of course, by now, almost everybody had heard about the raven's visit to the mission school at the end of last week. They'd also heard about Granny's carefully-prepared mixture of herbs and roots. "Smells plumb fearsome," Creed Allen had whispered to Mary when his mother had stopped by the O'Teale cabin to get some of Granny's "curse-chaser," as Granny called it. She placed a spoonful of the smelly mixture on a little piece of rag, then tied it up with a string. It was to be worn around the neck under your clothes—all the time, if you could stand it.

Mary thought Creed was right—the mixture did smell horrible—but Granny knew her potions well. And for whatever reason, nobody who'd been around Miz Christy had been hurt yet. Fact was, the tree hit by lightning hadn't done much damage, other than scaring some of the children. That very afternoon the preacher had boarded up the broken window.

Mary tossed the last of the corn to Lucybelle, her favorite chicken. She gazed toward the path that led to the school and let out a long sigh.

"Look at that face," Granny chided. "You look like you lost your last friend."

"Granny," Mary asked slowly, choosing her words with care, "if'n the raven and the lightning were signs that Miz Christy's cursed, how's come none of us were hurt at church last Sunday or the Sunday afore that? She was right there in a pew a-sittin'."

"It's the Lord's house on Sunday, child."

"But the children who keep a-goin' to school, they're still all right. Creed said so on Wednesday."

Granny considered. "Well, most all of 'em is wearin' your granny's secret curse-chaser, for one thing. And for another, that don't mean bad things can't still happen. Those parents is takin' an awful risk, if'n you ask me."

"Creed said his mama figures he'll be safe if'n he wears your recipe. She wants real bad for him to learn Latin, 'cause that's a proper education. So she's lettin' him and the other children keep a-goin' to school."

Granny held out her hand. Mary squeezed it gently.

"You don't need no schoolin' anyways, Mary," Granny said. "You're already smart as a whip."

Mary thought of Teacher's magic blue eyes as she'd read them the 24th Psalm the first day of school. Her voice had been magic, too. She'd promised them she would teach them how to read words out of real books, and how to write the way she did on the blackboard, with letters full of loops and curves. She'd talked of faraway places they would learn about, places with funny names that twisted on your tongue.

And she'd told them wonderful stories that came straight out of her own head—made-up, but real as could be. Sometimes Mary told Mountie stories like that, late at night when they were too cold or too hungry to get to sleep. What a gift it would be to write them down all nice and proper on a chalkboard, or maybe even on a piece of paper Mary could keep forever and ever.

Mary pulled on her herb necklace. "Granny," she asked, "can I take this off'n me sometimes? It stinks somethin' terrible and it itches me, too."

"That's its power," Granny said firmly. "You leave that right around your pretty neck."

"But Teacher's nowhere near here."

"You leave it on, just in case. She weren't too near Bob Allen when that tree nearly killed him, now, was she? A bad curse can travel a long ways."

"What would happen if Teacher found out I was wearin' this thing?"

"She ain't a-goin' to find out, because you ain't a-goin' anywheres near that school." Granny gave a playful tug on Mary's hair. She'd been in a fine mood the last couple of days, Mary had noticed. "And ain't you just as glad? Didn't you miss your ol' Granny, sittin' in that school all day long?"

"Sure I missed you, Granny," Mary hesitated. "But just for the sake of askin', what would happen if she done found out?"

"Then the curse would take over," Granny explained. "It's the *secret* of the recipe that gives it all its power." She winked. "How about a smile for your poor ol' granny, now?"

Mary did her best. "I gotta go get some more kindling," she said. "Fire's gettin' low."

"Ain't no need to fuss." Granny wriggled her bare feet. "Gonna be a warm 'un for Jan'ry. Now that the rain's done stopped."

Mary's mother peered out the cabin door. "Queerest weather I ever did see."

"It's the brought-on teacher," Granny said.

As she headed for the edge of the woods, Mary considered her Granny's words. Here in the mountains, strange weather was hardly unusual. And lightning strikes—well, they were as common as ticks on a hound. The McHones' cabin had nearly burned down last summer after being struck by lightning.

Mary bent down to pick up a stick. Everything was far too wet to make good kindling. There was no point in looking. Granny was right, anyway. It was going to be a warm one today.

Granny was right a lot, Mary thought. She'd known Miz Spencer's last baby was going to be a boy. Of course, that could have just been good guessing. She knew that corn should go in the ground when the dogwood whitens, but then, a lot of folks knew that. She said you should never step to the ground with one shoe on and one shoe off, because for each step, you'd pay with a day of bad luck. But that was just common sense.

Granny had told Mary not to climb to the top of the hickory tree near Blossom Ridge or she'd fall and break into a thousand pieces, but Mary had anyway, and she'd had a fine view of the sun coming up, all rosy and full of itself. She'd told Mary not to bother telling Mountie stories, because Mountie couldn't understand them, but Mary told them, anyway. And she knew from the way Mountie smiled at her that she always understood every word.

It wasn't that Granny didn't love Mountie, of course. You could see she did, from the way she rocked Mountie to sleep at night. It was just that sometimes even Granny was wrong.

It was a hard thing to be thinking. It made Mary feel mixed-up inside. She didn't like that feeling, not at all.

"Mama?" Mary called. "I'm a-goin' down to the Spencers' to see Zady."

"Take Mountie," her mother called back. "Mary? You hear me?"

But Mary was already winding her way through the trees. She headed, fast as her feet could carry her, down a path that didn't go anywhere near the Spencers' cabin.

It went straight to the mission school.

～ ～ ～

"Twelve, thirteen, fourteen." Christy sighed. Fourteen students today. At this rate, she'd be down to zero soon.

"Has anyone talked to the O'Teale children?"

she asked. "Or the McHones or the Holcombes?" Even Lundy Taylor and Wraight Holt were gone today. As strange as it seemed, she was sorry to lose them. "With the weather better today, I'd hoped to see more of you."

Christy's gaze fell on Creed. The little boy's neck was flushed, and his eyes were oddly bright.

"Creed, are you feeling all right?"

"Yes'm," he said in the same flat voice he'd been using all week. "Just a little scratchy on my chest and neck is all."

"You might be coming down with something," Christy said. She reached over to feel his forehead. The boy flinched at her touch.

"You do feel a little warm. Are you sure you feel all right?"

"Yes'm."

"What's that string around your neck?"

"Just a—for decoration, Teacher."

Christy shook her head. She'd noticed that several of the other children were wearing pieces of string or yarn around their necks. There seemed to be something attached to the strings, but since the children wore the necklaces under their clothing, she couldn't tell for sure. Whatever the odd necklaces were, Christy had begun to suspect that they were the source of the bitter medicine smell wafting through the room. By now, she'd almost grown used to the odor.

Even Ruby Mae had taken to wearing one of

the necklaces. Yesterday at dinner, it had been hard to ignore. "What is that awful odor?" Miss Ida had demanded.

"I don't smell nothin'," Ruby Mae had said quickly.

"You'd have to be missing your nose not to smell it," David had said.

But Ruby Mae had just smiled innocently. When she'd left the table, David had whispered, "Probably just some mountain remedy. A lot of the children seem to be wearing those obnoxious things around their necks. Just think of it as another teaching challenge!"

Christy had laughed, but today, breathing in the horrible smell, she wondered how much longer she could stand it. Of course, at the rate her class was disappearing, she wouldn't have to tolerate the smell much longer.

The door opened and Christy turned to see Mary O'Teale, standing breathlessly in the doorway. Mary stared at all the empty seats, then smiled shyly at Christy.

"Mary!" Christy cried. "What a nice surprise! We've missed you. Come on in. As you can see, there's plenty of room."

"I missed you too, Teacher," Mary said, touching her neck self-consciously. She hesitated, then sat down on the girls' side of the room next to Ruby Mae.

"Were you unable to come because of the weather?" Christy asked hopefully.

"Weather. Yes'm," Mary said. Her cheeks were flushed and damp. "For certain that was part of it."

"And will Mountie and your brothers be coming today?"

Mary shifted uneasily in her seat, scratching hard at her upper chest. "I can't rightly say."

"Mary," Christy asked. "Are you all right? You look like you might be getting some kind of rash."

"Just some itchin' that needs scratchin' is all," Mary assured her.

Christy wondered again if the children were coming down with something. She knew that because the mountain people shared their drinking water and lacked the most basic hygiene, disease often spread like wildfire through the Cove. Typhoid, a particularly deadly disease, had hit the area many times. Christy wondered if she should have Doctor MacNeill take a look at the children. She'd seen him over at the mission house earlier today, talking to Miss Alice.

"It could be you're coming down with something contagious, Mary," Christy said.

"I reckon I don't know what you mean by 'contagious,'" Mary admitted.

"That means a sickness that other people can catch," Christy explained. "Creed looks a little under the weather, and so do some of the others, come to think of it. Do you mind if I check your neck, Mary?"

Mary clutched at the string around her neck. "Oh, no, Teacher," she cried. "I be fine, really I am."

Christy bent down. She could see a horrible, bumpy red rash making its way up the little girl's neck. "Mary," she said softly, "what *is* that necklace you're wearing? I notice a lot of the children have them."

"Ain't nothin' special," Mary said, looking away.

Christy sighed. She was getting nowhere fast. Her class smelled like a medicine factory. Several of her students were growing peculiar rashes. Most of them were wearing strange necklaces they refused to discuss. school at all.

Christy had talked to Miss Alice and David about the diminishing student population. They were as mystified as she was, but both had reassured Christy that it was only a matter of time before the mountain people began to accept her. She just wasn't sure she could wait that long.

"I am going to ask you this just once," Christy said, in her no-nonsense teacher tone. "Someone has to tell me the truth. John? Creed? Mary? Ruby Mae?"

Ruby Mae leaned over and whispered something to Mary.

Mary whispered back. Both girls locked their eyes on Christy.

"Ruby Mae?

"Yes'm?"

"Is there anything you want to tell me?"

Ruby Mae twisted a strand of red hair around her finger. "No, Miz Christy, I reckon there ain't nothin' I *want* to tell you."

"But you're usually such a chatterbox."

"Yes'm, it's true. My mouth don't open just for feedin' baby birds," Ruby Mae agreed. "And I don't mean to be ornery, but I reckon there's not a solitary thing I want to be tellin' you right now."

"Fine," Christy said, struggling to rein in her anger. "At the noon recess, I'm going to have Doctor MacNeill and Miss Alice take a look at those odd rashes." She opened her tattered history book. "In the meantime, why don't I read you the story about George Washington and the cherry tree? Do you all know who George Washington was?"

Creed raised his hand.

"Yes, Creed?"

"I reckon he was Pa of the whole U-nited States."

"Father of our country. Very good, Creed. And one of the things he's most famous for is saying he could not tell a lie."

She studied the anxious faces of her audience. "Perhaps that's a lesson you could all learn from."

"I'm a-tellin you, these rashes is part o' the curse," Creed whispered in hushed tones behind the school during the noon recess. "I thought I'd be safe comin', what with Granny O'Teale's herbs and such." He kicked at a pebble with his bare foot. "Truth is, I kinda *like* comin' to school. And Teacher seems so all-fired nice and everything, even if'n she *is* a flatlander and talks right peculiar. But now—" he scratched frantically at his upper chest, "*now* I ain't so sure I'm ever comin' back. I itch somethin' fierce."

Ruby Mae leaned against the building, careful to avoid a brown tobacco stain. "I don't know what to think anymore. These rashes is plumb unnatural. Factually speakin', it makes me mighty nervous to be sharin' the same roof with someone who might just have a curse a-hangin' over her."

"Could be Teacher's found out about Granny's magic recipe," Creed suggested, eyes wide with fear. "Do you s'pose she's fightin' back with spells of her own?"

"Swear to Josh-way," Mary said, "I've had rashes like this before from Granny's potions. One time—" she lowered her voice, "she got to fussin' 'cause Smith saw a pure black skunk. Not a stripe on that animal anywheres. Granny said it was an omen. Said we was all a-goin' to come down with the typhoid. So she made up this mixture, with lard and bear grease and who knows what all-else in it. Smelled to high heaven, it did. She made us smear it all over ourselves for three days solid. Thought I'd like to die from the stink of it."

"So what happened?" Ruby Mae asked.

"Well, we'uns broke out with boils all over. You talk about itchin'? I tell you, I cried somethin' awful, it itched so bad. Worse than this, even," Mary said, pointing to her chest. "Course," she added, to be fair, "we never *did* come down with the typhoid, so maybe there was somethin' to Granny's potion, after all." She sighed. "I feel all switched-up inside, like there's two whole Mary's in there, argufyin' over whether to trust Teacher or not."

"I might just have a way to figure out the truth of things," Ruby Mae said. "You two can come if'n you want, but you gotta be quiet as mice."

"Will it tell us if'n Granny's wrong?" Mary asked.

"Could be. We're a-goin' to sneak into Miz Christy's room and find out the truth."

Mary nodded. "Let's do it, quick-like," she said. "I have to know if I'm right about Teacher, one way or the other."

❧ Seven ❧

"Miss Ida, have you seen Miss Alice?" Christy asked as she stepped inside the mission house.

Miss Ida looked up from the pie crust she was rolling out in careful, even strokes.

"I thought you were upstairs," she said, her brow knitted. "Didn't I just hear you—" She shrugged. "I must be imagining things. Miss Alice is in her cabin, I believe. She's meeting with Doctor MacNeill."

"Doctor MacNeill's still here?" Christy said. "That's wonderful. I need to have him look over some of the children." She hesitated. "Actually, I was wondering if I could recruit you for a minute or two. . . ."

"Me?" Miss Ida demanded. "I don't know the first thing about teaching!"

"I just need you to keep an eye on things while I go get Miss Alice and the doctor,"

Christy explained. "There aren't that many children to watch, actually."

Miss Ida sighed. "I'm right in the middle of an apple pie."

"Tell you what," Christy said. "I'll do all the cleaning up around here for the next couple of days, if you can just spare me ten minutes."

"No need," Miss Ida said, wiping her hands on her apron. "My work is never done around here, anyway. What would you all do without me, I wonder?"

"So do I," Christy said with a grateful smile.

As she headed across the main room toward the front door, Christy thought she heard whispering from the stairwell. She paused, listening. Nothing. But as soon as she started walking again, she was almost certain she heard a muffled giggle coming from the second story.

Christy crept up the stairs, careful to avoid the one near the top that squeaked. Her bedroom door was half-closed. She could hear the shuffle of feet, then whispering.

"Ruby Mae?" Christy asked, pushing the door open.

Someone screeched. Christy entered the room to see Ruby Mae standing near the bed, hands clasped behind her back. Mary O'Teale and Creed Allen were sitting at the foot of the bed.

"What on earth are you three doing in here?" Christy cried.

"We . . . uh, we was just a-lookin' for—" Mary's voice trailed off.

"For somethin'," Creed volunteered.

"That much is obvious," Christy said. She took a step forward and Ruby Mae instantly took a step back, tumbling onto the bed. "What's that behind your back, Ruby Mae?" Christy asked.

"Behind my back?" Ruby Mae repeated in a shrill voice not at all like her own. "Behind my back? Well, like as not, I 'spect that would be my fanny." She offered Christy a weak smile.

"Very funny, Ruby Mae." Christy put her hands on her hips. "You three do understand that this is my room, and that you do not just go poking around other people's property without their permission?"

All three slowly nodded.

Christy reached for Ruby Mae's arm. "Come on, Ruby Mae," she said gently, "hand it over."

"No!" Creed cried suddenly, leaping off the bed. "Don't hurt her, Teacher!"

"Creed, of course I wouldn't—"

Ruby Mae's face was white as she reached out a trembling hand. She was holding a black leather book.

"My diary?" Christy gasped. "You were reading my diary?"

"We was just tryin' to find out if you—" Ruby Mae seemed to lose her voice.

"If I what?" Christy pressed.

Ruby Mae looked at Creed. Creed looked at

Mary. Their faces were pale, their foreheads beaded with sweat.

Christy approached Mary. The little girl was trembling, but when Christy knelt beside her, Mary managed a small smile.

"If I what, Mary?" Christy asked in a whisper. She held out her hand and Mary reached for it. Her fingers were like tiny icicles.

"You know, Mary," Christy said, "I miss seeing Mountie. I miss all the children, of course, but I've especially missed seeing you two. When you came back today, I was so happy that I said a little prayer of thanks. Do you think Mountie misses me?"

Mary gave a tiny nod.

"And have you missed me, too?"

She answered with another nod.

"Whatever you tell me, Mary, you can trust me. I won't let any harm come to you. I'm your friend. I came here to help you. Do you believe me?"

Mary thought for a minute, her small mouth working. At last, she nodded again.

"Then you can tell me, Mary. What are you afraid of?"

"Don't, Mary!" Creed cried. "If'n you tell her, then the secret recipe won't work no more."

Mary bit her lip. She looked into Christy's eyes, as if she thought she could find something she needed there.

"Granny . . ."

"Yes?"

"Granny says . . ." Mary cleared her throat.

"Granny says what?" Christy encouraged.

"She says you're cursed," Mary blurted. "She says you brought bad things to Cutter Gap, and that we'uns shouldn't go to school no more!"

Christy blinked. So that was it. That explained the missing children. That explained the look of fear on the faces of the few students who still dared to come to school.

She pulled Mary close and gave her a hug. The bitter smell of herbs made her eyes burn. Gently Christy pulled on the yarn necklace around Mary's neck. At the bottom was a small piece of old cloth, filled with what felt like dried bits of plants.

"Did Granny make this necklace for you?" Christy asked.

"Yes'm."

"Why?"

"It's a curse-chaser. To ward off your bad spell and keep us safe."

Christy frowned at the awful rash on the little girl's neck. "Well, I'm not so sure she's accomplishing that." She looked over at Creed. "Are you wearing one, too?"

Creed nodded. "Most all of us are, Teacher. Ma said the only way she'd let me go to school was if'n I wore this and kept my distance. Course some parents just flat-out said no." He cocked his head at her, a confused look on his face.

"What's wrong?"

"Well, I figured you'd be sore as a skinned owl when Mary done told you. You ain't a-goin' to put a spell on us, is you?"

"Creed, of course not. That's nonsense." Christy could barely control the anger in her voice. "I don't understand how you children could believe such a silly notion—" She stopped herself.

It wasn't the children who deserved her anger. It was Granny O'Teale and the other adults who'd allowed such superstitious foolishness to fill the heads of these poor children.

"Thank you, Mary," Christy said gently, "for telling the truth."

"You won't tell on me to Granny, will you?" Mary asked in a quavering voice. "I weren't even supposed to be here."

"Of course not." Christy smiled. "Creed and Mary, I want you to come with me. Doctor MacNeill needs to take a look at those rashes."

As Christy started for the door, Ruby Mae rushed past, nearly knocking her aside.

"What's wrong, Ruby Mae?" Christy asked. "It's going to be all right. I'm not mad."

Ruby Mae paused in the doorway, glaring.

"Come on," Christy said. "You've hardly spoken a word."

"Reckon I ain't got nothin' to say," Ruby Mae muttered.

"Reckon that's the way you like it, anyways."

With that, she turned on her heel and ran down the stairs.

— ❦ —

"You won't believe what I'm about to tell you!" Christy cried as soon as Miss Alice opened the door to her cabin. Christy stomped inside, motioning for Creed and Mary to follow.

"Relax, Christy," Miss Alice urged. "I can see you're very upset."

"It's just that—well, do you have any idea what people in the Cove are saying about me?"

Doctor MacNeill was sitting in a rocker. "Hmm, let me see. That you're the finest teacher they've ever seen in these parts?"

Christy paced back and forth on the polished wooden floor, practically choking on her anger. "They—"

"Let me try again," the doctor interrupted with a grim smile. "They're saying you're cursed and that the only way to go near you is with a handful of foul-smelling herbs?"

Christy stopped in mid-stride. "You're telling me you *knew*?"

"Relax, Miss Huddleston," the doctor said. He paused to take a long puff on his pipe. "I only just heard myself." He nodded to Miss Alice.

"I stopped by the McHones' yesterday evening to check on that broken arm of Isaak's," Miss

212

Alice explained. "That's when I first got wind of Granny O'Teale's theory about you."

"Theory!" Christy practically spat out the word. "Look at that rash on Mary, Doctor. Creed has one, too. I think it's from Granny's herb concoction. I'll bet half the population of the Cove is breaking out!"

The doctor called Creed over and examined the little boy's rash. "How long have you had this, Creed?"

"I disremember exactly. Last couple days for sure."

"How about you, Mary?" Miss Alice asked gently.

"It don't bother me none, Miss Alice," Mary said. She took a nervous step backward. "You ain't a-goin' to tell Granny I told on her, are you?"

"Are you afraid she'll hurt you, Mary?" Christy asked.

"No'm. Mostly I'm afraid she'd be a-thinkin' I didn't believe."

"Believe?" Christy echoed.

"In her powers. Her second sight and such."

"Your secret is safe with us, Mary," the doctor assured the little girl.

"Why don't you two run on out to the schoolyard?" Miss Alice suggested. "The doctor and I will be by with some medicine to make that itching stop."

As soon as Miss Alice opened the door, Creed

ran outside. But Mary paused in the doorway. "Teacher?" she said softly.

"Yes, Mary?"

"I'm purty sure that Mountie misses you, too. She can't exactly say it just so, but I can tell."

Christy nodded. "Thank you, Mary."

Miss Alice closed the door and Christy sank into a chair. "Where on earth did that old woman come up with such a notion?" she demanded.

"Superstitions grow like weeds around these parts," the doctor said. Carefully he placed some fresh tobacco in the bowl of his pipe. "You've still got a lot to learn about the mountain people. Granny is known in the Cove as a fine herbalist. Some of her knowledge is sound enough, and some of it is nonsense. But her word is still gospel."

"But what made her turn on me? Why me?"

Miss Alice touched Christy's shoulder. "There's no use looking for a logical reason, Christy. Perhaps it was Bob's accident, or Mary's fall. Perhaps Granny just feels threatened by all the changes going on here in the Cove."

Christy jumped from her chair. "I need to reason with her. Maybe I can explain to her why she has nothing to fear from me."

The doctor laughed. "No use trying to use logic with someone like Granny. You can't fight mountain superstition. Remember right before Bob Allen's operation? His wife ran into the cabin where we were operating and swung an axe into the floor. Then she tied a string around Bob's wrist."

Christy nodded. She remembered all too well.

"Well, I could have argued with his wife till spring, telling her that a string won't keep disease away, and an axe won't keep a person from hemorrhaging. But meantime, Bob would have died." The doctor shook his pipe at Christy. "And if you try to argue these people out of their superstitions about you, your dreams for the school will die, too."

"But if I don't fight back somehow, there won't *be* a school," Christy cried. "I've lost most of my students already, Doctor. Pretty soon I'll be teaching a roomful of empty desks!"

Miss Alice added a log to the fire. "Christy," she said, rising, "our job here at the mission is to demonstrate that there's a better way than fear and superstition. We want to create an atmosphere where hearts can be changed. If we preach to the hearts of men and women, the fruits will follow. But it's no good tying apples onto a tree. Soon they'll be rotting apples."

Christy clenched her fists angrily. "But that could take forever, Miss Alice! The doctor's been here for years, and the mountain people still don't understand even the most basic principals of hygiene."

The doctor stiffened. "And you, Miss Huddleston, have been here two weeks, and

215

you think you can change the world?" He gave a dark laugh. "I wish you luck."

"Time," Miss Alice said, "is a great healer, Christy. Give Granny and the others time. They will come to trust you."

Christy took a deep breath. Maybe Miss Alice and the doctor were right. Or maybe they were just tired of fighting back. And in any case, *they* weren't "cursed." She was.

"Miss Alice," Christy said firmly, "I understand what you're saying, but I have to try to save my reputation. I'm going to the O'Teales'. I'll ask David to watch the class for the rest of the day."

"Miss Huddleston, I wouldn't—" the doctor began, but Christy shot him a determined look, and he held up his hands.

"Will you give me directions to the O'Teales' cabin?" Christy asked. "If not, I'll ask Mary to tell me the way."

"Of course I will," said Miss Alice. "I'd advise against this, but if you insist on going, I want you to remember one thing. For all her ignorance and superstitions, there's a good heart inside Granny O'Teale. There's a good heart inside all God's children. Look hard enough and you will find it."

"I've just one question," said Doctor MacNeill. "What are you going to say when you get there?"

Christy headed for the door. "Good question, Doctor. Guess I'll figure that out on the way."

❧ Eight ❧

As Christy trudged along the muddy path, she took in deep lungfuls of the mountain air, trying to let go of her anger. Again and again, Mary's fearful face came back to her. She thought of the way Creed had cringed at her touch, the way Vella had jumped when Christy touched her shoulder, the way Ruby Mae had glared at her so coldly.

Granny had done this. Granny O'Teale had, in the space of a few short days, managed to undo Christy's first halting attempts at befriending these children. And how? By playing on their fears and superstitions and ignorance.

Suddenly, just ahead of her down the path, Christy saw some dark blobs scattered over the snow for several yards. As she got closer, she realized the blobs were blood stains and bits of torn fur—some black, some reddish brown.

She gasped. Some poor little rabbit had been caught by another animal and torn to bits.

Quickly Christy carved a wide path around the dead animal's remains. She wished her mind were a blackboard, so she could wipe away what she had just seen. Why did nature have to be so vicious?

Why, she wondered, did *people* have to be so vicious?

The O'Teales' tobacco barn was just up ahead, so she knew their cabin wasn't far. Soon it came into view beyond a stand of pines. In the yard, the trampled-down, muddy snow was littered with rags and papers and junk. Pigs and chickens wandered at will. A big black pot was turned on its side, rusting. No effort had been made to stack the firewood. The logs lay in disarray where they had been tossed.

Christy paused at the edge of the yard. Suddenly she realized that the debris was even worse than it had looked from a distance. The yard was covered with filth—both human and animal filth. The chickens were pecking at it. The pigs were rolling in it and grunting. Christy lifted her skirts, picking her way across the yard. Wasn't there an outhouse in the backyard? Weren't they teaching the children anything?

Swannie O'Teale appeared on the crude porch. She was a tall, slender woman with stringy, dirty-looking blond hair. Her eyes looked dull and tired and sad. But there was something else there, too. Fear—that was it. It was the same look Christy had seen in her students' eyes.

"Mrs. O'Teale," Christy called. "I'm Christy Huddleston, the new teacher."

"I know who you are," Swannie O'Teale hissed. "And if you know what's good for you, you'll get. Granny's out gatherin' bark for her potions, and if'n she sees you . . ."

"I don't want to hurt you, Mrs. O'Teale. I want to help. You've got to trust me."

"Can't trust the likes of you. You be cursed. Granny said so," Mrs. O'Teale said, backing into the open doorway. "Get now." She clutched the yarn necklace around her neck. "Get now, I'm a-tellin' you!"

Christy took another step. Even from several feet away, the stench coming from the cabin was horrible. A low half-growl, half-screech met her ears. In the dim light beyond the door, she could make out a boy in his teens wearing a tattered sweater. Saliva drooled from the corners of his mouth and trickled through the grime on his chin.

"Ah . . . hello," Christy said.

"That be Wilmer, my first-born."

Christy remembered hearing that one of the O'Teale children was retarded and had epileptic seizures, or "fits," as the mountain people called them.

The boy pointed to a tin plate of cornbread on a table. "Unh-Um-humh. Ah-hmm."

"Hungry, Wilmer?" Mrs. O'Teale said wearily. "Don't go squawking."

What must it be like, to have to care for Wilmer and the other children in these awful surroundings? Christy wondered. Such poverty. Such misery. Staring into Mrs. O'Teale's weary, fearful eyes, Christy felt her anger drain away.

"Mrs. O'Teale," Christy said. "Where are the other children?"

"Out with Granny, 'cept for Smith. He's helpin' his daddy. And Mary, she done run off over to the Spencers' this mornin'. That girl can be a heap of trouble—" She caught herself. "I can't be a-talkin' to the likes of you."

"Mary's a sweet girl," Christy offered. "And the boys—"

Mrs. O'Teale scoffed. "Smith! You're plumb crazy if'n you think he's a sweet'un!"

"Well, he does get a little rambunctious," Christy conceded. She had the feeling that if she just kept talking about the children, she might get somewhere with Mrs. O'Teale. Despite her warnings to Christy, the woman seemed anxious to talk. "But I think more rowdy when he and Lundy Taylor get together. They sort of provoke each other."

"Those boys stick together like sap and bark," Mrs. O'Teale said. "I don't know how you manage with all those young'uns in one place."

"It must be hard for you, too," Christy said, glancing over Mrs. O'Teale's shoulder at Wilmer.

"Naw." Mrs. O'Teale considered. She seemed to be losing her fear. "Not too bad. I got Granny here to help me."

"And does she help?"

"Lord-amercy, yes! Loves these children more'n I do, I sometimes think. She's especially partial to the girls." She winked. "Though she won't let 'em know it, mind you. Don't want 'em gettin' all high and mighty with the boys. But many's the night I seen her watchin' Mary and Mountie when they're a-dreamin'—" She paused, straightening her faded calico skirt. "I . . . I shouldn't be lettin' my mouth run on like this." She lowered her voice. "I know you mean well, Miz Huddleston, and maybe you ain't cursed and maybe you is. But it'd be best if you get goin' right quick."

She couldn't go, not now. Christy could sense that she was making progress. If she could just win over Mrs. O'Teale, maybe Granny would follow.

"Mrs. O'Teale, do you think I could step inside for just a moment to sit? I'm not used to walking such long distances, and I could use a rest before I head back to the mission."

"I just don't rightly think—"

"A minute, that's all," Christy said, practically pushing her way inside.

"You're buyin' yourself one passel o' trouble," Mrs. O'Teale said, still holding her necklace. She watched warily as Christy sat down on one of the two chairs in the room. "Granny'll give you more trouble than ever you saw in all your born days."

"See?" Christy smiled, trying hard not to stare at the horrible filth or breathe in the stench. "Nothing's happened. No one's hurt. Mrs. O'Teale, there's been a terrible misunderstanding. I didn't come here to hurt your children. I want to help. I know what Granny's said about me being cursed, but that's not true."

A loud noise filled the room. Christy jumped. Wilmer had dropped his tin plate. He pointed to it and laughed as it rolled across the floor. Saliva poured down his chin. Christy looked away, then felt ashamed for her reaction.

"You're wrong about Granny," Mrs. O'Teale said. "She's got the second sight. Sees signs and portents where you and me just sees clouds or rain or embers in the fire. She's a wise 'un, Granny is. Knows things you and I plumb can't."

"I'm sure she does. But I wish she could give me another chance. Maybe I know one or two things, too. Maybe together we could help the children. I've been thinking about Mountie. If I worked with her, took some extra time, we might be able to help her speak."

A glimmer of hope sparked the woman's tired brown eyes, then faded. "You had me a-goin' there for a minute. But all the book-learnin' in the world ain't a-goin' to fix my Mountie."

"It wouldn't hurt to try, would it?"

Mrs. O'Teale started to answer, but suddenly her mouth dropped open. There, in the doorway, stood Granny O'Teale, flanked by Mountie, Orter Ball, George, and Thomas. The old woman pointed a shaking finger at Christy, her eyes flaring.

"Out!" she cried. "Out of here, or there'll be the devil to pay, you hear?"

"Granny," Mrs. O'Teale began, "she ain't hurt nobody—"

"What were ye thinkin', Swannie?" Granny demanded. "You gone as simple-minded as Wilmer? That girl has a curse on her as black as midnight."

Christy stood. When she reached the doorway, Granny and the children backed away. "Granny," Christy said, trying to keep her voice from revealing the anger she felt, "I came here to make peace with you, to show you that there's nothing to be afraid of." She stepped onto the porch.

Granny stood her ground a few feet away. Mountie clung to her hand, but the other children backed away into the filthy yard.

"I ain't afraid of you," Granny said. "I'm just protectin' what's mine."

"I don't want to harm the children," Christy persisted. "I came here to the Cove to help. To teach. Learning to read and write can't hurt Mountie or Mary or Smith or the others."

"It ain't the learning and such. It's you. You're the one hurt Bob Allen and little Mary. You're the one made the lightning hit."

"Those were accidents, that's all. I can't control the weather."

Granny's eyes narrowed to slits. "How do you explain the raven, then? Surest sign of a curse I heard of in all my days."

Christy glanced back at Mrs. O'Teale. She was standing in the doorway, her face blank. Behind her, Wilmer grunted and drooled. Near Christy's feet, a chicken pecked at what looked like human waste.

Suddenly a feeling of overwhelming weariness filled Christy, weighing her down like a great, impossible burden. What was she thinking, standing here in filth and horrible poverty, trying to reason with a frightened old woman? Miss Alice and the doctor had been right. Christy couldn't change generations' worth of ignorance with a few well-chosen words. She'd been a fool to think she had that kind of power. She'd been a fool to think she could leave her comfortable life in Asheville and make a difference here. What did she, Christy Huddleston, have to offer these desperate, unhappy people?

"I just wanted to help, Granny," Christy whispered. Tears came to her eyes, and she wiped them away with the back of her hand.

"Don't need no help from some city-gal with a curse on her head," Granny said, but her voice had softened just a touch, as if she sensed that she'd finally won.

"I wish I understood what you're so afraid of," Christy said. She knelt down beside Mountie. Granny tugged on the girl's arm, but Mountie didn't budge, and at last Granny gave in.

"Mountie, I just want you to know how much I'll miss you," Christy said. The little girl stared at her, eyes wide and unblinking. Christy reached over and gently pulled Mountie's shabby coat closed. "You take care of yourself, you hear?" She stood and smiled at the other children. "I'll miss all of you," she said.

Granny tightened her grip on Mountie, pulling her close. Miss Alice had said there was good in Granny's heart, good in all of God's children. But perhaps Miss Alice could see what others couldn't. When Christy looked at Granny, all she saw was fear and ignorance and hate.

"All right," Christy said. "All right, Granny. You win."

She ran across the yard to the path. Her long skirt tore on a holly bush, but she didn't stop running until the O'Teale cabin had vanished from sight. She made a wide detour around the dead rabbit.

Halfway to the mission house, Christy heard someone approaching. It was Mary O'Teale, heading home. Christy hid behind a tree until the little girl had passed.

She had failed Mary, failed all her children. She didn't want to have to face her—not now, not ever again.

❧ Nine ❧

At the mission house, Christy dashed up the stairs directly to her bedroom. There she changed all her clothes and brushed her long hair by a wide open window so that the clean mountain air could pour through it. She washed her face, first in warm water, then in cold, scrubbing her hands over and over. But try as she might, she could not scrub out the memory of what she had seen at the O'Teales' cabin.

Miss Alice, David, Ruby Mae, and Miss Ida were at the dinner table by the time Christy made it downstairs. She felt woozy, but she forced a smile as she sat next to Ruby Mae.

Miss Ida passed plates of salmon croquettes and hash-browned potatoes. She was a fine cook, and normally Christy would have enjoyed the food. But tonight her stomach was churning.

"I hear you went to the O'Teales'. How did your visit go?" David asked.

Christy reached for her fork and stabbed half-heartedly at the salmon. "Let's just say that Miss Alice and Doctor MacNeill were right. It was a waste of time."

"I'm sorry it wasn't what you'd hoped for," Miss Alice said gently.

"Not what I'd hoped—" Christy choked on the words, then caught herself. Her head was spinning. "I'd rather not talk about it."

"I understand," Miss Alice said.

Silence fell over the table. A sullen Ruby Mae stared at her plate.

"Aren't you going to eat, Ruby Mae?" Miss Ida chided. "I can always count on you to take seconds, goodness knows."

"I don't want to be no bundle," Ruby Mae muttered. She glared at Christy, then down at her plate.

"What are you talking about, dear?" Miss Alice asked.

"Don't pay me no mind. I just talk for the sake o' talkin'."

Miss Ida cleared her throat. "I've forgotten my cooked apples," she said, rushing off to the kitchen. A moment later she returned with a steaming bowl. "Here, David," she said. "Your favorite. Lots of cinnamon."

"Well," said Miss Alice, "I'm happy to report that the doctor says Granny's herb concoction is indeed the cause of those mysterious rashes. He treated all the children who were affected. I believe David and I managed to convince them that if they insist on carrying her herb mixture around, they need to put it in a pocket and keep it away from their skin."

"I done tied mine around my waist, see?" Ruby Mae said to Christy, eyeing her angrily.

"She doesn't need to see it. She can *smell* it," David said. He took a sip of milk. "Don't you understand what nonsense all that superstitious stuff is, Ruby Mae? I'd have hoped to have at least gotten through to you, of all people. After all, you live right here with Christy."

"All the more reason for me to protect myself," Ruby Mae countered, accepting the bowl of apples from David. "Don't know when she might spread the curse to me."

Ruby Mae shoved the apples toward Christy. The steam wafted up toward Christy's face. She swallowed back the sour taste in her mouth.

"I just don't know why we can't get through to you, Ruby Mae!" David cried in exasperation.

"Don't bother, David," Christy said bitterly. "There isn't any point in trying to reach her. There isn't any point in trying to reach any of them—" Suddenly her stomach did a wild flip and she knew she was going to be sick. "Excuse me," she managed to blurt.

She dashed out of the dining room and out into the yard. Moments later she felt Miss

Alice's firm, cool hands supporting her head. "Go ahead, Christy," she said. "Get rid of everything. You'll feel better now."

"I—I haven't been so sick since I was a little girl. . . ."

"No, don't try to talk."

Finally it was over. Christy stood on unsteady feet. "I . . . I have to go think. . . ."

"You go on upstairs," Miss Alice said gently. "I'll come by later and we can talk."

Christy sat on her bed, staring bleakly at her lesson plans. When she heard a soft knock on the door, she knew who it was. "Come on in, Miss Alice."

"How are you feeling?" Miss Alice sat down on the edge of the bed.

"All right, physically . . . but . . ." Christy fought back the tears burning her eyes. "But I'm so confused, Miss Alice. I think maybe Father and Mother were right. Everyone was right, all the people who said I don't belong here. I wasn't willing to listen. I thought I could come here and be welcomed with open arms. I thought I could make a difference." She began to sob. "I . . . I can't fight the ignorance and superstition. I can't."

She cried for several minutes, sobbing while Miss Alice listened quietly. At last Christy lifted her head to look at the peaceful woman. Suddenly she needed to know what Miss Alice was thinking.

"Am I wrong to feel this way?" Christy asked.

"Any sensitive person would feel exactly as you feel." Miss Alice's voice was matter-of-fact. "Maybe it's just as well all this has happened. Now is as good a time as any to decide whether you'll go home or not—provided you make your decision on a true basis."

"What do you mean—a true basis?"

"The way life really is."

"Not much of life can be as bad as what I saw this afternoon," Christy said.

"You'd be surprised. Every bit of life, every single one of us has a dark side," Miss Alice replied. "When you decided to leave home and take this teaching job, you were leaving the safety and security you'd known all your life. I was the same way. I know. Then we get our first good look at the way life really is, and a lot of us want to run back to shelter in a hurry."

Christy hugged her pillow. "You? Even you?"

"Yes, certainly."

Christy thought of the horrible conditions at the O'Teale cabin, of Wilmer, of poor Mountie . . . even of the little rabbit that had never had a chance. How could there be such suffering? How could she fight such horrible things?

"But why did you stay?" Christy asked.

"When you wanted to leave? When you saw all the evil here?"

Miss Alice considered for a moment. "I believe that you've got to see life the way it really is before you can do anything about evil, Christy. Certainly, people like you are more sensitive than others. But if we're going to work on God's side, we have to decide to open our hearts to the griefs and pain all around us. It's not an easy decision."

"Miss Alice, even if you're right . . . how can I fight back against the things Granny has said? I can't reach the children if they fear me." Christy gave a bitter laugh. "And I can't be a teacher if I don't have any students."

Miss Alice fell silent for a moment. "I can tell you this. There's a healing power in love, Christy," she said at last. "I've seen it work miracles."

Miss Alice had such peace about her, such a sense of being at home no matter where she was. Christy wanted that feeling, but it seemed as far away as her family and her cozy bedroom back in Asheville.

"I just don't know," Christy whispered at last.

"Know what?"

"If I should stay. If there's any point in it."

Miss Alice nodded, as if she'd asked herself the same question, once upon a time. "First, ask yourself this, Christy. Who are you?"

"I wish I knew."

"But you can know. You're important, terribly important. Each of us is. You're unique. So is David. And Miss Ida. And Ruby Mae and Doctor MacNeill. No one else in all the world can fill David's place, or mine, or yours. Other teachers may come here to Cutter Gap, but you and you alone have a special gift to offer these people. If you don't do the work that God has given you to do, that work may never be done."

She rose to go. "It's late and you're tired. But here's the question for you to sleep on. Were you supposed to come here, Christy? Or were you just running away from home?"

Christy watched the door close behind Miss Alice. After a while, she retrieved her diary off the dresser.

Was I supposed to come here? Christy wondered. She wanted someone to tell her the answer—someone, anyone. But the only person who could answer that question was Christy herself. And she was afraid she already knew the answer.

She opened her diary and scanned the last lines she'd written. *Today braids. Tomorrow, the world!*

How hopeful and foolish that sounded now.

Her eyes fell on another passage. *Well, like it or not, Ruby Mae is clearly going to be my bundle.*

Christy groaned. Had Ruby Mae read those

words today? That would explain her sullen behavior at the dinner table. She must be feeling terribly hurt and angry. Christy knew she should go to Ruby Mae and explain that she hadn't meant anything when she'd written those words. Certainly the last thing she'd intended to do was to hurt Ruby Mae.

Christy started for the door, then stopped herself. What was the point? To begin with, the girl shouldn't have been snooping in Christy's diary. And in any case, Ruby Mae was still wearing Granny's herbs—still apparently convinced that Christy was cursed.

Why bother trying to console Ruby Mae? There was no point.

Then, Christy realized that she already knew the answer to Miss Alice's question. Tomorrow, she would start packing.

It was time to go home.

❧ Ten ❧

On Saturday morning, someone knocked on Christy's door while she was packing. Quickly Christy set aside the blouse she had been folding. "Come in," she called.

Ruby Mae stuck her head inside the door. "You're sure now?" she said sullenly. "I don't want to be a-steppin' on your *privacy* or nothin'."

"Ruby Mae," Christy said, "when I wrote that, I didn't mean that I didn't like having you around. I only meant that sometimes a person wants to be alone. Can you understand that?"

"I just come up 'cause Miz Ida done made me. Said the buckwheat cakes she made are gettin' cold."

"Oh. Would you mind telling her I'm not hungry this morning?"

Ruby Mae put her hands on her hips. "Where's all your things?"

"What—oh, you mean the things on my dresser? I just . . . I was just rearranging things." There was no point in telling Ruby Mae she was packing. If Ruby Mae knew, the entire Cove would know by this afternoon.

"Well, I best be goin'. Don't want to talk your ears plumb off."

Christy ran to Ruby Mae and took her by the arm. Granny's pouch of herbs was still tied around her waist. "Ruby Mae," Christy said gently, "have you ever said something that just came out wrong? Something that hurt somebody when you didn't mean it to?"

"Sure." Ruby Mae crossed her arms over her chest. "I say the wrong things regular as a clock a-strikin' the hour. You know for yourself I can't keep my mouth shut for more than a minute or two. Dumb things is bound and certain to come out."

The pain in Ruby Mae's voice made Christy wince. Part of her was angry at Ruby Mae, the way she was angry with all the mountain people. After all, this girl was standing in Christy's room, just inches away, wearing a pouch of foul-smelling herbs, just in case Christy was cursed.

And yet, she also felt pity for Ruby Mae, a confused teenager who'd thought she'd found a new friend in Christy. However unintentionally, Christy had repaid that friendship with hurt.

"I have something for you." Christy went to

her trunk and pulled out her diary. She opened it and yanked out the first few pages filled with her careful handwriting.

"What in tarnation are you doin'?" Ruby Mae cried.

Christy held out the black leather book. "I want you to have this."

Ruby Mae's eyes went wide. "Oh, no, Miz Christy, I couldn't rightly—"

"Why? Because it's cursed?" Christy demanded, surprised by the bitterness in her own voice.

Slowly Ruby Mae shook her head. "I just . . . it's yours. It's your private book."

"Now it's yours. I want you to write in it every day."

"I ain't no writer. What could the likes of me ever write in a fancy book?"

"Just pretend it's a friend. A friend you can talk to when no one else will listen."

A slow smile dawned on Ruby Mae's face as she accepted the book. "A friend?"

"Maybe you should even give it a name. How about . . . hmmm. How about Rose? I've always liked that name."

"Rose." Ruby Mae tried the name on for size. "That's a fine name, Miz Christy." She stroked the leather cover tenderly.

"Here. You'll need a pen, too. And remember. Whatever you write in there is private. That means you can say anything you want, even if it doesn't always come out just the way you meant it to."

Ruby Mae gave a small nod. "Thank you, Miz Christy."

"Now run and tell Miss Ida I won't be having breakfast."

When she was alone again, Christy scanned the pages she'd ripped from the diary—the chronicle of her magnificent adventure in the mountains. A sentence on the first page caught her attention:

> *I have begun my great adventure this day, and although things have not gone exactly as I had hoped, I am still committed to my dream of teaching at the mission.*

Well, she was not committed to her dream anymore, that much was certain. She stuffed the pages in her trunk—all except the last one. It was her letter of resignation, the letter she would give to Miss Alice tomorrow, after David's sermon. She would ask him to accompany her back to the train station at El Pano. Perhaps they could borrow Miss Alice's horse. It would be a long, hard trip, but when it was over, she'd be on her way back home. Home, where she would once again be safe and secure and loved.

～ ～ ～

The service was over. The crowd was gone, the schoolroom deserted.

Christy stood in the middle of the room, breathing in the now-familiar smells of chalk dust, fresh paint, and wood smoke.

She fingered the resignation letter in her skirt pocket. She still hadn't told David or Miss Alice that she planned to leave today. She'd tried to—a hundred times, it seemed—but each time she'd opened her mouth to say the words, a choked sob had come out instead.

Besides, her letter said all that needed to be said:

> *Effective immediately, I will be resigning from my post as teacher at the Cutter Gap mission school. I am deeply sorry that I must leave, but I have determined that I am not suited to the position.*
> *Sincerely,*
> *Christy Rudd Huddleston*

Not suited to the position. Not suited because she was weak and afraid. Not suited because her stomach revolted at the sight of her students' homes. Not suited because she could not find a way to fight evil and ignorance, not the way someone like Miss Alice could.

She should find David. He was probably down at his bunkhouse. She wanted to tell him first, since David would be easier than Miss Alice. Miss Alice would not be able to hide her disappointment in Christy. Just imagining the look in her eyes made Christy ache inside.

She ran her fingers over the worn surface of her desk. It was almost funny, when you thought about it. A silly raven had landed here and changed her life forever.

She turned to leave. Near the door, she spied a ragged brown coat lying on a desk. It was Mountie's. Christy would recognize the shabby, oversized thing anywhere. It was still unseasonably warm out, and it had been hot today during the service. Mountie must have left the coat behind by accident.

Christy touched the dirty brown fabric. It had been patched and repatched a dozen times. All the buttons were missing. How many times had she seen Mountie clutching the lapels to keep out the winter wind?

Poor Mountie. Christy could practically hear the mean chant of the boys at the noon recess, taunting the speechless little girl:

Mush-mouthed Millie,
Can't even speak,
Jabber jabber jaybird
Marbles in the beak.

Suddenly an idea came to her. At least she could do one small thing before she abandoned Mountie for good.

With the coat in hand, Christy headed for the mission house. Everyone was gone, probably having tea at Miss Alice's cabin. She selected four gold buttons from Miss Ida's sewing box in the kitchen cupboard, along with a needle and thread.

One by one, Christy sewed the buttons onto Mountie's coat. She was just tying the last knot when Ruby Mae appeared at the kitchen door.

"Fine sermon today," she commented, joining Christy at the table. She was still wearing the herb pouch around her waist.

"Yes, David's a wonderful speaker."

"What's that you're up to?"

"Mountie left her coat behind in the schoolroom. I'm just sewing some buttons on it."

Ruby Mae rolled her eyes. "Granny'll like *that.*"

Christy winced. "Oh, no! What was I thinking? She'll probably assume I'm trying to put some kind of curse on Mountie, won't she?" Angrily, she tossed the coat onto the table. "I can't even sew on some buttons without getting into trouble."

With grim determination, Christy found a pair of scissors in Miss Ida's box. She grabbed the coat.

"What are you doin'?" Ruby Mae cried.

"I'm taking off the buttons. Mountie needs this coat. If Granny thinks I've been near it, she won't let Mountie wear it." The horrible unfairness of it all burned in her heart.

Ruby Mae grabbed the scissors. "There's no need for her to know, now, is there? S'posin' I put it back in the school? Anyone asks, I'll say I sewed on the buttons."

"What if the coat *is* cursed?" Christy challenged. "How do you know it isn't?"

Ruby Mae gave a shrug. "In January—" she smiled, "buttons win out over curses."

Clutching the little coat, Christy followed Ruby Mae outside. As they walked along, Ruby Mae chattered away, just like she always did. "You know," she said, "there's somethin' you got to understand, Miz Christy. Granny's just lookin' out for her family."

Christy didn't answer. She had other things on her mind, and was only half-listening. What if David couldn't take her to the station today? What if Miss Alice refused to accept her resignation?

"I s'pose when school got a-goin'," Ruby Mae was saying, "she sort of felt all left behind. Granny's right partial to Mary and Mountie, 'specially Mountie."

Christy stopped in her tracks, as Ruby Mae's words finally began to register. Maybe that was it. Maybe Granny was so afraid of Christy because it meant losing the company of her great-grandchildren.

She touched Ruby Mae's shoulder. "You know, Ruby Mae," she said, "I'm beginning to think I should have listened to you more while I had the chance."

"I don't rightly get what you're aimin' at, Miz Christy."

"Never mind. I'm just sorry, that's all." She

started to hand the coat to Ruby Mae, but a noise coming from the edge of the woods made her pause. It was Granny, with Mary and Mountie, no doubt returning for the missing coat.

Granny froze. She scowled at the coat in Christy's hands. But before Granny could say a word, Mountie was dashing over to retrieve the coat.

Christy handed it to her. It took Mountie a moment before she noticed the new buttons. Her little face seemed to transform. Her expression was a mixture of awe and pure joy. She let out a strange, musical giggle.

"Mountie," Christy asked softly, "what's funny?"

Gleefully, Mountie held up the coat for Mary and Granny to see.

"What have you done to that coat?" Granny snapped.

Mountie tugged on Christy's sleeve.

"What is it, Mountie?" Christy asked.

Mountie screwed her face into a look of pure concentration. "Look at my buttons!" she suddenly blurted. "Look at my buttons!"

Silence fell. A bird chirped from its perch on the mission house roof. Wind rustled the bare-limbed trees.

"Mountie," Christy whispered, "what did you say?"

"Teacher, look! Look at my buttons! See how pretty?"

Christy blinked in disbelief at the beautiful

words coming from the little girl's mouth. They were a little slurred, perhaps, but to Christy they sounded as clear and joyful as the peals of a church bell.

"Did you hear what I heard?" she asked Ruby Mae.

Ruby Mae nodded, eyes wide. "I'm as plumb mystified as you, Miz Christy."

Christy looked over at Granny. Even from a distance, she could tell that the old woman had tears in her eyes. Mary wore a smile so big it seemed to take up her whole face.

Mountie grabbed Christy's hand. "Teacher! See them?"

Christy knelt down. "I see them, Mountie."

Mary broke free of Granny and ran over to hug her big sister. "See my buttons, Mary?" Mountie said.

"I see 'em. They's shiny as real gold. And I heard you, all the ways over there, Mountie!" Mary smiled shyly at Christy. "Thank you, Miz Christy," she whispered. "You done a good thing, I reckon."

She had done a good thing. A small thing, yes. But a thing that might help change Mountie's life.

What if Mountie was part of God's plan for Christy? Part of the work, as Miss Alice had said, that only Christy could do?

What if she had left yesterday, and those buttons had remained forever in Miss Ida's sewing box?

If Christy left Cutter Gap now, superstition and ignorance would have triumphed. If she stayed, maybe there would be other Mounties—other small miracles.

Christy reached into her pocket and slowly crumpled up her resignation letter.

"Come on, girls," Granny called. "Get away from her."

"I just want you to know something, Granny," Christy said, moving closer. "I'm staying. I almost left because of you and the things you've been saying about me. But I'm staying. And nothing you can say will change my mind. I'm staying because I care about Mountie and Mary and the rest of these children." She paused, then smiled, remembering what Ruby Mae had said about Granny. "Just like you do."

Granny worked her mouth, as if she were searching for words. Mountie rushed over to her. "Granny, see my buttons?"

Granny squeezed the girl's hand. "I see, child." She looked over at Christy. For the first time, Christy thought she saw something more than fear and anger there—maybe even a glimmer of respect.

But after a long moment, Granny turned away without another word, pulling Mountie along.

Mary turned back to Christy. "Thank you," she whispered again, and then she, too, was gone.

❧ Eleven ❧

On Monday morning, Christy made her way over the plank walk across the muddy school yard. She clutched her lesson plan to her chest. She'd worked on it all last evening, although she wasn't sure why. How many children would even come today? Ten? Five? None?

Miss Alice and David had told her to keep showing up every day, no matter what. Eventually, they said, she'd have her students back. She hadn't told them about her resignation letter. It was still crumpled in her pocket.

Inside the schoolroom, a fire already burned in the old stove. David had come in earlier to start it, although it was still strangely warm outside. Christy took the ball of paper out of her pocket and tossed it into the potbellied stove. It was a satisfying feeling, watching it crackle and burn, then vanish.

She went to her desk and set down her lesson book. She turned to the last roll call. Just a handful of students. She'd never have dreamed she'd miss having all sixty-seven of them, but she did.

As she started to sit, she noticed a familiar book lying open on her chair. It was her diary. She picked it up, smiling at the childish scrawl, marred by cross-outs. It filled the page in huge letters, too big to ignore:

Miz Cristy is right trubling sometimz. She'z alwayz makin me wash my fas and brush the mous nests outa my har. And she gits thez feraway looks in her eyz sometimz. Won't listn a-tall. Still and all, even if shez fer shure cursd, I'm prowd and onered to call her my frend.

"Ain't you never heard of a thing called privacy?"

Christy jumped, nearly dropping the diary. "Ruby Mae! I was just—"

Ruby Mae stood in the doorway, tapping her foot. "Just readin' my Rose, I'm a-guessin'."

"I apologize, really I do. It's just that it was sitting right there, in my chair, where I could hardly miss it—"

"Imagine that." Ruby Mae grinned. "Wonder how it got there?"

Christy closed the diary and passed it to

Ruby Mae. "I'm proud and honored to call you my friend, too," she said softly.

Ruby Mae blushed and went quickly to one of the windows.

Christy was surprised to see that she was no longer wearing Granny's herbs.

"Ruby Mae," Christy said, "do you think anyone will show up today?"

"Ain't you looked outside?"

Christy joined her at the window. Coming up the hill, she saw Lundy Taylor and Wraight Holt, trailed by several others. "The Holts are coming!" she exclaimed. "And there's Isaak McHone!"

"Yes'm. I reckon you'll have your hands full today. Everybody's a-comin'."

"But why? Why are they all coming back?"

Ruby Mae rolled her eyes. "It's a good thing you got me to keep you up on Cove gossip, Miz Christy. Don't you even know that Granny says you're uncursed?"

"*Un*cursed?"

"Yes'm. As of yesterday. Everybody knows."

"Except me. The one who's cursed." Christy narrowed her eyes. "I don't believe it. You're telling me *Granny* changed her mind about me? How is that possible?"

"Don't rightly know. All I knows is she says she saw a sign yesterday."

"A sign," Christy repeated, torn between laughing and groaning and crying.

Just then, she saw two little girls appear out of the dark woods. An old woman with a cane followed behind.

"It's Mountie and Mary," Christy whispered. "They're back. They're all coming back!" She hugged Ruby Mae until the girl pulled away, gasping for breath.

"Watch out for my braids, now," Ruby Mae scolded. "You know it done took me half the night to get 'em just so."

Granny paused at the edge of the schoolyard as Mary and Mountie dashed ahead. The old woman met Christy's eyes and gave a small nod.

"So Granny saw a sign," Christy said. "I wonder what it was?"

"Search me. But I heard it had something to do with four golden coins that fell from heaven."

Christy looked at Ruby Mae. Ruby Mae looked back with a sly grin. "Can't imagine what she meant, Miz Christy," she said. "Can you?"

The Angry
Intruder

The Characters

CHRISTY RUDD HUDDLESTON, a nineteen-year-old girl.

CHRISTY'S STUDENTS:
    ROB ALLEN, age fourteen.
    CREED ALLEN, age nine.
    LITTLE BURL ALLEN, age six.
    BESSIE COBURN, age twelve.
    LIZETTE HOLCOMBE, age fifteen.
    WRAIGHT HOLT, age seventeen.
    ZACHARIAS HOLT, age nine.
    VELLA HOLT, age five.
    SMITH O'TEALE, age fifteen.
    MOUNTIE O'TEALE, age ten.
    MARY O'TEALE, age eight.
    RUBY MAE MORRISON, age thirteen.
    JOHN SPENCER, age fifteen.
    CLARA SPENCER, age twelve.
    ZADY SPENCER, age ten.
    LULU SPENCER, age six.
    LUNDY TAYLOR, age seventeen.

BEN PENTLAND, the mailman.

PRINCE, black stallion donated to the mission.
GOLDIE, mare belonging to Miss Alice Henderson.

OLD THEO, crippled mule owned by the mission.

LUCY MAE FURNAM, Prince's former owner.
CHARLES FURNAM, her husband.

OZIAS HOLT, a mountain man.
   (Father of Christy's students Wraight, Zacharais, and Vella.)
GEORGIA HOLT, Ozias' sister.

DAVID GRANTLAND, the young minister.
IDA GRANTLAND, David's sister.

ALICE HENDERSON, a Quaker mission worker from Ardmore, Pennsylvania.

FAIRLIGHT SPENCER, a mountain woman.
JEB SPENCER, her husband.
   (Parents of Little Guy and Christy's students John, Clara, Zady, and Lulu.)

BOB ALLEN, a mountain man.

DR. NEIL MACNEILL, the physician of the Cove.

GRANNY O'TEALE, a superstitious mountain woman.
   (Great-grandmother of Christy's students Smith, Mountie, and Mary.)

❧ One ❧

Special delivery from the U-nited States Postal Service for Miss Christy Rudd Huddleston!"

Ben Pentland, the mailman, waved from the doorway of the one-room schoolhouse where Christy taught. Her students—all sixty-seven of them—whispered excitedly. The arrival of the mail was always a big event in this remote section of the Great Smoky Mountains.

"Thank you, Mr. Pentland," Christy called. "Why don't you just leave it by the door?"

"Well, Miz Christy, I don't mean to be ornery—" Mr. Pentland stroked his whiskered chin, "but I reckon that's not such a good idea."

"As you can see, we're in the middle of an arithmetic lesson, Mr. Pentland," Christy explained. She pointed to the blackboard, where fifteen-year-old John Spencer was carefully adding a long column of numbers.

"I'm sorry to interrupt your learnin'," Mr. Pentland said, shifting his mail bag from one shoulder to the other, "but this is what you might call a mighty big special delivery."

The students murmured excitedly. "Go on and get it, why don't you, Teacher?" urged Ruby Mae Morrison, a red-haired thirteen-year-old who was the school's biggest gossip.

"We have more important matters to attend to, Ruby Mae," Christy said in a professional tone. But the truth was, she couldn't help wondering what Mr. Pentland had brought. Could it be a package from her parents, back in North Carolina? In her letters home, she had urged them to help her locate much-needed supplies for the mission school. Christy's mother had promised to talk to the women's group at their church about gathering clothing and shoes for the poor mountain children.

Christy had even written several companies about the mission's desperate need for supplies, requesting donations of mattresses, soap, food, window shades, and cleaning supplies. She'd contacted the Bell Telephone Company, asking them to donate wires and equipment for a telephone, since nobody in the area owned one. And although she knew they probably wouldn't answer, she'd even written the Lyon and Healy Company, in the hope of obtaining a piano for the mission.

Although weeks had passed, none of the companies had responded. Perhaps, Christy thought excitedly, this delivery today was the first answer to her letters!

"I have to admit I'm curious about the delivery, Mr. Pentland," Christy said, "but it would be wrong to interrupt John in the middle of his arithmetic work." John was a gifted student who was especially strong in mathematics. Even before the school had opened, he'd managed to do all the problems in a worn old geometry textbook by himself.

"Miz Christy," John said, "I could hold off on my figurin', if'n you want to see about the special delivery."

"No, John," Christy replied, "you go ahead and add that last column. By the way, you've done a great job so far. I'm proud of you." She turned to Mr. Pentland. "I'll deal with the mail during the noon recess, Mr. Pentland."

"Truth to tell," Mr. Pentland said, his deep-set eyes gleaming, "I'm not rightly sure the mail will wait that long."

"Is it a big package?" Christy asked.

Mr. Pentland nodded slowly. "Biggest I ever did deliver."

"Where is it now?"

"Over to the back side of the school."

"I wonder if it's from one of the businesses I wrote," Christy said.

"Looks like a donation for the mission, near as I can figure."

"It's not a mattress, is it?"

"No'm." Mr. Pentland grinned. "Although like as not you could sit on it, if'n it were willin'."

"I don't understand—"

"Come on, Teacher," cried Creed Allen, a freckled nine-year-old. "I'm like to burst wide open if'n I don't see what it is!"

"All right, then. Let's just finish up these problems first. John, you let me know when you're done. Meanwhile, have the rest of you come up with an answer to the arithmetic problem I assigned? When we add two and four together, we get . . ."

She pointed to Lundy Taylor, a burly seventeen-year-old who was the class bully. "Lundy, if I add two apples and four apples together, how many apples do I have?"

Lundy shrugged. "Enough for a good-sized pie, I reckon."

The class broke into laughter. Mr. Pentland rubbed his mouth, not quite hiding a smile.

"Well, to tell you the truth, Lundy, I'm not much of a cook myself," Christy said, "so I'll have to take your word for it. But what I'm looking for now is a number."

Lundy stared at the floor.

"Lordamercy!" Creed cried. "Even *I* know this one, Teacher!"

"Wraight?" Christy asked. Wraight Holt, also seventeen, was one of Lundy's best friends. "How about you?"

Wraight shifted uncomfortably in his seat.

"Count it out on your fingers. Two plus four. It won't hurt to try. Nobody will laugh at you if you're wrong. Can you at least give me a guess?"

Wraight just rolled his eyes. He had always been sullen and stubborn, but lately, he'd been acting even more difficult than usual. About the only time Christy had ever seen Wraight smile was when he was playing his battered old dulcimer, a stringed musical instrument. He'd brought it to school with him for a while, but she hadn't seen him with it lately.

"Teacher, I'm done with my figurin'," John announced.

"Just a second, John," Christy said. "Wraight? Imagine the four strings on your dulcimer. What if you added two more? How many would you have then?"

"Ain't never had no extra strings on my dulcimer."

"Pretend, then."

Wraight's nine-year-old brother, Zach, leaned over. Holding his dirty red cap in front of his mouth, he whispered something to Wraight.

Wraight glared at Christy. "I reckon there'd be six."

"That's right, Wraight," Christy said with a tolerant smile. "Or perhaps I should say Zach. Don't worry, those of you who are still having trouble with numbers. Soon you'll be adding just as fast as John does."

As she turned back to her desk, Christy sighed. Usually David Grantland, the mission's young minister, handled math and Bible study classes. But he was busy today with church matters, so Christy had agreed to teach all the classes. It was going to be a very long day.

Christy found teaching students in so many different grades very difficult. When she'd volunteered to teach here at the mission in Cutter Gap, Tennessee, she hadn't realized that her classroom would be filled with over five dozen children, ranging in age from five to seventeen. She had a few gifted students, who had already been exposed to some schooling—students like John Spencer and Lizette Holcombe, a tall, dark-haired girl of fifteen with intelligent brown eyes.

But she also had many students like Lundy Taylor and Wraight Holt, who had never set foot in a classroom before. Christy didn't want to bore the more advanced students. On the other hand, she didn't want to discourage the ones who'd never been to school before.

"John, let's go over those figures in a moment," Christy said. She smiled at Mr. Pentland.

"I suppose our curiosity is getting the better of us. Why don't you bring the package in here so we can all take a look at it?"

"You're sure about wantin' it in here?"

"If it's a donation for the mission, why not? The children will enjoy seeing what you've brought."

"Oh, I reckon they'll enjoy it, all right." Chuckling softly to himself, Mr. Pentland set down his bag and headed off.

Christy couldn't help feeling proud of herself. After only two months of teaching, she'd managed to obtain much-needed supplies for the mission school—and all on her own! Even Miss Alice Henderson, who'd helped found the school, hadn't thought of writing to companies for donations. Miss Alice was going to be very impressed when she saw the results of Christy's efforts.

It would be nice, Christy thought, *if this first package contained donated books. Won't it be wonderful for each child to have a fresh, new book to hold.* . . . Suddenly, she gasped.

Mr. Pentland stood in the doorway, grinning from ear to ear. "Like I said, biggest delivery I ever did make. Hungriest, too. Ate half my lunch on the way here."

Slowly Mr. Pentland entered the room. He was pulling on a rope. Attached to the rope was a huge black stallion with a white star on his brow. The horse had a silky mane and a long, flowing tail. On his back was a beautiful leather saddle.

The horse had to lower his proud head to come in through the door. His hooves pounded on the wooden floor. When he tossed his tail, it whipped back and forth across the faces of the students on the last row. Gazing curiously at the class, he snorted twice. His ears twitched. Then he leaned down to nuzzle Ruby Mae's hair.

"Her hair's so red, he most likely figures it's carrots," Mr. Pentland joked.

"Mr. Pentland," Christy said when she finally managed to recover her voice, "there must be some mistake. This is . . . this is a *horse!*"

Mr. Pentland grinned. "For a city-gal, you sure do pick things up quick-like. Bet you can even tell which end of the horse is which."

"Well, I *am* a city-gal," Christy said with a laugh, "but I'm pretty sure you feed the end without a tail." She shook her head. "But I still say there's got to be some mistake. When I requested donations, I didn't ask for a horse. Did he come with a note, or any kind of explanation?"

"Just that tag on his saddle with your name on it."

"But Teacher," said Zach, "the mission needs a horse bad. All you got is that half-crippled mule, Old Theo."

It was true. Miss Alice owned a horse, but she was often gone on long trips. Without any transportation, it was very difficult for David to visit families living in remote areas.

"You're right, Zach," Christy agreed. "But we still can't keep this horse."

The entire class moaned in disappointment. As if he understood what was going on, the horse stepped closer to Christy's desk, his horseshoes clopping loudly on the floor. He nudged Christy's shoulder.

"I reckon he likes you, Teacher," said Mary O'Teale, a gentle eight-year-old with wide, green eyes. The horse's tail swished over her face as he tossed it to and fro.

"I'm sure you're a very nice horse," Christy said to the stallion, "but we can't keep you without knowing where you came from."

"I plumb forgot!" Mr. Pentland exclaimed. "You've got a couple letters, too. Had a monstrous big pile of mail this week. Eight whole letters!" He stroked the horse's neck. "Nine, if'n you count this big, hairy one."

Christy smiled. She still couldn't get over living in a world where eight letters meant a "big pile of mail!"

Mr. Pentland handed Christy the letters. One was from her mother. The other had a North Carolina postmark, too, but Christy didn't recognize the name on the envelope.

She opened it and read:

February 8, 1912

Dear Miss Huddleston:

I hope that you will forgive a stranger writing to you. Let me explain that I have just returned from Asheville, where I was visiting my sister.

At a tea she gave in my honor, I met your mother. She spoke most charmingly about the contents of some of your recent letters, your fascinating pupils, and their needs.

When she mentioned the mission's need for a good horse, my heart soared, for I knew of the perfect animal. My husband, Charles, having developed rheumatism this past year, has been unable to give our fine stallion, Prince, the exercise and attention he properly deserves. I trust that the mission will find him the loving friend and companion that we have.

> *Sincerely,*
> *Lucy Mae Furnam*

Christy stroked the horse's glossy mane. "Well, Prince," she said, "it looks like you have a new home."

"You're a-keepin' him for sure and certain?" Ruby Mae cried.

"It seems he is a gift," Christy explained, "from some people back in my home state. His name is Prince."

"And he looks like one, don't he, Teacher?"

asked Little Burl Allen, a sweet, red-haired six-year-old.

"Yes, he does, Little Burl," Christy agreed. "Very majestic. All he needs is a crown."

"Can Ruby Mae and me ride him double-like?" asked Bessie Coburn. Twelve-year-old Bessie was Ruby Mae's best friend.

"I think what Prince needs right now is a little rest after his long journey," Christy said.

But just then, Prince reared up on his hind legs.

"Look out!" Ruby Mae yelled.

The horse's black head nearly touched the rafters as he pawed the air with his forelegs.

"Whoa, there, boy," Mr. Pentland soothed, pulling on the lead rope.

At last Prince lowered his legs. He stood calmly, as if nothing unusual had happened.

"No, ma'am," Little Burl said, shaking his head. "I don't reckon he is tired."

Christy laughed, a little flustered by the sudden display. "Well, we'd better take Prince outside."

Ruby Mae and Bessie jumped up to grab the lead rope. Prince, with his head still high, allowed himself to be led through the door. Christy, Mr. Pentland, and the rest of the children followed behind.

As soon as he was out on the snow-covered grass, the horse yanked free of the girls' grasp and took off at a gallop. He ran in a great, wide circle, tossing his head back and forth and kicking up sprays of snow. Finally, after several minutes, he meekly returned to the children.

"Thank you, Mr. Pentland, for bringing him all this way," Christy said. "He really is a beauty."

"All part of bein' a U-nited States mailman," Mr. Pentland said with a tip of his worn hat. "Anyways, kind of liked having a critter around for company. By the way, I 'spect there's more surprises a-comin'. Big delivery come into El Pano yesterday. Should be here soon."

Ruby Mae tugged on Mr. Pentland's sleeve. "Another horse?"

"Nope," he said with a sly grin.

"We'll let it be a surprise," Christy said. "Just tell me this, so I can prepare myself—does it breathe?"

"Nope. Don't breathe," said Mr. Pentland. "Course it do make noise. . . ." With a mysterious smile, he was on his way.

As Christy watched him go, she realized she felt a real fondness for the gentle mailman. Mr. Pentland had escorted Christy on her seven-mile journey through the mountains when she came to Cutter Gap two months ago. It had been a rough trip, ending with Christy's fall into a dangerous, icy river. Through it all, Mr. Pentland had been a kind friend when she'd needed one.

"Ruby Mae," Christy said, "why don't you and Bessie take Prince over to the mission house? I believe I saw Mr. Grantland over there. He'll take care of our new friend."

Christy turned back toward the school. A snowball fight had already started. If she didn't get everyone back into the classroom soon, she'd lose what little control she had.

"All right, now," Christy called loudly. "Back to John's math problems."

The children responded with loud groans. A few of her more willing students, like John and Lizette, rushed up the steps to the schoolhouse. Wouldn't it be wonderful, Christy thought, if all her students were so eager and quick to learn? Unfortunately, most of them had never even handled a pencil or a piece of chalk or a real book. And without the necessary supplies, there were days when Christy wondered if she would ever make a difference in the lives of her young students.

Still, Prince's unexpected arrival had filled her with hope. She couldn't exactly take credit for the beautiful horse—he was a surprise gift, after all. But if some of the other donations she'd requested came through, think of all the changes she could make to the mission school! She couldn't wait to see what the next delivery would bring.

"Miz Christy! Come quick!" Lizette called from the doorway.

"What is it, Lizette?"

"Somebody's done erased all of John's figurin'. And there's ink spilled all over your papers!"

Rounding up the last few stragglers, Christy hurried inside the school. A deep blue puddle of ink covered her attendance book. Ink flowed to the edge of her desk, where it dripped like a tiny waterfall onto the rough, wood floor. John stood by the blackboard, staring in dismay at the smeared remains of his addition problems. The ghosts of a few numbers were still visible, but most of his work had been completely erased.

Christy wondered if Prince had somehow knocked over her inkwell. But no, the horse hadn't been near her desk when he'd reared up. And he certainly hadn't erased the board.

"Sit down, all of you!" Christy cried. Reining in her anger, she lowered her voice. "Please, go to your seats. I need to get to the bottom of this."

She heard snickers outside. She leaned out the door to see a group of the older boys—Lundy Taylor, Smith O'Teale, Wraight Holt, and Wraight's little brother, Zach—hovering near the steps, whispering.

"Inside, now!" Christy ordered.

The boys sauntered in, taking their time. Zach, a thin boy with curly blond hair, cast a nervous glance in Christy's direction, then slipped into his seat. Lundy chuckled as he walked to his desk.

"I'm glad you find this so amusing, Lundy," Christy said. "But I'm afraid I do not. John worked very hard on those math problems. And as for my attendance book, it's ruined. Do you realize how difficult it is for us to obtain supplies? Ink and paper and chalk cost money."

Christy paced up and down the aisles of the small classroom. An uneasy quiet fell over the class. Some students hung their heads. Others looked out the windows. Lundy, Wraight, and Smith avoided her gaze.

"I want to know who did this," Christy said. "And I want to know right now."

She was not surprised when no one answered.

After a tense moment, John raised his hand. "Miz Christy, I can do the figurin' again. It ain't no problem."

"That's not the point, John. I need to find out who is responsible for this."

Actually, Christy had a pretty good idea who the culprit was—Lundy Taylor. Although she'd never been able to prove it, she was certain that Lundy had thrown a rock at five-year-old Vella Holt on the first day of school. It was also likely that he'd tripped Mary O'Teale at the top of an icy slide, causing her to tumble down a steep slope and hurt her arm and head. But no one would ever directly accuse Lundy of anything. He was big and hulking and mean, and even Christy was a little afraid of him.

"Lundy, do you have anything to say?" Christy asked.

"I'd say you got yourself one big mess up yonder on that desk," Lundy said with a smirk.

Christy clenched her hands. She took a deep breath. She was determined not to lose her temper.

"It's just some spilled ink," she said. "I'll clean it up. John will redo his arithmetic. And that's that. But if I ever catch one of you vandalizing the school again, I'll . . ." She lowered her voice. "This is *your* school. It belongs to you. You should treat it with respect and love."

Christy put a fresh column of numbers on the blackboard for John. But as she wrote, she couldn't help glancing back at Lundy. He glared back with steely dark eyes. What else was Lundy capable of doing to the school?

It's just a prank, nothing more, Christy told herself, but she couldn't quite bring herself to believe it.

❧ TWO ❧

When school was over, Lizette offered to stay behind and help clean up the classroom. "I'd be glad for the help," said Christy, "and the company." Lizette couldn't help beaming.

She loved the way Miz Christy talked, so nice and citified. And she had a sweetness to her that Lizette admired. She often tried to picture herself as a teacher someday, just like Miz Christy, with fine clothes and pleasant manners and so much learning inside her head.

Lizette took the blackboard erasers outside to bang them together. The chalk dust exploded in big puffs and floated away on the breeze.

Just then, she spotted a scene that sent her heart leaping straight into her throat. Lundy, Smith, and Wraight were standing shoulder-to-shoulder by the edge of the woods. Wraight's little brother, Zach, stood a few steps back, looking worried.

John Spencer stood alone, facing the three older boys.

Lizette strained to listen. She could hear the sound of angry voices—especially Lundy's.

"I'll knock you good, if'n you don't keep your trap shut," Lundy was saying.

John said something in response, but Lizette couldn't tell what it was. She wondered if she should go back inside and get Miz Christy. It looked like things could turn ugly, right quick. No doubt Miz Christy could put an end to it all with a few words. But Teacher wouldn't always be around every time Lundy Taylor decided to act like a bully.

Lizette made up her mind. Trying to look as tough as Miz Christy did when she had words with Lundy, she strode over to the boys.

Lundy saw her coming and gave a nasty laugh. "Look'a here, John. Lizette is a-comin' to rescue you."

John did not turn around. He just scowled and stood his ground. But Lizette could tell he was plenty scared. She tried to meet Wraight's gaze. But Wraight was looking straight ahead, his eyes dark with anger.

Why does Wraight get so angry sometimes? Lizette wondered. Wraight wasn't like Lundy. Not really, not deep down.

"John, Teacher was wonderin' if'n you was still here, and if maybe you could go back and help her with somethin'," Lizette lied in a shaky voice.

"Maybe you'd best run along and hide behind Teacher's skirts, John," Lundy sneered.

"I'm just warning you, Lundy," John said. "You shouldn't go messin' up Teacher's things."

Lundy stepped closer, until his chest was right up against John's. "You're warnin' me? I'll do what I please with Teacher. If'n I want, I might just get rid of her, permanent-like. That city-gal's got no business here in the Cove. You hear me, boy?" He balled up his fist, ready to strike. "I believe it's time you was taught a real lesson."

"Lundy, don't!" Lizette cried.

"Lundy, don't! Lundy, don't!" Lundy mocked her.

Suddenly the glint of anger in Wraight's eyes flickered. He glanced at Lizette. "Let him go, Lundy," he said in a low voice.

Lizette sent him a grateful look.

"Let him go?" Lundy demanded. "Well, Wraight, it was you who was made a fool of by this little teacher's pet, a-showin' off in class. Him and all his figurin'."

Now, the black anger raged in Wraight's eyes. He seemed to be fighting with it. "It weren't John's fault," he said at last. He jerked his head back toward the schoolhouse. "It's that flatlander teacher who's got everything all mixed up."

Lundy looked annoyed. He shoved John away with both hands. "I reckon you get to live another day, teacher's pet. Run on to Miz Christy now. That's where you belong."

Lizette could tell how angry John was. But it was clear he saw no point in starting a fight he was sure to lose.

Slowly, John turned away.

"You'd best go, too, Lizette," Lundy said with a sneer. "Two of a kind, you and John. Two little teacher's pets." With a last snort, Lundy turned away, followed by Smith.

Wraight began to follow them, but Lizette grabbed his arm. He looked at her, surprised.

Silently, so that only Wraight would know what she said, she mouthed the words, "Thank you."

For a second, the anger in Wraight's eyes was truly gone. In its place was something gentler, a look Lizette had seen before.

"Lizette?" Miz Christy called.

Wraight looked past Lizette to the schoolhouse. Once more, the dark shadow settled over his face. He turned and followed Lundy and Smith into the woods, followed at a distance by his little brother.

Late that night, Christy awoke to the sound of pounding. She sat up in bed, rubbing her eyes. *Tap. Tap. Tap.* No doubt about it. It was the steady, sharp sound of a hammer hitting a nail.

She ran to her window and pulled back the curtain. The wooden floor was icy. The light of a full moon spilled over the snow-covered mission yard.

Who could be hammering in the middle of the night? Was David doing some kind of emergency repair on the school?

Just beyond the school, Christy noticed a small figure dashing into the thick trees. It looked like a little boy. Christy couldn't tell who it was, but she did catch a glimpse of the red cap the boy was wearing.

Zach Holt? What could he be doing here, in the middle of the night? Perhaps someone in the Holt family was sick, or hurt. Christy had heard that Ozias Holt, Zach's father, sometimes drank too much. Maybe it wasn't hammering she'd heard. Maybe Zach had been pounding at the front door, trying to get Christy to wake up. But why had he given up and run away so quickly?

Christy put on her robe and slippers. She met Miss Ida, David's older, no-nonsense sister, at the top of the stairs. She was carrying a lamp and wearing a nightgown, with a knitted shawl draped over her shoulders. It seemed strange to see Miss Ida's gray hair hanging loose. Usually she wore it in a tight bun.

"What on earth was that banging?" Miss Ida asked, rubbing her eyes.

"I thought I saw one of my students by the schoolhouse," Christy said. "Let's go take a look."

Miss Ida led the way down the stairs. The lamp cast long, dancing shadows on the walls. Walking side by side, Christy and Miss Ida crossed the main room.

The mission house was a white three-story frame building with a screened porch on either side. Miss Ida and Christy lived there, along with Ruby Mae, who had been having problems at home and needed a temporary place to stay. Miss Alice had her own cabin, and David had a bunkhouse nearby. The house was primitive, with no electricity, telephone, or indoor plumbing, and only the barest of furnishings. Still, Christy had already begun to think of it as her real home.

"I thought maybe someone was knocking on the door," Christy said. "Maybe Zach needed help, and when no one answered, he ran off."

"No," Miss Ida said firmly. "That was hammering I heard, I'm certain of it."

"Maybe David was doing some repairs on the schoolhouse."

"In the middle of the night? Nonsense."

Christy opened the front door. Cold air slapped at her like an icy hand. It was March, but the mountain nights were nearly as bitter as they had been in January, when Christy had first arrived at the mission.

She stepped out onto the porch. The yard was covered with muddy patches of snow. Up the hill stood the newly built schoolhouse, which also served as a church on Sundays. In the silvery moonlight, the freshly painted building practically glowed. A gust of wind set the tree branches chattering.

"I don't see anything," Miss Ida said.

"Or anyone," Christy added in a whisper. She turned to Miss Ida. "You wait here. It's awfully cold. I'll go take a look."

"Take my shawl," Miss Ida said. "And be careful."

Slowly Christy crossed the yard. The snow patches were crusty and packed. *I wish I'd worn my boots*, she thought. Instantly she felt guilty. The little footprints of her students filled the yard. Few of the children owned shoes. Even in the coldest weather, they walked to school barefoot.

The sight of an especially small set of footprints, glowing in the moonlight, filled Christy with a mixture of love and awe. The school meant so much to these children that they would walk for miles through snow-covered mountains just to spend a few hours here. It showed just how much they wanted to learn.

Suddenly, Christy froze in place as the front of the school came clearly into view. "No!" she cried in outrage.

The message was scrawled across the front of the school, in huge, dripping, brown letters:

GIT AWA TEECHR

Hugging Miss Ida's shawl to her, Christy stared in disbelief at the crude writing. *Get away Teacher*, she whispered, nearly choking on the words.

She stepped closer, touching her index finger to one of the letters. It wasn't paint. But it was an oily, smelly goop that certainly wouldn't wash off easily.

She heard steps behind her and spun around, her heart racing.

"Christy?" came a familiar voice. "What is it?"

Miss Alice walked across the yard. She was wearing a blue coat over her nightgown. Her long, thick hair, sprinkled with gray, hung down past her shoulders. Even now, awakened from sleep in the middle of the night, she walked like a magnificent queen, tall and dignified.

Miss Alice shook her head sadly as she draped her arm around Christy's shoulders. "It's terrible," she murmured. "Just terrible."

"Isn't it?" Christy cried. "How could someone do such a thing?"

Miss Alice gave a wry smile. "No, I meant the spelling."

"How can you make jokes?" Christy moaned.

"I find that laughter is almost always the best way to deal with a difficult problem," Miss Alice said. She climbed the steps to the front door and pointed. "This explains the hammering."

For the first time, Christy noticed the long piece of wood nailed across the door frame.

"But why would anyone do that?" Christy cried.

"To keep us out, I imagine," Miss Alice said calmly. "It's a simple enough thing to remove the nails, of course. Not a very well-planned prank."

"Is that all you think it is?" Christy asked. "A prank?"

Miss Alice examined the nailed board. "Most likely."

"Are you all right?" a male voice called from the distance.

Christy craned her neck. It was David, dashing across the yard. He was wearing big boots and long johns. His black hair was a tangled mess. She couldn't help grinning. He looked a little ridiculous.

"David to the rescue," Christy teased.

David rushed up the stairs, panting. He combed a hand through his snarled hair, but one stubborn lock still poked into the air. "It's a long way from the bunkhouse, you know," he said sheepishly. "I came as fast as I could."

"Nice outfit," Christy said. "A little flashy for Cutter Gap."

David started to respond, but just then he noticed the words scrawled over the schoolhouse. "What—" He rubbed his eyes. His mouth hung open.

"Miss Alice thinks it's a prank," Christy said.

David ran a finger over one of the letters. "What *is* this stuff?"

"A mixture of things, probably," Miss Alice said. "Goodness knows no one around here can afford paint. I'd guess some lard, some mud, maybe some of the homemade dye the women use for coloring yarn. Could be any number of things."

"My beautiful paint job," David moaned.

"They nailed the door shut, too," Christy said.

David rolled his eyes. "Well, that's easy enough to remedy, at least."

"Let's get inside before we all end up with frostbite," Miss Alice said. "We can take care of this mess before school starts in the morning."

Christy shook her head. "I don't want to clean it off."

"But we have to," David insisted.

"No. I want the children to see what someone has done to their school."

"Come to think of it, that's probably a good idea, Christy," David agreed. "Maybe someone will even confess. I doubt it, though."

"Let's get over to the house and warm up with some tea," Miss Alice urged.

"First I want to check on Prince," David said. "It's his first night here, and I want to make sure he's doing all right."

"I'll go, too," Christy said.

Miss Alice grinned. "Might as well make a night of it."

The little shed that served as a barn was dark and cozy. It smelled of leather and hay, a soothing, warm smell. Christy went over to Prince, who eyed her sleepily. She stroked his velvety muzzle.

"How do you like your new home, Prince?" she asked.

"Seems to like it fine," David said. "He and Goldie are already good friends. Old Theo, I'm not so sure about."

"Isn't he beautiful, Miss Alice?" Christy asked.

"He is indeed," Miss Alice said.

Christy rubbed her cheek against the stallion's warm neck. What an unexpected gift he was! His arrival had made Christy all the more anxious to receive responses to her letters. Miss Alice was going to be so surprised. She didn't know about the letters Christy had sent requesting donations from businesses.

It wasn't that Christy wanted to keep them from Miss Alice. But there was no point in discussing her plan, she told herself, until she saw the results. Then it would be a real surprise. Christy's thoughts turned back to tonight's disturbing incident.

"Well, it looks as if everything's in order here," David said. "Let's go have that tea."

"It'll be dawn soon," Miss Alice said. "Perhaps we should just have breakfast."

"Coming, Christy?" David asked from the doorway of the shed.

Christy stroked Prince's ear distractedly. "Oh—yes. Sorry. I was just thinking about the writing on the school. Why would someone write that about me? It's hard not to take it personally. I keep thinking about Zach, wondering if I've hurt him in some way. . . ."

"Zach Holt?" David repeated. "Why him?"

"I thought I saw him running from the school," Christy explained. "Or at least I saw his red cap. But the more I think about it, the more I can't believe it was Zach. For one thing, some of those letters are very high. A fairly tall person had to write them."

David nodded. "Good point. Unless, of

course, Zach was sitting on the shoulders of a friend."

"Or using stilts," Miss Alice added with a grin.

"There's another reason I doubt it was Zach," Christy said.

"And what is that, Sherlock Holmes?" David inquired, arms crossed over his chest.

"Elementary, my dear Watson. Zach Holt just happens to be a very fine speller. He would never spell 'Teacher' with two *E's*."

Miss Alice laughed. "With you on the case, we're sure to get to the bottom of this prank."

"I hope that's all it is," David said, his voice tense.

"What do you mean, David?"

"Well, Zach's been spending a lot of time with the older troublemakers—his brother, Wraight, as well as Lundy and Smith. They're capable of making more than simple mischief." He stared at Christy thoughtfully. "I just think you should be careful for the next few days."

Christy smiled. It was sweet, and a little flattering, that David was acting so protective. Still, she could take care of herself. "I'll be fine, David. I'm a big girl."

"After all those problems with Granny O'Teale, though," David said, "there may still be some bad feelings about you."

Christy shuddered at the memory. She had only been teaching for a week when Granny O'Teale, the great-grandmother of the six O'Teale children, had started a terrible rumor about Christy. She'd decided that Christy was cursed, after a big black raven flew into the schoolroom and perched next to Christy on her desk.

"Let's not jump to any conclusions, David," Miss Alice advised. "Maybe this is just a one-time incident. Has anything else happened at school like this?"

"No . . ." Christy began. She hesitated. "Well, come to think of it, today someone erased some of John Spencer's arithmetic problems off the board and spilled ink on my attendance book."

"You be careful, Christy," David said. "These aren't all just innocent children. The mountain people have been raised to think that feuding and fighting are part of daily life."

"There is good in all these people, David," Miss Alice chided gently. "And in all God's creatures. Sometimes we just have to look a little harder."

David nodded. "I know that, Miss Alice. But that doesn't mean Christy shouldn't watch herself. Things could get out of hand, even if this prankster doesn't mean for them to."

"Stop worrying, David," Christy said with a wave of her hand. "I'll take care of myself, I promise. Besides, I have more important things to worry about."

"Such as?" David asked.

"Such as how I'm ever going to teach these children how to spell correctly!"

"See how things go today," Miss Alice said. "We'll talk more after school at dinner."

"Oh, that reminds me," Christy said. "I promised Fairlight Spencer I'd start teaching her reading this afternoon. I may be a little late getting home." Fairlight Spencer was the mother of four of Christy's students—John, Clara, Zady, and Lulu.

"Well, just be careful coming home from the Spencers' cabin," David advised. "That's a long walk, and it gets dark early, you know. Maybe I should walk you home."

"I'll have John walk me home," Christy promised.

"All right, then," David agreed.

The three of them left the shed and made their way across the yard. Christy glanced back over her shoulder at the school. *Get away, Teacher*, she murmured.

Prank or not, the words still stung.

❧ Three ❧

By the time the children arrived for school that morning, David had removed the plank nailed across the schoolhouse door. As the students read the message scrawled on the front of the school, Christy watched their expressions, hoping to get a clue about the culprit. She kept a careful eye on Lundy, Smith, and Wraight. Lundy seemed to find the message especially funny, but that was hardly proof he was involved.

When Zach arrived, trailing behind the older boys, he just glanced at the message for a moment, then turned away. He pulled his dirty red cap down so low that his eyes were almost hidden.

"It's the most all-fired rotten thing I ever did see, Miz Christy," cried Lizette. Her wide brown eyes glistened with tears. "Makes me madder'n a peeled rattler to see something like that on our brand-spankin' new school. Who do you think done it?"

Christy patted Lizette's shoulder. "I'm not sure, Lizette," she said. "But I intend to find out."

"Let's clean it off," John suggested.

"We will," Christy said, "but first I want everybody to have a look."

A tiny, cold hand reached for Christy's. It was Mountie O'Teale, a shy ten-year-old who, with Christy's help, was learning to overcome a speech problem that had left her nearly silent.

"But Teacher," Mountie said softly, "i—it was so purty and clean."

Christy smiled. Every time Mountie spoke, it still seemed like a small miracle. "I know, Mountie," she said. "But we'll fix the school. Don't worry, sweetheart. Soon it'll be good as new."

When all the students had arrived, Christy signaled for them to quiet down and gather by the school. "First things first," she said to her hushed audience. She knelt down and dipped her hand into a slushy spot of half-frozen mud near the steps, scooping up a big handful.

"What in tarnation are you doin', Miz Christy?" Ruby Mae cried.

"Mud fight!" Creed yelled, and some of the other boys cheered.

"Nice try, Creed," Christy said. "But this mud is for another purpose."

Lifting her long skirt, Christy picked her way along the edge of the building through the snow and mud.

"She's gone plumb crazy, I 'spect," Ruby Mae whispered loudly.

Christy turned to the group. *Laughter is almost always the best way to deal with a difficult problem*, Miss Alice had said.

"I want to say that while I appreciate the effort that went into this . . . this little writing exercise, I am very disappointed in the spelling." Christy turned to the wall. "To begin with, it's *get*, not *git*."

Using the cold mud, Christy carefully drew three small horizontal lines extending from the letter *I*. Behind her, the children watched, murmuring and whispering in amazement. A few giggled.

"And the rest of this is no better." Christy corrected the remaining message as well as she could. She glanced back at her students. Most of them were staring at her mud-covered hand.

"And frankly, I don't much care for the punctuation," Christy added. "I would add a comma here, after *away*. And how about an exclamation point at the end? That way—" she paused to smile, "it's clear that you're serious about wanting me to leave."

Christy stepped back to admire her work:

GET AWAY, TEACHER!

"There," she said with satisfaction. "Much better. I want to thank the person responsible for providing us with such an excellent opportunity for a spelling lesson. Next time, however, if it's not too much trouble, I'd prefer to work on grammar."

Christy motioned to the door. "Time to head inside."

"But Teacher," came a small voice.

Christy felt a tug at her skirt. It was Little Burl.

"What is it, Little Burl?"

"Ain't you mad? About the writin'?"

Christy smiled. "Sometimes getting mad just gets in the way, Little Burl. I'm disappointed that somebody hurt the new school. And I'm sad to think that someone is angry at me, because I would never want to hurt one of you in any way. Not ever."

"But what about the mess?" Creed asked. "Who's a-goin' to clean it off?"

Christy winked. "Guess what we're going to be doing during noon recess?"

Everyone groaned. "If I ever get my hands on the person who did this, I'll whop him good!" Creed said.

"I appreciate the offer, Creed," Christy said.

"But I don't think that'll be necessary. The person who did this knows that it was wrong. And I hope that he—or she—will reconsider before pulling a similar stunt. Now I want all of you to get inside. I'll be there in a minute. I've got to wash off my hand in the snow."

While the children made their way up the steps, Christy knelt down and wiped off her muddy hand in a patch of snow. When Zach passed by, she motioned for him to join her. He grimaced, glanced over at his brother, then reluctantly shuffled over. Wraight, Lundy, and Smith waited for him by the door, scowling at Christy.

"Zach," Christy said in a soft voice, so the others wouldn't hear, "you know that I would never accuse you of something unless I had a very good reason, don't you?"

Zach shrugged. He kicked at a mound of snow with his bare foot.

"The thing is, I thought I saw someone running away from the school last night. He was about your size, and he had on a red cap, just like the one you're wearing."

Zach touched his cap. His cheeks were flushed. "Don't mean nothin'," he finally said. "Sure don't mean I done it."

Christy stood, drying her hand on her skirt. "No, it doesn't. As a matter of fact, I happen to know from your work that you're an excellent speller, Zach. You would never spell *Teacher* the way it was written on the wall."

A small smile lit up Zach's thin face. "Got to admit it ain't the best spellin' I ever seen, that's for certain."

"How did you learn to spell so well, Zach?"

"My Aunt Georgia came a-visitin' last summer. She had a real, live book with her. Taught me some of the words. Little ones, leastways."

"That's wonderful. You should be very proud."

Zach shifted from one foot to the other. He glanced nervously toward the door of the schoolhouse. "I reckon so. But just 'cause a feller can't spell and such, that don't mean he's worthless or nothin'."

Christy nodded thoughtfully. Was Zach trying to tell her something? "Zach, I don't think you wrote that, but I do think you might know who did. Can you tell me who it was?"

"Don't know nothin' about that."

"Are you sure?"

Again Zach stole a fearful glance toward the steps, where the older boys were waiting. "Yep."

"Is someone making you afraid, Zach? One of the older boys?"

"I ain't afraid of nobody!" Zach cried. "Now can I go in?"

Christy sighed. "Of course you can."

She watched the boy march into the school. "Lundy," Christy called.

Lundy glared at her. "You be wantin' somethin'?"

"I want to know if you have anything to say about the writing on the school wall."

"I ain't got nothin' to say to you," he spat. Wraight and Smith came to stand beside Lundy.

By now, Christy was used to Lundy's angry outbursts. From the first day of school, he'd been this way. But the sneer on his face today was almost more than she could bear. Still, she reminded herself, she wasn't going to get anywhere by yelling at Lundy—even if she did suspect he was responsible for the vandalism.

"I'm just going to ask once. Do you boys know anything about that writing?" Christy asked calmly.

"Why are you blamin' us?" Wraight demanded. He was a taller version of Zach, with the same gray-blue eyes and tangled blond hair. But there was something troubling in his gaze.

"I'm not blaming you, I just—"

"Why don't you ask Rob Allen or John Spencer if'n they done it?" Wraight pressed, his anger growing.

"'Cause *they* can spell," Smith said with a snort. "Myself, I don't take no stock in spellin' and such. Can't feed an empty stomach with no spellin' words."

"Boys," Christy said. "I thought you might know something—"

"You know we don't know nothin'," Wraight shot back. His words burned with angry sarcasm. "Nothin'. Can't add, can't spell. Can't do nothin', ain't worth nothin'."

"Course," Lundy said with a dark smile, "we can shoot the eye out of a deer half a mile aways, quicker than you can spit and holler howdy."

"True enough," Smith agreed.

"What do you think of that, Teacher?" Lundy demanded.

"I think," Christy said with all the quiet force she could muster, "that it's time for you boys to go inside."

As they slowly entered the school, big and sullen and full of anger, Christy suddenly felt very small and afraid. She shivered, but she knew it wasn't because of the cold.

~ ~ ~

Lizette just couldn't understand it. If she were the teacher, she would have been angry with the person who'd ruined the front of the school that way. But Miz Christy was sitting at her desk like always, acting as if nothing out of the ordinary had happened. She was reading from a book about a boy named Huckleberry Finn. It was a mighty funny book, and Lizette loved listening to the pretty words. Miz Christy spun them out like pure music.

But Lizette had other things on her mind today. She glanced down at her little blackboard. She'd carefully drawn a heart, with fancy frills along the outside. It was a little lopsided, but still, it wasn't a bad-looking heart, not at all.

John Spencer had carved a heart just like it, on the big spruce near the bridge over Big Spoon Creek. He'd worked on it for two afternoons to get it just so. At least, that's what he'd told Lizette. Inside the heart he'd put big letters—*J. S. + L. H.* It had taken her a minute to realize that the *L. H.* stood for her—Lizette Holcombe.

John had been so proud of his work that Lizette hadn't known what to say. She hated to hurt anyone's feelings, least of all John's. He was probably the nicest boy this side of the Mississippi. But it had taken her by surprise to learn he was sweet on her.

After all, she and John had known each other all their lives. They'd always been friends—just friends. Always liked the same sorts of things, too—dreaming about the future, or staring up at the night sky when the stars were just starting to peek out at you.

Both of them loved learning, too. Since school had started, they'd spent long hours talking about how exciting it all was, the arithmetic and history and English Miz Christy was going to teach them.

And it wasn't that John wasn't a fine-looking boy. He had that curly blond hair, and light brown eyes that smiled a lot. Still, he wasn't the one she couldn't seem to stop thinking about.

Lizette fingered her chalk, considering. In the center of the heart, she wrote *L. H. + W. H.*

Ruby Mae leaned over. "What's that you're writin'?" she whispered.

"Nothin'," Lizette said quickly. She wiped away the initials with her palm.

When John had showed her the heart in the spruce tree, his face had turned as red as an apple. "I guess you can tell I'm sweet on you, Lizette," he'd said, all shy and soft.

What could she say? After a while, she'd said, "I like you, too, I reckon, John," because they'd seemed like words that wouldn't hurt his feelings. But on the way home, when he'd tried to hold her hand, she'd stuffed it in her skirt pocket as fast as lightning. He hadn't tried again, after that.

She couldn't have said the real truth of it, that she had her eyes on another boy. To begin with, John probably wouldn't have believed her. Wraight Holt was as different from Lizette as night was from day—on the outside, anyway. Where she liked to talk, he was gruff and shy. Where she loved to learn, he didn't much seem to like school at all. And though it pained her to say it, he wasn't very quick at picking up things, not the way she and John were.

Of course, she'd spent a little bit of time last year at the school way over in Low Gap. The school year only lasted four months there, but that was something, anyway. Wraight hadn't gone to the Low Gap school. His pa wasn't much for learning, from what Lizette could figure. He'd only let the Holt children go to school this year because Wraight's ma had talked him into it.

But Lizette knew that Wraight was smart. Maybe he wasn't the quickest study when it came to letters and numbers and such. Many times, she'd seen how angry he got when he looked foolish in class. But Wraight was special in other ways.

He'd long been famous around these parts for his hunting. He'd shot a deer at two hundred yards. And once he'd even brought down a bear that was charging straight at him. Other children had looked up to him after that. Even the men would nod their heads and say, "That Wraight's a tough one, he is, and a mighty fine shot."

But that wasn't all. When Wraight played his dulcimer and sang in a voice so pure it could melt a frozen river, that's when Lizette knew for sure how different he was from all the other boys. And when he smiled at her in a way that made her toes curl up just so, she was even more certain.

Lizette looked up and was surprised to see Miz Christy had finished her reading. When she got to thinking about Wraight like that, Lizette often lost track of time.

Miz Christy was so beautiful. Lizette would give anything to have eyes that blue and a smile that bright. She had a feeling the preacher thought Miz Christy was special, too. When he came in the afternoon to teach math and Bible studies, he always had an extra-wide grin for Miz Christy. Anybody with a lick of romance in them could see it there, plain as day.

Ruby Mae had told Lizette that she thought Dr. MacNeill was sweet on Miz Christy, too. Of course, Ruby Mae was full of crazy gossip half the time, but she might just be right about the doctor. She'd sounded pretty sure of herself.

"I have a special announcement to make," Miz Christy said. "I am going to appoint three Junior Teachers today. This is a very special honor. Junior Teachers will help me work with the other students." She held up a small piece of cloth in the shape of a shield. It was trimmed with fancy golden braids and beads. "This is a special badge I made. Each of the Junior Teachers will wear one."

Lizette sat up a little straighter and crossed her fingers.

She had never seen anything as beautiful as that badge. Oh, how she wanted to be a Junior Teacher! It was all she could do to keep from waving her hand in the air and begging Miz Christy for the honor.

"John Spencer," Miz Christy announced. John looked over at Lizette and smiled.

"Rob Allen."

Lizette closed her eyes. *Please, please, let it be me,* she whispered.

"And Lizette Holcombe," Miz Christy finished. "Come on up and accept your badges."

Lizette gasped. Had Miz Christy really called her name?

"Go on up," Ruby Mae said to Lizette.

Her cheeks flushed, Lizette joined John and Rob at the front of the room. Miz Christy pinned a badge on each of them. John winked at Lizette and nudged her with his elbow. She smiled back, but most of her attention was on her new badge. Miz Christy had made them herself, she'd said. The beads and spangles were as pretty as real diamonds, and worth much more to Lizette.

As the Junior Teachers returned to their seats, the class applauded. Lizette glanced toward the back of the room, where she knew Wraight was sitting. Her heart jumped when she realized he was looking right at her. But he didn't return her smile, and he and Lundy and the other boys at the back were not applauding.

Lizette sat down with a sigh. Maybe she was crazy to think Wraight could ever like her. All he'd ever done was throw snowballs at her, or tease her a little now and then. But there was that one time he'd sung to her at recess. It had been a song about love and broken hearts and sweet pain, and she'd been *almost* sure he'd felt something then.

Of course, that was a while back. Wraight hadn't brought his dulcimer to school in quite a spell. For that matter, he hadn't even thrown a snowball at her lately. There'd been a dark cloud over Wraight, it seemed, these last few weeks. He'd been spending more and more time with Lundy and Smith and they were not the best kind of friends to have. Those boys were trouble.

She wondered if maybe Lundy wasn't the one who'd written that awful message on the school wall. Of course, Lizette hadn't said anything to Miz Christy. She didn't exactly have any proof. And Lundy wasn't the kind of boy you wanted to tangle with, that was for sure.

Slowly Lizette turned around again. Wraight was still staring at her. She smiled, and this time, she thought maybe—just maybe—she saw him smile back. But when Lundy whispered something to Wraight, his smile vanished.

Lizette picked up her chalk and made another heart. *L.H. +*, she wrote.

She left the rest of the heart empty.

❧ Four ❧

That afternoon, Christy walked to the Spencers' cabin. The Spencer children— John, Zady, Clara, and Lulu—went with her. Lizette Holcombe came along, too. As official Junior Teachers, John and Lizette were anxious to talk about ways they could help the younger students. As she listened to their discussion, Christy felt very pleased. Her Junior Teacher idea was obviously going to be a big success.

As they walked through the sun-dappled woods, filled with the clean scent of pine and balsam, Christy could almost forget the ugly message on the schoolhouse. Even with the help of her students, it had taken most of the noon recess to scrub off the messy letters.

The Spencers' cabin came into view at the top of a ridge. Christy thought back to the first time she'd met the Spencer family. When no one had been at the train station to greet her, Christy had decided to set off on the seven-mile journey to the mission with Mr. Pentland as he delivered the mail. They'd stopped at the Spencers' cabin to warm themselves. But almost as soon as they'd sat down before the fire, a man named Bob Allen had been carried into the cabin on a homemade stretcher. Mr. Allen had been on his way to meet Christy at the station when a tree had fallen on his head. He was very badly hurt.

Before long, the local doctor, Neil MacNeill, had arrived to perform risky brain surgery right there in the Spencers' simple cabin. Christy had actually assisted the doctor during the operation. He was a big handsome man, if a little gruff. Christy had been amazed at his skill, not to mention his ability to remain calm under tremendous pressure.

Fortunately, Bob had survived. But she had felt terribly guilty about his accident—after all, he'd been on his way to meet her when it had happened.

During the anxious moments before and after the operation, Fairlight Spencer had offered Christy a gentle voice and a kind smile. She was graceful woman, with delicate features and lovely eyes. Somehow she hadn't seemed to belong in that primitive cabin, tucked far away in the woods. Christy had liked Fairlight instantly, and she had the feeling they would grow to be good friends.

Jeb Spencer, Fairlight's husband, was in the yard, chopping wood. When he heard the children coming, he set his axe down and opened his arms to hug Lulu, his six-year-old daughter, who was running to greet him. Two of the dogs raced over to John, yapping eagerly.

"And how was school today, you rascal?" Jeb asked Lulu. Jeb had deep-set blue eyes and a red beard. The front of his hat was pinned up with a long thorn. A sprig of balsam stuck out from the hat band like a feather. In spite of his ragged clothing, there was something dashing about him.

"Pa, we brought Teacher home with us!" Lulu cried proudly.

"So I see," Jeb said. He removed his hat and gave Christy a little bow. "Howdy-do, Miz Christy. Fairlight's been so excited about your comin', she ain't sat still all day long."

Fairlight was waiting at the door of the cabin. Little Guy, a chubby-faced toddler, clutched at her worn calico skirt. "I'm so glad you come, Miz Christy," Fairlight said, her face glowing. "I was half-afraid you wouldn't. Jeb's right. I've been so all-fired excited, I've been buzzin' around this cabin like a hungry bee a-huntin' for honey."

Christy laughed. "Of course I came, Fairlight. I've been looking forward to starting our lessons. I'm just sorry we couldn't start sooner. It's taken me a while to get settled in."

"With all those young'uns to teach, I should say so!" Fairlight exclaimed. "Come on in. You children, too, but mind your manners. There's gingerbread I made fresh, but don't be eatin' it all. We have company."

The Spencer cabin was just two rooms: a kitchen area, and a main room that served as dining room, living room, and bedroom. A narrow ladder led to a hole in the ceiling, where a sleeping loft was located. The floor was bare. Clothes and a worn saddle hung off pegs on the wall. Across an elk-horn rack rested a long-barreled rifle.

The first time Christy had seen this cabin, she'd been shocked at the primitive conditions. The Spencers had no running water, no phone, and no electricity. Stepping into their home was almost like stepping into another century, back to the days of the American frontier.

But since then, Christy had visited some of the other cabins in the area. Now she saw how much Fairlight had done to make this simple home special. She'd made the cabin warm and inviting by adding little touches of beauty. The rickety table by the fire, for example, was covered by a worn piece of delicately embroidered fabric. A chipped ceramic bowl sat on top of the table. Fairlight had carefully arranged sprigs of pine and balsam in it, then added the first delicate crocuses of the spring for a bit of color. Next to the bowl was a plate piled high with gingerbread, still warm.

Christy sat down at the table. On the floor beside her, she placed the box of teaching materials she'd brought along. Little Guy climbed into her lap. He seemed to be fascinated, like all the children, with her soft red sweater. She accepted a piece of gingerbread from Fairlight and gave half of it to Little Guy.

Christy took a bite of the spicy bread. "Fairlight, this is wonderful!" she exclaimed.

John grabbed two pieces of gingerbread. When Fairlight sent him a warning look, he quickly said, "One's for Lizette."

"What are those fancy things you two are wearing?" Fairlight asked, pointing to John's badge.

"We're Junior Teachers," John said proudly. "Me and Lizette and Rob Allen. We get to help Miz Christy with the young'uns."

"Well, that's mighty impressive," Fairlight said, winking at Christy. "I'm proud of you, John. And just to give you a little extra practice, you can keep an eye on Lulu and Little Guy while Miz Christy and me are a-studyin'."

John groaned. "We don't mind," Lizette

said with a grin. "Come on, Little Guy." She reached for the toddler and lifted him off Christy's lap.

As she passed the fireplace, Lizette's gaze fell on the dulcimer that belonged to Jeb. "John," she said thoughtfully, "did you ever think of learnin' to play the dulcimer like your pa does?"

John shrugged. "Naw. Pa plays enough for all of us. You know how he loves his ballad-singin'."

"Wraight plays," Lizette said.

"So?" John asked.

"So . . . nothin'. Have you ever heard him?" Her eyes had a faraway look in them.

"Nope. Don't want to, neither. I 'spect Wraight Holt has a voice like a bullfrog with the sniffles."

Lizette smiled wistfully. "You'd 'spect so. But when that boy takes a notion to sing, he's got more music in him than a treeful of birds."

"What are we talking about Wraight for, anyways?" John demanded. "He's trouble."

"No, he ain't," Lizette said.

"Well, he and Lundy and Smith are friends. And those other two ain't exactly angels. Look at what happened today at school. And yesterday."

"That don't mean Wraight had anything to—"

"Come on," John said gruffly. "We've got work to do."

Fairlight watched John and Lizette head over to the far corner of the room. She leaned close to Christy. "Near as I can figure, John's got a real hankerin' for Lizette. Lately, he's been walkin' around all moony-eyed." She lowered her voice. "But I have a feelin' Lizette don't feel the same way about John. I'm just guessin', mind you, but I think she's got her heart set on Wraight Holt."

Christy nodded. "It does sound that way, doesn't it?"

"What was John talkin' about?" Fairlight asked, reaching for a piece of gingerbread. "Did somethin' happen at the school?"

"Someone wrote *Get away, Teacher* on the side of the schoolhouse," Christy said with a sigh. "Not only that, they nailed the front door shut."

Fairlight blinked in disbelief. "Who done it, do you figure?"

"I wish I knew. Naturally, I suspect Lundy Taylor. But I don't have any proof. And I *thought* I saw Zach Holt running from the school. . . ."

"Zach's such a good boy," Fairlight said. "I reckon it wasn't him, unless one of the big boys put him up to it."

"Well, whoever it was, he wasn't a good speller." Christy smiled. "And speaking of spelling, we have more important things to be talking about! Shall we start?"

"I can't wait," Fairlight said. Her eyes were wide with excitement.

Christy opened the box she'd brought. Inside was a copy of the alphabet printed in large, clear letters; a Bible; a fresh, ruled pad; and some pictures Christy had cut out from old magazines. Some were of landscapes. Others were figures of men, women, and children, pasted onto cardboard bases so they could be stood upright, the way Christy used to do with paper dolls when she was a little girl. She was hoping to find a new and interesting way to teach Fairlight. She didn't want to use the same simple books she used for children beginning to read—the ones that began with sentences like "The rat ran from the cat."

Christy picked up the Bible. "There are lots and lots of words in this book."

"How soon will I be able to read it, Miz Christy?"

"In no time! And I'll tell you why. All the words in this book use only twenty-six English letters." She pointed to the alphabet. "After you've learned how to put the letters together, then, with some practice, you'll be able to read."

Fairlight's eyes shone. "I'd like that the best in the world."

After they had read through the alphabet twice, Fairlight began studying the letters with such concentration that she seemed to forget Christy was even there. After a while, she looked up. "Think I've got it," she announced. "A—B—C—D . . ." She went all the way through the alphabet, only making one mistake.

John and Lizette applauded. "Ma, that was wonderful!" John exclaimed.

"Isn't she the smartest ma in the whole wide world, Miz Christy?" cried twelve-year-old Clara, who was playing by the fire with her younger sister, Zady.

"Fairlight, I can tell you are going to be a wonderful student," Christy said. She felt almost as excited as Fairlight clearly was. She propped up one of the background pictures of a landscape drenched in sunlight. "Now, Fairlight, you pick out one of the paper people from this pile."

Fairlight selected a well-dressed young man and stood him up before the landscape. Christy taught her the word *man*, and Fairlight eagerly practiced saying it and forming the letters. Soon they'd moved on to *tree*, *sun*, *grass*, *sky*, and *light*. Before long, Fairlight had mastered ten words.

Christy opened the Bible to the first chapter of Genesis. "Now, Fairlight, look at this," she said. "The words on this page are just ideas marching along. Like this one—'And God said, Let there be light—'"

"L-I-G-H-T!" Fairlight cried. "There it is! *Light!* Just like in my own name. I *see* it!" She turned to Clara and Zady. "Look, girls. L-I-G-H-T, *light.*"

Christy couldn't help beaming. It was such a thrill to be able to open up a whole new world of reading to someone like Fairlight, who was so grateful for the chance to learn.

"Before long, you'll be reading the Bible to the children," Christy said. "I must say, Fairlight, you're a joy to teach."

Zady pulled on Christy's sleeve. "How about us, Teacher?" she asked, her black eyes wide. "Are we joys, too?"

"You are a joy to teach, too," Christy said, patting Zady on the head. "All my students are."

"Even Wraight and Lundy and Smith?" John asked from the corner.

"Even them," Christy said. Although the truth was, there had been many days when she'd wished the older boys weren't at school, trying her patience and testing her will.

Fairlight turned toward the only window. "What was that?" she asked, frowning.

"What?" Christy asked.

"Thought I heard somethin' at the window."

"Probably just Pa," John said, standing. "But I'll go check."

Outside the window, the shadows had grown long. Already the sun was vanishing behind the mountains. "I should get going," Christy said. "Miss Ida frets so if I'm late for dinner."

"John'll walk you," Fairlight said.

Christy shook her head. "Oh, there's no need."

"I'll walk with you part way, Miz Christy," Lizette volunteered. "Time for me to get goin', anyhow."

"John'll walk you both," Fairlight insisted.

"All right, then," Christy said, recalling her promise to David that morning.

John appeared in the doorway. "Ain't nothin', Ma," he reported. "Pa stackin' logs, most likely. He says he didn't see or hear nothin'."

"Probably just my ears playin' tricks on me," Fairlight said. "John, I want you to walk Miz Christy and Lizette on home. It's gettin' on toward dark, and I'm afraid I took up way too much time with my schoolin'."

"Don't be silly, Fairlight," Christy assured her. "I enjoyed every minute. In fact, I can't wait for us to get together again for another lesson. I'll leave that box of materials for you to work on."

"Meantime, maybe I can get me some help from my very own Junior Teacher," Fairlight said, giving John a hug.

John blushed, glancing over at Lizette. "We'd best get goin'," he said, pulling out of his mother's grasp.

"Thank you again, Miz Christy. I'm goin' to practice my letters till I know 'em backwards and forwards and inside out."

After Christy said goodbye to the children and to Jeb, she and Lizette and John set out along the rough path toward the mission. They took a slight detour that led to Lizette's cabin. When Lizette was safely inside, John and Christy resumed their walk to the mission.

After a few minutes of silence, John turned to Christy. "Have you ever been . . ."

"Ever been what, John?"

"You know." He picked up the pace. "You know, sweet on somebody?"

Christy hurried to catch up. "Well, once or twice, I suppose."

"Lizette says the preacher's sweet on you."

"Oh, she does, does she?"

John gave a terse nod. "S'posin' the preacher were sweet on you, but you weren't sweet on him?"

Christy felt herself blushing. She wasn't "sweet on" David, exactly. After all, she'd only known him a little while. But she had to admit she did look forward to his sly smiles and silly jokes.

"Miz Christy?"

Christy cleared her throat. "All right, then.

Let's suppose. As long as you understand we're *just* supposing."

"Well, s'posin'—" Suddenly John stopped in his tracks. "You hear somethin'?"

Christy paused, straining to hear. "No."

"Bushes cracklin'."

"No, I don't hear anything."

Christy glanced over her shoulder. The trees cast long, black shadows. The edges of the sky were tinged with pink, but the sun had vanished.

"Hearin' things, I guess. Sorry."

"So, John, you were saying?" Christy asked as they started walking again.

"Oh. That. I guess I was just wonderin' if there's a way to get a girl to be sweet on you when maybe she ain't."

"That's a good question. I suppose you should just be the person you really are, John. And if Liz . . . I mean, this girl . . . isn't the right one for you, trust me, someone else will come along who sees how special you really are."

John gave a small, hopeful smile. "You reckon?"

"I'm sure of it."

After a few more minutes, they reached the last ridge before the mission. The first stars had begun to glimmer.

"You go on home, now, John," Christy said. "If you head back now, you might not miss dinner."

"No'm. I promised I'd take you all the way."

"John," Christy said firmly. "I insist. Otherwise I'll have to worry about you."

John hesitated. "I don't mind, Miz Christy—"

"But I do. The mission is just over the next ridge, and I don't want you going home in complete darkness." She put her hands on her hips. "Now, go home. That's an order. After all, you may be a Junior Teacher. But I'm the Senior Teacher."

John laughed. "All right, then. You take care to go straight over the ridge so you don't get sidetracked. The path is hard to follow when it gets this dark." He started to turn, then hesitated. "Miz Christy?"

"Yes, John?"

"Thanks for the . . . uh, the advice."

"Any time."

Christy smiled as she started up the crude path. John was a nice boy. She wondered why Lizette was interested in Wraight—if she really was. Well, love was funny that way. Maybe Lizette saw something in Wraight that Christy couldn't see.

She climbed up the path, taking careful steps because of the patches of snow and mud. After a while, the path seemed to disappear in the twilight gloom. Hadn't it been better marked? The hill was steeper than she'd remembered it, too.

She stopped. Had she lost the trail, just as

John had warned her not to do? It had been here a minute ago—

Behind her, something cracked. It was the distinct, loud crunch of a dry stick breaking.

An animal, Christy told herself. She turned, straining her eyes to see if she could make out anything. John had long since vanished. She saw no animals. Nothing. In the near darkness, the trees blended into one another, forming a lacy, black curtain. She gazed back up toward the top of the ridge. Above her, a stand of pines lurked like a group of menacing giants.

Hoo—hoo—oo—hoo—hoo.

Christy started. It was an owl, that much she knew. She wasn't such a "city-gal" that she'd never heard an owl before. But it seemed to be coming from deep in the bushes, just a few yards to her left. Shouldn't any self-respecting owl be up in a tree?

You're almost home, Christy, she told herself. *Relax.*

It was just like Fairlight had said—her ears were playing tricks on her.

Christy quickened her pace, but the snow was hard and icy in spots. She'd only gained a few feet when she slipped and fell. She landed on the cold ground with a thud. As she struggled to untangle her long skirts, a deep, horrifying howling noise seemed to fill the whole woods. It was the cry of a wolf, so close it might have been just inches away.

Christy froze in place. Her heart galloped in her chest. If he saw her move, he might attack.

The howl came again, a long, sad wail. It was close, too close. She was sure she could hear the wild, dangerous animal breathing.

Whatever you do, she told herself, *don't move.*

On the other hand, she couldn't sit here all night in the cold, could she? They'd find her here tomorrow, stiff as a statue, with a look of terror permanently frozen on her face.

No, that was too awful to think about. One way or another, she had to take her chances.

Christy stumbled slowly to her feet. There was no point in looking for the path now. She'd just aim for the top of the ridge, where the dark blue sky glistened with a dusting of stars. She couldn't run up the steep, bramble-covered hill, even if she'd wanted to. Instead she grabbed at limbs and bushes wherever she could, pulling herself toward the top.

Christy held her breath as she made her way past the spot where she'd imagined the wolf—or whatever the source of that horrible howl—was hiding. She tried to be quiet, but every step meant the sound of cracking branches or crunching snow.

Nothing happened. No knife-toothed creature leapt from the darkness to tear at her throat. The only sound was the gentle creak and moan of an old tree nearby, fighting the wind.

See? Christy told herself. *You let your imagination get the better of you. Now, relax. You've lost the path, but once you reach the top of the ridge, the mission will be in view. In a few more minutes, you'll be sitting at the dinner table, laughing about your imaginary "wolf."*

Step, grab. Step, grab. It was slow going, but she was almost to the top. The trees had grown so thick that she had to squeeze between some of them. The smell of pine trees perfumed the night air. Their needles made a soft, swishing noise, like whispering voices. The bare branches of other trees clicked and cracked, but Christy told herself it was just the wind.

Near the top of the ridge, the trees thinned out a bit. Christy was panting. She paused to lean against a tall pine. "You're almost there," she said aloud. "Just a few more—"

Suddenly, she heard something falling from the tree. Christy screamed as it glanced off her shoulder before landing on the ground. Whatever it was, it was wet and soft and small. Swallowing back her fear, Christy knelt down.

It was a rat, a dead one. Starlight shone in its glassy eyes. Christy shuddered and backed away. She stared up into the pine tree.

Just then, a shadowy figure leapt out from behind a nearby tree, and once again, with all her might, Christy screamed.

✎ Five ✎

The figure moved closer and closer.

Christy backed against the pine. Her heart hammered in her chest. Her fists were clenched.

"Miz Christy, don't be scared. It's me."

Christy blinked. She didn't recognize the boy's voice. But she did recognize the red cap.

"Zach Holt?" she said in a trembling voice. "Is that you, Zach?"

The little boy came close and extended his hand. Even in near-darkness, she could see that his forehead was beaded with sweat. Pine needles stuck to his ragged, patched coat. A small stick was caught on his cap.

"Zach, what are you doing here? You weren't . . . following me, were you?"

"Me?" Zach cried. "No'm. Not me. I was just—" he hesitated, "I was just out huntin' possum."

"With your bare hands?"

Zach swallowed. "It's a special trick my pa taught me," he said quickly. "You corner 'em, and then when they play possum—you know, all curled up like they's dead, you whomp 'em on the head with a stick."

"I see." Christy crossed her arms over her chest. Now that her fear was fading, she was left with far too many questions. "I heard noises before," she said. "Branches cracking, that sort of thing. It sounded like somebody was following me."

With great care, Zach examined some pine needles on his coat.

"And I heard a wolf. At least, I thought it was a wolf."

"Could'a been." Zach nodded. "There's lots of wolves around these here parts. They get real mean this time of year. Hungry, too."

Christy nudged the dead rat on the ground with her toe. "Are there lots of tree rats in the area, too?"

Zach gulped. "Tree rats? Ain't never heard of no tree rats, Ma'am."

"I haven't, either. So how do you explain this one? It fell out of this pine tree. And nearly scared me to death, I might add."

Zach glanced up quickly at the upper branches of the tree, then met Christy's eyes. "Just can't mortally explain it, Miz Christy."

Christy stared up at the tree. She saw nothing but a blur of dark branches.

"Could be that's not a ground rat, factually speaking," Zach suggested. "Could be one of them there flyin' rats."

"Ah. Those must be very rare. I've never heard of them."

"Well, you're from the city. Ain't no flyin' rats in the city. They hate cars and such."

"I see."

"You heard of flyin' squirrels?"

"Yes. Now that you mention it, I believe I have." Christy tried not to smile. She was torn between her anger at having been scared, and her amusement at Zach's desperate attempt to explain the rat.

"Flyin' rats is the same thing. Only instead of big fuzzy tails, they got scrawny ones."

"Well, then. Thank you for clearing that up, Zach."

He pointed to the top of the ridge. "If'n you like, I could walk you the rest of the way home."

"Actually, I'm more worried about you getting home, safe and sound."

"Oh, don't fret about me none. I got company—" Zach swallowed hard. "What I mean to say is, I got me the stars and the trees for company. I know these woods like the back of my own hand, anyways."

"I'd be pleased to have you as an escort, then, Zach," Christy said.

They climbed in silence. At last they reached the top of the ridge. Below them, the mission house was a welcome sight. Yellow light glowed in the windows, and Christy could just make out the figure of Miss Ida inside, bustling to and fro.

Christy brushed the snow off a fallen log and sat down. She motioned for Zach to join her there. "I'd like to rest up, Zach, before I go the rest of the way. Maybe you could keep me company for a moment."

"Well . . ." Zach sat down, looking very uncomfortable. "My pa gets ornery if'n I'm out too long. I oughta be gettin' on. That is, if'n you don't need me to es-squirt you the rest of the way."

"Escort." Christy smiled. "Are you close to your pa, Zach?"

"Close?"

"You know. Do you two like to talk? Go hunting and fishing together, that sort of thing?"

"Not a whole heap. He talks some, I s'pose." Zach kicked at a stone. "Pa's got kind of a mean streak in him, when he gets to drinkin' moonshine."

Christy nodded. Miss Alice had told her that illegal liquor was a big problem here in the mountains.

"That must be hard for you, when he gets like that," she said gently.

"Ain't so hard. I'm used to it. Wraight, he—" Zach stopped himself.

"What, Zach?"

"Nothin'. It's just . . . now and again, he gets riled up somethin' fierce about Pa. Wraight's got a temper, see, and so does Pa." He gave a little shrug. "Course it's not *real* feudin', mind you. Not like the Taylors and the Allens or nothin'."

"I've heard that the Taylor and Allen families have been fighting each other for a long, long time," Christy said. "Why are they still fighting, do you think?"

Zach looked at her in confusion, as if he couldn't understand why she'd even bother asking. "Way back when, the Taylors and Allens got to shootin' each other, and they ain't never stopped. Could be over moonshinin'." He shrugged. "Could be over nothin'."

Once again, Christy felt a deep sadness for mountain children like Zach. They were so used to hate and fighting and killing. It wasn't fair. They grew up far too fast.

"Zach," she asked casually, "do you like Lundy?"

"He's all right enough, I s'pose."

"But you're friends with him, aren't you?"

"I'm too little. Wraight's his friend, more'n I am."

Christy stared up at the starry sky. "I guess Lundy can be kind of a bully, can't he?"

Zach answered with a small nod.

"I can see how it might be hard for someone

—especially someone smaller—to say no to Lundy."

"Right hard," Zach agreed.

Christy sighed. This was tougher than she'd thought it would be. She was almost certain that Lundy was putting Zach up to these pranks. But could she ever get the little boy to admit it, as long as he was so afraid of Lundy?

She decided to try the direct approach. "Zach, did Lundy make you follow me this evening, to try to scare me?"

"No'm," Zach said, leaping off the log. "Don't be gettin' Lundy all mixed up in this. It'll just make things worse!"

"Zach, what are you talking about?"

"I got to go, Miz Christy. My pa and all. Will you be all right the rest of the way over to the mission?"

"Of course I will. And thank you, Zach, for taking me this far."

With an awkward tip of his little red cap, Zach slipped into the trees and vanished.

— — —

The next day at school, Christy didn't say anything to Zach about the incident in the woods. She noticed that he seemed even quieter than usual. Wraight and Lundy, on the other hand, were especially bad-tempered and rude. Twice she'd had to scold them during reading lessons.

It had been a frustrating day, even with the help of her new Junior Teachers. When Lizette had tried to help Wraight with his spelling, he'd snapped at her so gruffly that she'd practically cried.

Christy was glad when the school day finally ended. As she stood in the doorway, saying goodbye to the children, she was surprised to see Mr. Pentland appear at the top of the ridge.

"Back so soon?" Christy called.

"Not just me," Mr. Pentland yelled back. He jerked his thumb back toward the woods. "Got some delivery folks a-comin', too. Mighty big load."

"Oh, that's wonderful!" Christy exclaimed. "Donations for the mission?"

"Yep. All of it's for the mission, near as I can tell. Been piling up at the train station for a while now."

Soon a big wagon, pulled by two pairs of strong oxen, lumbered into the schoolyard. It was piled high with crates and boxes. Some were covered with a large tarp.

Christy ran to greet the wagon. So her letter-writing campaign had worked, after all! What would David and Miss Alice say when they saw how well her plan had worked?

Most of the children, who'd been about to

head home, stayed to watch as the two delivery men began unloading large boxes.

Only Zach, Lundy, Wraight, and Smith hung back on the porch, as sullen and watchful as ever.

"My, it's Christmas in March!" David exclaimed, rushing over to help the delivery men. "Are you sure they're in the right place, Mr. Pentland?"

"Yep. Took two days to get here over those rutted roads. But they figured better now than when the spring thaw comes and the mud with it. It's all for the mission. Oh— 'ceptin' this package for you, Miz Christy." Mr. Pentland reached into his bag and handed her a small package. It was wrapped in brown paper and tied with a string. "Mighty big week for deliveries."

The careful handwriting on the package told Christy it was from her mother.

"Ain't you goin' to open it, Teacher?" Ruby Mae asked.

"I'll save it for later," Christy said. "We've got enough to open, don't you think?"

David borrowed a hammer from one of the delivery men and began to open a large wooden crate. "This says to Miss Christy Rudd Huddleston," David said. "From the Martin Textile Company in Charlotte, North Carolina." He grinned at her. "You have connections in Charlotte?"

"Well, not exactly," Christy said. "It's a long story."

The top of the crate popped off. "Blankets!" Ruby Mae cried. She and Bessie began pulling out the fresh wool blankets, one by one. David opened another crate from the same company, this one filled with pillows.

One by one, David revealed the contents of the other crates. Each time, the children gathered around, gasping in surprise at the bounty inside. Christy beamed as she watched the donations pile up. All of it was so desperately needed—sheets, towels, rugs, cleaning supplies, medicine. And all of it was the result of Christy's letter-writing campaign, with the exception of two barrels of secondhand clothing, sent by her mother's church. The Bell Company had even come through with a large donation of telephone wire and a telephone.

David stared at the wire, frowning in disbelief. "And how exactly am I going to hook up telephone lines?" he asked.

"Well, you built an entire schoolhouse, didn't you?" Christy said with a wink. "How hard will it be to install one little telephone?"

"It has to be connected up, you know. Two ends, something to carry the voice."

"A telephone!" Ruby Mae exclaimed. "Wouldn't that just be the most all-fired amazin' thing Cutter Gap ever seen? How long will it take you to hook it up, Preacher?"

David rolled his eyes. "I wouldn't hold your breath, Ruby Mae. It may be a very long wait. In spite of your teacher's confidence in me."

"But David—" Christy began, stinging a little from the sarcasm in his voice. After all, she'd gone to a lot of trouble to get the telephone equipment. Couldn't he at least show a little gratitude?

"Well, well. This is quite a sight," Miss Alice called from her cabin porch. But the look on her face was not exactly what Christy had hoped to see. She'd expected Miss Alice to be as thrilled as she was about the donations. Instead, she almost looked annoyed.

"Looky here, Miss Alice," Little Burl said, running to grab her hand as she approached. "There's pillows in that there crate, soft as can be!"

"So I see."

Miss Alice met Christy's eyes. Now Christy was certain of it. Her heart sank a little. Miss Alice was not pleased.

David held up the wire. "Christy apparently thinks that with my magical skills, I'll be able to string up a telephone wire. She seems to have forgotten that the wire has to go over two mountains, not to mention a river."

Just then, John cried out. "Ooo-wee! Will you look at this!" He and Creed had managed to open a large cardboard box.

Christy recognized the printing on the top

of the box. It was from a textbook supplier she'd written. Could it be?

John held up a brand-new history textbook. "Real, live books!" he cried. "Have you ever seen somethin' so all-fired pretty?"

Christy joined the boys. The other children crowded close. It was more than she'd ever dreamed possible—maps, books, even a globe and an American flag!

"Oh, Miss Alice!" Christy cried. "Isn't it wonderful?"

"I'm glad, for the sake of the children," Miss Alice said quietly, "but I do think we need to have a talk, Christy."

Before Christy could respond, Little Burl grabbed her arm. "Teacher," he said urgently, "what's under the big blanket over yonder on the wagon? Those are the biggest boxes I ever did see!"

Christy was almost afraid to ask. Judging from Miss Alice's stern look, she had made some kind of terrible mistake. Still, she had no choice but to ask.

"Mr. Pentland," she said, "what's under the tarp? More boxes? Or maybe mattresses?"

"No'm. I reckon you remember how I told you somethin' was a-comin' that could make noise?" He signaled to the two delivery men, who yanked the tarp free.

Everyone gasped, but no one was more stunned than Christy.

A beautiful, brand-new, gleaming, grand piano sat on its side in the wagon.

"Oh, my!" Christy said, her hand to her mouth.

"Oh, my, indeed," said Miss Alice.

"Mercy, Teacher!" whispered Creed. "What *is* it?"

"It's a piano, Creed. A concert grand piano. It makes beautiful music."

Even Lundy and his friends ran over, staring at the piano in awe. Wraight reached out and touched the shiny black piano bench, his jaw slightly ajar.

"Ain't it just purty?" Ruby Mae said to Wraight.

He gave a small nod, his fingers lingering on the smooth wood.

Christy turned to Miss Alice and David. "Well," she said a little sheepishly, "surprise!"

David slowly shook his head. He could not seem to find the right words.

"Christy," he said at last, "that may be the understatement of the year."

❧ Six ❧

But I thought you'd be pleased," Christy said after dinner that night. She was sitting at the dining room table with David, Miss Alice, and Miss Ida. Ruby Mae was in the kitchen, cleaning up the dishes.

The boxes of donations sat in the living room, along with the grand piano. It had taken David, Mr. Pentland, and the two delivery men several frustrating hours to get it into the mission house.

Miss Ida pursed her lips. "Miss Alice doesn't like begging," she said primly.

"But I didn't beg, exactly," Christy said lamely. "I just wrote a nice letter to some companies. I explained the mission's desperate need for supplies. And I told them about the children. That's all."

"Now's the time for me to explain the

mission's philosophy of fundraising," Miss Alice said. She paused to pour a fresh cup of tea from a steaming pot. "We believe that only one reason is good enough for a person to give—because that person, without pressure, freely chooses to make the gift. Money pried out of people won't be blessed for the work we need to do, anyway. Donations must come from the heart."

Christy hung her head. "I understand. At least, I think I do."

"As much as we need those supplies, you risked putting the mission in a bad light, Christy," Miss Alice continued. "I honestly don't think going ahead on your own like this was even good teamwork."

Christy nodded. She thought of many explanations for her behavior, but she knew Miss Alice was right. "I guess sometimes I do go running off on my own," she admitted.

"Independence can be a good thing," Miss Alice said. "But you've only been here a brief time. Before you go changing the world, take things a little more slowly, and consult David and me. Sometimes it's hard to see the whole picture. For example, these donations are going to cause some unintended problems."

"But how could they? The mission desperately needs everything that was sent." Christy paused. David was gazing at the piano, grinning widely. "With the possible exception of the grand piano," she added.

"The thing is, Christy, we can't simply give these items away to the mountain people." Miss Alice sat back in her chair. "There's a strong mountain code, you see. No one wants to owe anyone for anything. These people don't respect anyone who can't earn his own way."

"But all the clothes!" Christy cried. "We can't just let them sit there in the barrels, untouched. There are lots of shoes in good condition, Miss Alice. You know how badly the children need shoes."

"You're right. But do you see my point?" Miss Alice asked gently. "You need to understand the mountain people before you can help them. Your intentions were good. But the result was not precisely what you'd hoped. If you simply give away all these items, then people will feel like the few things they've worked so hard for are worth less. We must always remember that this mission represents a change for Cutter Gap. We hope it will be a change for the better. But change can be frightening, too. And frightened people can become angry people."

For a moment, everyone sat quietly, contemplating the boxes and barrels stacked high in the parlor.

Suddenly, David snapped his fingers. "I have an idea!" he exclaimed. "Suppose we sell the clothes? Priced very low, of course. We could set up a little store. Charge something like seventy-five cents for a good suit, five cents for a vest. That sort of thing."

"That's a wonderful idea," Christy said, relieved that the donations might not have to go to waste. "And maybe we could accept vegetables or other things as payment, instead of money. That way, all the mountain people would have a chance to get what they need, no matter how poor they are."

"I think that's a fine solution to a tricky problem," Miss Alice pronounced.

Ruby Mae came in, drying her hands on a dish towel. "I been meanin' to ask you," she said. "Are we goin' to have some kind of jollification, now that we have that giant piano-thing right there in the middle of the parlor, just a-waitin' for some playin'?"

"Another fine idea!" Miss Alice said. "How about an open house?"

"Ruby Mae, you're brilliant," David said. "We could have a party here, with music and dancing, and invite everyone from Cutter Gap. Jeb can play his dulcimer, and I'll play my ukelele."

"I play a little piano," Christy said. "Not very well, but I could give it a try."

"Wonderful," said Miss Alice. "How about Saturday night? Ruby Mae, you spread the word."

"I'll get right on that, Miz Alice," Ruby Mae said excitedly. "Be tickled to death to help out."

"With Ruby Mae on the job, everyone in Cutter Gap will know about it within an hour," David teased. Ruby Mae rolled her eyes, then slapped at David playfully with the dish towel.

Miss Alice leaned over to Miss Ida, whose brow was creased with a deep frown. "What's wrong, Miss Ida?"

"I was just thinking about what a mess an open house like that will make!" Miss Ida groaned. "I'll be cleaning up for a month or more."

"Don't worry, Miss Ida," Christy said. "I'll get the children to help."

Miss Ida seemed to relax a little. "Don't you fret none, Miss Ida," Ruby Mae said, patting her on the shoulder. "Last jollification I went to, over at the Holcombes', it weren't hardly any mess at all." She shrugged. "Unless, of course, you count that broken window. Or when the kitchen caught on fire . . ."

Miss Ida groaned, dropping her head into her hands.

Christy winked at Ruby Mae. "You've probably reassured Miss Ida enough for one evening, Ruby Mae."

"Well, now," David said to Christy. "It seems everything worked out for the best. We've found a way to deal with all these donations, and we even managed to get that piano inside. One of these days, I may even figure out how to hook up that telephone of yours."

"Still, I'm sorry about all this," Christy said. "I only meant to help, but I can see now that I went a little too fast." She sighed. "Sometimes I wonder if I'll ever really understand these people. Take last night, when I thought I was being chased on my way home from the Spencers' cabin. I ran into Zach Holt, but when I tried to question him—"

"Did you just say 'when I thought I was being chased'?" David interrupted. "What are you talking about? I thought John Spencer walked you home."

"He did. And it's nothing, really, David," Christy said with a wave of her hand. "That's why I didn't mention it yesterday when I got home. I heard some noises, a dead rat dropped out of a pine tree—"

"A *what*?" David cried.

"I'm sure it was just more of the same. Another prank, that's all. The odd thing was that Zach suddenly appeared, out of nowhere. But try as I might, I couldn't get him to admit that Lundy has been putting him up to these things. And I'm sure that's what's going on."

"I don't like this, not at all," David said. "This is getting out of hand."

Miss Alice shook her head. "One thing's clear, anyway. That message on the school is not going to be the end of these pranks."

"You've got to be more careful, Christy," David said sternly.

"I will, I promise—"

"No, I don't think you understand. This is just like the situation with the donations. You think you understand these people, but you don't—not yet. They can be violent. Very violent. People in Cutter Gap have been shot for no reason."

"But if this prankster is just one of the children . . ." Christy's voice trailed off. "I can't believe any of them would be capable of real violence."

"Don't be too sure," Miss Ida warned.

"It can't hurt to be careful, Christy," Miss Alice said. "To begin with, you're not completely sure that one of the children is responsible. Until we can put a stop to this, I think you should stay close to the mission for a while, and be very careful."

"I understand," Christy said. "But it sure seems to me like you're worrying over nothing."

Miss Alice seemed surprised by Christy's reaction. "Don't forget what I told you. In these mountains, anything new and strange poses a threat. And here we have a new schoolhouse, a new starry-eyed teacher, and now, new books. . . . For some, that may add up to a threat to the only way of life they've ever known. Don't forget all the mischief Granny O'Teale was able to make when she decided you were cursed."

Christy gave a wry laugh. "How could I? Still, I hate to think one of the children feels that way." She pushed back her chair and stood. "Did you ever have one of those days when you felt like you couldn't do anything right?"

"Don't be silly," Miss Alice said, reaching over to pat Christy's arm. "You're doing so much right. You've made great strides with the children already. And I know you're going to do much more, with time."

"That will only be possible if they'll let me."

A smile tugged at the corners of Miss Alice's mouth. "Remember Matthew 19:26, Christy: '. . . with God all things are possible.'"

___

Up in her room, Christy settled on her bed and carefully opened the package Mr. Pentland had brought her today. Inside was a note written in her mother's careful handwriting and a gift, about the size of a book, wrapped in pretty blue tissue paper. Carefully, Christy tore off the paper. She wanted to save as much as she could. Perhaps she could use it for an art project at school.

Inside, to her surprise, was a brand-new

leather-covered diary and a new fountain pen. Christy had told her mother how she'd given her old diary away to Ruby Mae after Christy had caught her snooping in it. Christy had torn out the few pages where she'd written about her journey to Cutter Gap. Most of the diary was untouched, and Ruby had been thrilled at the idea of having a private place all her own where she could write down her thoughts and dreams. As hard as it had been to part with the diary, Christy had never regretted giving it away.

Now, here was her chance to start fresh. Something told her it was important to record everything that happened to her here at the mission. She knew she was on an important adventure, even if she had no idea how it would all unfold.

Christy opened to the first page. On it, her mother had written:

February 21, 1912
For my lovely and brave daughter,
to record all her adventures.

All my love,
Mother

A hot lump formed in Christy's throat. There were many days when she missed her parents and her brother George so much that it felt like she could hardly bear it.

Even though her parents had at first argued against her coming here, once Christy had made up her mind to teach in Cutter Gap, they had been completely supportive. She traced her fingers over her mother's message. Christy could almost hear her talking to the women's group at the church about her daughter's wonderful work in the mountains. She could imagine her as she carefully folded each sweater and dress into the donation barrels that had arrived today.

But was Christy's work here so wonderful? Sometimes she wondered. Obviously, she had disappointed Miss Alice today. And she'd angered someone enough to cause a string of angry pranks.

Christy reached for the pen and began to write.

Wednesday, March 13, 1912

My first entry in my new diary. As I continue my adventures in Cutter Gap, I pray that I won't let down my parents, Miss Alice, David, or the children. And most importantly, perhaps, I pray I won't let myself down.

I can be far too stubborn, too vain, too independent. I often try to do too much, too fast. I sometimes assume I know everything, when in fact I know so little. Today, the day the donations arrived, I saw plenty of evidence of these facts.

But perhaps knowing my failings is at least a beginning. I can only have faith that I will learn and grow, and that I will become a stronger, better person here, despite the disappointments and hardships . . . not to mention the "flying rats"!

Christy closed her diary. It had been quite a day. She thought of the grand piano in the main room downstairs and smiled. She knew Miss Alice was right about the donations. But now that they *had* the piano, Christy was awfully glad they were going to get a chance to use it.

A party—a "jollification," as Ruby Mae called it—would be just the thing to distract the children from the recent pranks and to show them that they had nothing to fear from the mission. Perhaps she'd invite the children over to the mission house after school on Friday to help decorate for the party.

Maybe after that, Christy thought hopefully, the strange pranks would end at last, for once and for all.

❧ Seven ❧

She was so beautiful, Wraight thought.
Lizette Holcombe had to be the prettiest girl
in the whole, wide state of Tennessee.

He stood in the corner of the mission house
parlor with Lundy and Zach and Smith. Miz
Christy had invited all the students in after
school finished today, so they could help her
decorate for the big jollification tomorrow
night.

He didn't see as there was any point in going to the party. He couldn't dance worth a
hoot. And with his dulcimer all broken to
bits, he couldn't play along with Jeb and the
preacher and the other music-makers. Besides,
Lizette would be so beautiful that everyone
would want to dance with her. John Spencer,
for one. Wraight knew John was sweet on her.

Wraight wondered if John knew pretty

things to say to Lizette, the things girls liked. Fancy words about flowers and birds and love. Wraight didn't know any of that sugar-sweet romancing talk. About the only thing he knew to get Lizette's attention was to throw snowballs at her. That always made her laugh, all right.

He'd gone and made a fool of himself when she was trying to help him with his spelling. He'd growled at her like an old bear because he couldn't understand what she was trying to explain.

When that happened—and it happened a whole lot at school—he felt all tight and coiled up inside. He got angry and did things he didn't mean to do, just like his Pa did things he didn't mean to do sometimes.

Wraight watched while Lizette and Bessie and Ruby Mae tried on hats out of the barrel of clothes the mission had for sale. Lizette put on a big floppy straw one with a pink flower on it.

"What do you think, Wraight?" she called to him. "Do I look like a city-gal?"

"You look . . . " Wraight hesitated. He glanced over to Lundy for help, but Lundy just gave his usual smirk. "You look fine," Wraight managed.

Lizette sort of half-smiled, and Wraight breathed a sigh of relief. She was talking to him, at least, so that must mean she wasn't still mad about the way he'd practically bitten her head off when she'd tried to help him with his spelling.

Well, that was something, anyway.

Lundy elbowed him. "Why is it you get all tongue-tied 'round Lizette? You sweet on her or somethin'?"

"I ain't sweet on nobody."

"John Spencer's got his eye on her, anyways," Lundy said. "Course, why she'd pay any mind to that puny little varmint—"

"Don't talk that way about John," Zach spoke up. "He ain't so bad."

Lundy socked Zach in the shoulder, hard. "Hush up, weasel face. I ain't talkin' to you."

"Don't hit Zach," Wraight said, clenching his fist. "Never."

Lundy stepped closer, until he was just inches from Wraight's face. "You a-tellin' me what to do?"

Wraight stared past Lundy. He clenched his teeth. The anger boiled up inside him. But he didn't say a word.

"Thought so."

Wraight leaned back against the wall. Lundy was three inches taller than he was, and much heavier. He never lost a fight, never, and Wraight knew there was no point in starting one now. Lundy was mean. And he was a good shot. Too good, though not as good as Wraight. Still, around the school, what Lundy wanted, Lundy got. Everybody did what he said, even Wraight. That's just the way it was.

Across the room, Lizette and Ruby Mae were dancing with each other, giggling and carrying on the way girls did. Miz Christy was helping some of the littlest children hang up drawings they'd made for decorations. Miss Ida, the grouchy one with the sharp tongue, was rushing about with a feather duster.

"Want to dance, Wraight?" Lizette called as she whirled past, nearly knocking over a hat rack. She had a scarf around her neck. It flowed behind her, just like a flag in the wind. It was the color of her eyes, as dark and big as night itself.

He wanted to say something just right, when she whirled past again, but all he could think of was, "I can't dance."

He wished so badly that he still had his dulcimer. He'd played it for her once, under a tree during recess. He'd sung a ballad his ma had taught him, one with all the fancy words about love and such that he didn't know how to say himself. When he was singing or playing his music, everything made sense.

He felt smart when he sang, like his feelings got shaped into notes. He couldn't spell, couldn't add, but he could make the four strings of his dulcimer sing as sweet as the first spring bluebird. And he wasn't exactly sure, but it had seemed to him that when he played, Lizette had looked at him in a different way. His heart got all stirred up, just remembering it.

Of course, he didn't have his dulcimer, not anymore. His pa had smashed it good, one night when the moonshine had gotten the better of him. Wraight could still remember that night like it had just happened. It made him knot up inside, just thinking about it.

Wraight's pa had been mad at him because Wraight hadn't chopped enough wood to keep the fire going. "You ain't got a lick of sense in you, boy," he'd screamed, and then he'd grabbed the dulcimer right out of Wraight's hands. He'd held it high up in the air, waving it back and forth. "I'll get me some firewood right quick," he'd said, his voice all slow and dark with the moonshine.

Then, while Wraight had watched in horror, he'd slammed the little dulcimer against a table. It had broken into a hundred pieces. Splinters of wood covered the floor. It was like watching a living thing die, right before your eyes.

Wraight had tossed the pieces of wood in the fireplace for kindling. He hadn't cried. Hadn't said a word. There wasn't any point in crying.

He'd kept the strings, though. Why, he didn't know. He just couldn't let them go.

He gazed over at the new piano. Miz Christy had been mighty proud about getting it for the mission. She'd said the piano was full of wires inside, long ones. When you pushed on one of the little white or black boxes in a long row—she'd called them keys—a sound happened.

It would pleasure him something fierce to be able to play that big instrument. If he could get a sound out of it, even learn a song or two, maybe then Lizette would listen. Maybe she'd remember how he'd sung and played for her before.

He made his way over to the piano bench. "What are you up to, Wraight Holt?" Lundy called.

Wraight cringed. Lundy was like a dark shadow he could never get rid of. Always causing trouble, always looking to make life harder than it already was. Lundy hated the other students, hated the school, hated Miz Christy. Come to think of it, there wasn't much Lundy Taylor did seem to like. How many times had Wraight heard Lundy talk about getting rid of the school, and Miz Christy with it?

But the truth was, sometimes Wraight felt that way, too.

"I'm just lookin', is all," Wraight called back to Lundy. "Let me be."

He eased onto the bench. It was slippery. He let his fingers slide over the white keys. They were smooth, too. Miz Christy had said they were made of ivory, from elephants' tusks, but he hardly saw how that was possible. She'd said tusks were sharp, like knives. And these keys were as smooth and cool as ice.

Gently he pressed down on a key. Nothing happened. No sound. Nothing like the sweet, sad twang of a dulcimer string.

He pressed again. This time a sound did come, a low, smooth, easy sound that made him start. It came from deep in the belly of the piano, far from his touch. How could that be?

He moved his hand far up the keys. Again he pushed. This time, the sound was sweet and high as a raindrop in a pool of water. He blinked. It was a plain and simple miracle, near as he could figure.

"Miss Ida," Lundy's taunting voice met his ears. "Wraight Holt is playing on that there music-maker."

Miss Ida bustled over and slapped at Wraight's hand. "Get away from there," she said. "That's for people who know how to play. People who've had lessons, which I venture to say you have not."

She slammed down the black lid and the magic keys disappeared from view, as if they'd never been there. Behind him, Wraight heard Lundy's snarling laugh.

Wraight glanced across the room. Lizette

was standing with John. She was watching Wraight, and the look in her eyes was nothing like the look he remembered from that day under the tree.

He knew all too well what that look was. Her eyes said she felt sorry for him.

$$\sim\!\!\sim\!\!\sim$$

"Isn't this the perfect evening for a party?" Christy said to David as they walked along the porch of the mission house.

It was late Saturday afternoon, and the open house was already getting underway. The sun had just begun to sink. Its brilliant red rays seemed to set the mission house windows on fire. The day had been surprisingly warm for March. Patches of snow still remained, but much of it had melted, turning the yard to mud. Nevertheless, families were already gathering in the yard, laughing and hugging and gossiping.

"Jeb Spencer's already got his dulcimer going," David said. "I'm going to have to round up my ukelele so we can get a duet started."

"The yard's not exactly the best place for dancing," Christy pointed out. "I'd planned on the party taking place inside." She grinned. "Of course, I'm sure Miss Ida would be very relieved if everybody stayed out here."

"The temperature will drop soon enough,"

David said. "Then everyone will head inside." He paused to gaze at her, just long enough that Christy felt a blush creep up her neck. "By the way," David said, "have I mentioned how very nice you look tonight?"

Christy adjusted the blue bow in her hair. "You look pretty nice, yourself," she said shyly, just as Ruby Mae came out the front door.

David cleared his throat. "Well, I guess I should go find my ukelele," he said. He nudged Christy with his elbow. "Think later on we could talk you into playing a tune or two on the piano?"

"I'm not so sure that's a good idea, Preacher," Ruby Mae said. "Miz Christy was a-practicin' this afternoon. Scraped my eardrums somethin' fierce."

Christy laughed. "I am a little rusty."

"After all the work it took getting that piano inside the mission house, I can't bear to think it's going to go to waste," David said. "We'd better find somebody around here who can play it!"

While David went to find his ukelele, Ruby Mae and Christy watched the party from the porch. Soon Fairlight joined them.

She was wearing a lavender crocus in her hair. Little Guy dozed peacefully in her arms, his head on her shoulder.

"Listen to this," she said to Christy. "F-A-I-R-L-I-G-H-T."

"Fairlight, that's wonderful!" Christy exclaimed. "You really are a quick study."

"I can already spell all the names in the family. 'Cept I keep forgettin' to put that there *H* in *JOHN*."

"Where is John, anyway?" Christy asked. "I haven't seen him."

"Over yonder," Ruby Mae said. She pointed toward the schoolhouse. "Moonin' over Lizette, like always."

"Poor John," Fairlight said. "I fear he's pinin' for her bad."

"Crazy thing is," Ruby Mae said, lowering her voice, "Bessie Coburn's had her eye on John ever since school started. Told me every time he says howdy to her she plumb near walks on air the rest of the day."

"Are you sure?" Fairlight asked.

"Course I'm sure. Bessie's my best friend, and she told me after I promised never to breathe a word of it to nobody—" Suddenly Ruby Mae's eyes went wide. "Confound it all! I'd best be movin' on, before my mouth gets me into any more trouble."

Without another word, she dashed off. Fairlight and Christy laughed as they watched her go. "Looks like David found his ukelele," Christy said, pointing across the yard.

David and Jeb were sitting next to each other on two overturned crates. As they strummed and sang, more and more people

347

began to clap and dance, wheeling in circles on the muddy grass.

"Jeb loves that dizzifyin' music," Fairlight said. "He'll strum all night long, if'n we let him."

"I have the feeling David will, too," Christy said.

Miss Alice poked her head out the door. "This seems to have turned into an outdoor party," she said.

"Oh, they'll be in soon enough, Miz Alice," Fairlight said. "Once the dark falls and the air starts a-chillin'."

A tiny, bent woman passed by the porch. She was leaning on a wooden walking stick for support. She paused, tapping her stick on the porch railing to get Christy's attention.

"Granny O'Teale!" Christy exclaimed. Not too long ago, Granny would never have dared set foot at the mission. Christy was very pleased to see her here tonight.

"For a city-gal," Granny said, "you give a mighty fine jollification."

"Thank you, Granny," Christy said. "I'm awfully glad you came."

"There's food and such a-comin', right?"

"Oh, yes. Lots of it."

"Then I reckon I'm glad I came, too."

Christy watched Granny hobble off. "Wasn't this a wonderful idea, Miss Alice?" Christy asked.

"Yes, it was," Miss Alice agreed. "A fine idea. By the way, I'll be back in the kitchen with Miss Ida, if you need me."

Watching the children and adults clapping and dancing, their voices raised in song, Christy felt a warm glow. Cutter Gap may have seen its share of feuds and fighting over the years, but on a night like tonight, with the stars glistening and the music soaring, it seemed as if nothing could go wrong.

"Who's that over yonder?" Fairlight asked. She pointed to the bottom of the ridge, where four figures had emerged from the trees. They were barely visible in the waning light.

"Looks like Wraight and Zach," Christy said.

"Lundy and Smith, too," Fairlight said. "Hope they're not here to make trouble."

The four boys marched slowly across the yard. Lizette caught sight of Wraight and waved. "Wraight!" she called out. "I didn't think you'd come!"

Near the edge of the circle of dancers, Wraight paused to see where the voice was coming from. "Lizette?" he called, peering into the darkening twilight.

"Over here!" Lizette called from the school-house.

Wraight spun around in the direction of her voice. As he turned, he bumped shoulders with one of the dancers and lost his balance. He landed on his hands and knees in a patch of thick mud.

Instantly, the music and dancing stopped. Everyone turned to stare at Wraight. After a moment, the whole group broke into gales of laughter.

"That a new dance step, Wraight?" called Bob Allen.

Wraight tried to wipe his hair out of eyes, but he only succeeded in drawing a stripe of mud across his cheek and starting a whole new round of laughter.

"He never were much for dancin'," said Ruby Mae, giggling so hard she had to wipe tears from her eyes.

Christy could see how embarrassed poor Wraight was. As he struggled to his feet, his legs and hands caked with mud, she ran over to help him.

"Don't pay any attention to them, Wraight," she said, taking his arm. "Let's go on inside. I'll get you a towel and you can clean up."

"Don't need none of your help!" Wraight cried, yanking free of her grasp. His eyes burned. "Get away from me!"

"Really," Christy said gently, "I'll get you a towel and you'll be good as new, I promise. Don't be embarrassed. By the end of the evening, I'll bet you almost everybody will have some mud on them."

"I ain't embarrassed," Wraight shot back. He glared at her with such fury that Christy backed away a step. Without another word, he stomped off toward the mission house.

After a few moments of silence, Jeb and

David started playing again. Before long, the dancing was in full swing, and Wraight's fall was forgotten.

But no matter how hard she tried, Christy could not forget the look of anger in his eyes.

❧ Eight ❧

Wraight ran into the mission house because it was the only place he could think of where he could hide from the laughter and the stares. He'd looked like a complete fool out there, in front of all of Cutter Gap. Worst of all, he'd looked like a fool in front of Lizette.

He felt the rage inside him like a wild animal clawing to come out. He wanted to hurt something, or maybe even somebody.

He knew it was wrong to feel like this. But he couldn't seem to help it.

There were noises coming from the kitchen. He heard women's voices. The parlor was empty. He leaned against the wall, trying to catch his breath. He was covered with mud. It was on the floor, on the wall, anywhere he touched. What a sight he must have made out there in the yard! Was it any wonder they'd all laughed?

It didn't used to be this way. For as long as Wraight could remember, he'd been the one the other children had looked up to—not the one they laughed at. They'd pat him on the back, shake his hand, try to be his friend. He could hunt better, and shoot better, and play the dulcimer better than any of them, and they all knew it.

But ever since the mission school had come around, things had changed. Not a day went by that Miz Christy, with her numbers and her letters and her books, didn't manage to make him feel like a fool. When he felt like that, the anger boiled in him like a kettle on a fire, so hot it burned inside.

He'd known he shouldn't have come to the open house tonight. He'd told Lundy a thousand times he didn't want to. But Lundy had told Wraight he was coming, like it or not. Lundy was hoping to get hold of some moonshine and have a time of it.

Besides, Zach had wanted to come so bad. Their ma and pa weren't coming, and the only way Zach could come was if Wraight did, too. He'd practically begged Wraight. How could Wraight have said no? He would do anything for Zach, and Zach would do anything for him. So that was that. Wraight had agreed to come.

He glanced down at his legs. His feet and hands were covered with mud. He wiped his hands on his shirt, but that just made things worse. He had to get out of here. He'd grab Zach and make him head on home. He wondered, if he went back outside, if the laughter would start all over again.

Wraight's eyes fell on the big, gleaming piano. The top was propped open with some kind of stick. He started for the door, but something held him back, like a hand grabbing hold of his thoughts.

If he went over to that piano, he'd see the insides. See what made it work.

Slowly Wraight approached the piano, as if it were something alive. His feet left big footprints of mud. He glanced toward the kitchen. He was safe. No one was coming. Miss Ida, who'd shooed him away yesterday, was nowhere around.

He looked inside the piano and gasped. He saw wires, more than anyone could count, tight and long. He touched one with a muddy finger. So many more strings than his dulcimer!

Wraight stepped over to the bench. Even that was a sight to behold, all shiny and smooth. He sat down, almost without knowing what he was doing.

The little key things were lined up like soldiers. Black were thinner than white. He rested a finger on one, then slowly let it sink down. A soft whisper of a sound, like a dove's coo, came out of the piano's insides.

Another key, this one black. He touched it softly, too, not wanting to draw attention. This time the sound was a low grumble, like thunder at the end of a storm.

Something inside him changed. The boiling kettle of anger cooled. His guts weren't all twisted and tight anymore. He could feel the hate dripping away, the way it always did when he played his music.

How many times had he gone to his dulcimer when he'd felt angry? He remembered all those times he and his pa had nearly come to blows. The only thing that would make everything go away was playing and playing till you forgot what it was that had you so riled. He missed that. He hadn't known how much, till just now.

Wraight ran his fingers gently up and down the whole keyboard. It was sweet, the way the keys gave way and then popped back up, ready for more. With his eyes closed, he did it again, so softly that only a few notes sounded. When he opened his eyes, he looked down in horror to see that he'd left a long trail of mud on the beautiful white keys.

Just then, the front door opened and Miz Christy came in. The preacher was with her, and John Spencer's mama, and a whole lot of others, too.

"And here's our new pride and joy," Miz Christy said gaily. "The mission's very own grand piano!"

Then Wraight saw her. Lizette. She was standing at the edge of the group, staring at his muddy clothes with wide, shocked eyes.

Wraight gulped. He had to get out of here, and he had to get out fast. He pushed back the bench and leapt up.

"Wraight!" Miz Christy exclaimed. "There you are." Her eyes dropped to the floor. "Oh, no! Miss Ida's going to have a fit when she sees these footprints!" She rolled her eyes when she noticed the mud on the piano keys. "Wraight," she moaned. "Couldn't you at least have cleaned yourself up first?"

"I—I just wanted to . . ." Wraight muttered.

"I 'spect he thought he could play us all a tune," somebody said, and the laughter started all over again.

"I could play, if'n I had the chance!" Wraight cried. The blood was rushing to his head. He clenched his hands. His stomach churned.

"Well, before you play us a tune, wash up those hands," Miz Christy said. She was smiling, but Wraight knew it wasn't a friendly smile. It was the kind of smile you made when you were laughing on the inside.

He stepped back. The bench fell, crashing to the floor. Wraight pushed his way through the crowd and out the door. He could feel

Lizette's eyes on him. He wanted to hurt something again. And he wanted to run.

For now, he would run. Later—tonight, maybe—there would be plenty of time for the hurting.

$$\sim\!\!\sim\!\!\sim$$

Christy lay in bed, tossing and turning. It was two in the morning, but she couldn't seem to get to sleep.

Maybe it was the excitement of the open house. It had lasted into the wee hours, and everyone had agreed it was a huge success. To her relief, no windows had been broken, nothing had caught on fire, no fights had started. And there'd been no pranks, thank goodness—just lots of joking and laughing and dancing.

Christy had even danced a couple dances with Dr. MacNeill. Surprisingly, he was a good dancer. And she had to admit he'd looked very dashing this evening, in his fancy coat and tie. His hair was even neatly combed—for once.

After they were done dancing, Fairlight had whispered that she'd seen David watching Christy and the doctor very carefully. "If I didn't know better, Miz Christy," she'd said, "I'd swear to you that grumpy look on the preacher's face was pure green envy!"

Christy wondered if Fairlight could be right. Probably not. Christy and David were just friends—weren't they? And as for the doctor . . . well, he couldn't possibly be interested in Christy romantically. At least, she didn't think so.

Well, she could worry about that another day. The important thing was that the party had been a success. Everyone had danced and sung and told tall tales, and just generally seemed to enjoy the company of their neighbors. She had even played a few tunes — badly—on the piano, along with Jeb and David and some of the others.

The thought of the piano made her sigh out loud. Why hadn't she handled things better with Wraight this evening? She hadn't meant to embarrass him about getting the piano dirty, but clearly she had.

Lizette, who was spending the night here at the mission house with Ruby Mae and Bessie, had told Christy not to worry. She'd said that lately, Wraight seemed to have a temper that could flare up like a bonfire. "It isn't your fault, Miz Christy," she'd said sadly. "Near as I can figure, it's nobody's fault."

Well, maybe so. But Christy was the teacher, and she should have known better than to humiliate Wraight, when he'd already been embarrassed in front of everyone once that night. Monday, she'd be sure to apologize to him. Not that her apology would probably change anything. But she had to try.

She rolled over onto her side and tried to count sheep. She was on number eighteen when she heard a loud thump. She sat up in bed, waiting to see if she heard anything else.

No, nothing. It was probably Ruby Mae and her two friends, creeping around and making mischief.

Christy closed her eyes and started counting again. This time she made it to sheep number twenty-one before she heard another thud.

She threw back her covers. Those girls were going to keep her up all night, unless she put a stop to this. Ruby Mae had promised she and the others would be on their best behavior. Christy smiled as she donned her robe. Come to think of it, this probably *was* their best behavior.

Christy opened her door. She didn't have a lamp with her, but the moonlight through the hall window was bright. She heard a creak coming from downstairs, the sound of a footstep on wood. The girls were probably in the kitchen, searching for the last of Miss Ida's oatmeal cookies.

Christy eased open the door to Ruby Mae's bedroom. To her shock, all three girls were sleeping peacefully. Ruby Mae was snoring away.

Her hand trembling slightly, Christy closed

the door. Across the hall, Miss Ida's door was closed, which probably meant she was sound asleep, too. She'd said she was exhausted, after all the frantic preparations for the open house.

From somewhere downstairs came another thump. Christy's heart raced. If it wasn't Miss Ida, and it wasn't the girls, who could be downstairs at this hour?

Slowly, as quietly as she could, Christy crept down the stairs. Each step brought her a little closer to her fear.

She heard a creak. "Miss Ida?" she called in a hoarse whisper.

No one answered. Christy tried to swallow, but her throat was tight and dry.

At last she reached the bottom of the stairs. Moonlight filled the parlor with a milky glow. Nothing moved. No one seemed to be there.

She took two steps across the cold, wooden floor. She held her breath, and then she heard it—someone else's breathing.

Christy spun around.

Near the piano, she saw him. He was tall and menacing, his face hidden in shadow. She could just make out the glimmer of a silver knife, poised high in the air over the open piano.

The knife came down, in slow motion, and disappeared deep inside the piano. There was a sharp, metallic noise as it sliced through a wire.

"No!" Without thinking, Christy dashed toward the figure. Suddenly she realized who it was. She came to an abrupt stop inches away from the intruder.

"Wraight?" she whispered.

His eyes shone in the moonlight with a terrible anger, like nothing she'd ever seen before. He lifted the knife again, high over Christy's head.

"No, Wraight!" she cried, and as the knife came down, she grabbed for his arm with all her might.

✎ Nine ✎

Christy locked her hands onto Wraight's strong arm. The knife gleamed in the eerie light.

"It's been you all along, Wraight, hasn't it?" she whispered.

She felt his arm go limp. His eyes filled with tears.

"Don't do it, Wraight!" a boy's voice cried.

Christy spun around to see Zach, climbing through a half-open window on the other side of the room. He dashed across the room and threw himself against his big brother, sobbing frantically.

Wraight let the knife drop to the floor. "I told you not to follow me again," he said softly.

Zach clung to Wraight, his arms tight around the older boy's waist. "He wouldn't never hurt you, Miz Christy," Zach said. Tears streamed down his face. "He was just mad, is all. Like the other times."

Christy stared into Wraight's face, hoping to find an explanation there. But all she saw was a confused, unhappy boy.

"Was it you all those times, Wraight?" she asked. "The ink and the message on the school?"

He hung his head, but didn't answer.

"And that time I was walking home from the Spencers'—was that you, too?"

Wraight nodded slightly.

"But I was sure it was Zach," Christy said. "I thought Lundy was putting him up to it—"

Wraight looked up. He had a grim half-smile on his face. "Do sound like Lundy, don't it?"

Christy touched Zach's shoulder gently. "But Zach, why were you always there? I saw you at the schoolhouse, the night that message was left. And out in the woods . . ."

Wraight held his brother close. "It weren't him. It were me, every time. Zach, he's like my twin or something. Or my—what is it the preacher calls it?—my conch . . . uh, my—"

"Conscience," Christy said.

"He knew I was up to no good, and when I wouldn't listen to nothing he had to say, he started following me around." He touched Zach's red cap. "Followed me tonight, too, even though I told him if'n he did I'd make him do my chores for a month."

"Christy?" Miss Ida called from the top of the stairwell. "Do I hear voices down there?"

"Wait here," Christy told the boys. She went to the stairs. Ruby Mae, Bessie, and Lizette were sitting on the top steps, yawning and rubbing their eyes.

"Everything's under control, Miss Ida. Go back to sleep," Christy said. "That goes for you girls, too."

"Can't sleep," Ruby Mae said firmly. "You've got us all a-wondering what's goin' on."

"I can sleep just fine, thank you," said Miss Ida. She turned on her heel and went back to her room.

"You girls wait there," Christy instructed.

She went back to Zach and Wraight. "Zach," she said, kneeling down, "I need to talk to your brother for a few minutes, all right? You go on up to the top of the stairs and wait. Some of your school friends are up there."

"Is they . . . girls?"

"I'm afraid so."

Zach moaned. "See what you got me into?" he said to Wraight. He turned to Christy. "He ain't in big trouble, is he, Teacher?"

"Well, he's in trouble," Christy said. "But I wouldn't worry, if I were you."

"If you whop him with a birch switch, he won't cry a lick," Zach said proudly.

"I don't think that will be necessary, Zach," Christy said with a smile. "Now, you go on up."

Zach headed upstairs, and Christy motioned for Wraight to join her on the piano bench. He gazed at her doubtfully.

"Come on, Wraight," Christy said. "We need to talk."

After a moment, he sat down awkwardly beside her.

Christy took a deep breath, trying to clear her thoughts. Moonlight flowed over the piano like liquid silver. Wraight's sharp knife still lay on the floor. She could hear the soft whispers of Zach and the girls on the stairs.

She thought of the spilled ink and the erased chalkboard. She thought of the angry message on the schoolhouse. She thought of her fear— that night in the woods—and again tonight.

She was angry at Wraight. She wanted to tell him that. Part of her even wanted to scare him, the way he'd scared her.

But when she looked at the quiet boy sitting beside her, staring at the piano keys as if they were bars of gold, she wondered if getting angry was the answer. She wanted to help Wraight, more than she wanted to get angry at him.

Miss Alice had said that Christy had to understand the mountain people before she would ever be able to help them.

Why would Wraight have turned on Christy? Why, when he seemed so entranced by the piano, would he try to hurt it?

"You know, Wraight," Christy said, "I'll let you in on a little secret. Ever since I came here to the mission, I keep making mistakes. Sometimes I feel like a real fool."

Wraight stared at her, mystified, as if she were speaking in a foreign language. "You?" he said at last. "Make mistakes? Ain't likely."

"It's true," Christy insisted. "Like those donations I got for the mission. I thought they were a good idea, but it turned out Miss Alice was pretty unhappy with me. The way I asked for them wasn't right. And we ended up with things we're going to have a hard time using, like telephone wire—" she ran her fingers over the keys, "and, of course, this piano."

"This piano ain't no mistake," Wraight said firmly. "It's the most amazin' thing Cutter Gap ever seen. It's like . . ."

He threw open his arms, searching for the right word. "Like the biggest dulcimer in the whole, wide world, right here, just a-waitin' for someone to help it sing."

Christy played a soft chord, three notes together that lingered in the air. "Then why did you cut that wire, Wraight? Why did you want to hurt the piano?"

For a long time, Wraight sat silently, staring at the keyboard. "Sometimes," he said at last, "when you can't have something . . . it just makes you so mad, you feel like you're going to bust up inside."

"But if you'd wanted lessons on the piano, I would have been glad to teach you, Wraight. Not that I'm much of a piano player, mind you. But all you had to do was ask."

Wraight gave a hard laugh. "And make more of a fool of myself than I have already? Not hardly."

"What are you talking about?"

"Like it ain't as plain as the nose on my face."

Christy touched him on the shoulder. "I don't understand, Wraight. Really, I don't. Try to explain it to me."

Wraight thought for a while. "I can't step inside that there schoolhouse," he said, avoiding her gaze, "without sayin' or doin' somethin' so all-fired stupid that I sound like the biggest fool this side of Coldsprings Mountain. The way you're always goin' on about numbers and letters and such, it's enough to make me—"

"What? Make you angry?" Christy asked. At last she was beginning to understand.

"Well, if'n you want the whole truth—" Wraight's voice was harsh, "some days it makes me want to burn that whole school right to the ground."

Christy nodded. "Sometimes fear makes a person do things he doesn't want to do," she said. "Things he knows are wrong."

Wraight pushed down a key with his index finger and listened. "I reckon," he finally said.

"Lizette tells me you're quite a dulcimer player," Christy said.

"Don't have no dulcimer no more."

"I never could play the piano very well," Christy said. "I took lessons growing up, but no matter how hard I tried, my fingers just couldn't keep up with the notes." She laughed softly. "One year, when I was eight, we had a recital. All the parents came to hear us. It seemed to me like all of Asheville, North Carolina, was there. Well, my teacher wanted me to play something simple—you know, like 'Twinkle, Twinkle, Little Star.' You've heard that, haven't you?"

Christy plunked out the first few notes of the song, and Wraight nodded.

"But of course, I had other things on my mind. I wanted to impress everyone with my incredible talent. So I decided to play one of my favorite hymns—'What a Friend We Have in Jesus.'"

This time she played the first notes of the hymn. Wraight watched her fingers, fascinated.

"Well, needless to say, I got up there to play, and I froze. I played about three notes, looked out at all those faces in the audience, and the fear just took over."

"What happened then?" Wraight asked.

"I'm very embarrassed to report that I threw up all over my piano teacher's favorite rug."

Wraight burst out laughing. "Miz Christy, that is the saddest tale I ever did hear! You wouldn't tell me a whopper, now, would you?"

"Cross my heart. It's the truth. And the *really* sad thing is that I stopped taking lessons after that. I was so afraid of failing that I just gave up. I've always regretted it." She sighed. "Now it seems like I can hardly get a note out of this piano."

"Try," Wraight said softly. His voice was almost pleading.

Christy cleared her throat. "Well, here goes nothing."

Slowly and painfully, she began to play "What a Friend We Have in Jesus." All too often, she hit a wrong note that made her wince, but she kept going because Wraight seemed to want her to. He was watching her fingers as if he were in a trance.

Halfway through, she struggled again and again with the same chord, but she simply couldn't find the right note.

"Maybe that's enough. I don't want to ruin your hearing," she said. "I'm sorry. I just can't seem to get it right."

"Could I . . . could I give it a whirl?" Wraight whispered.

Christy slid off the bench. "Be my guest."

Wraight stared at the keys, deep in concentration. He arranged his fingers carefully, then pressed them all down at once.

The first chord of the old gospel hymn rang out. Wraight closed his eyes as if he'd witnessed a miracle. Then, slowly and with great care, he began to play the same piece Christy had struggled through. He only missed a few notes.

Christy watched in amazement. She felt the way she had when she was teaching Fairlight Spencer to read—as if all she'd had to do was open a door, and send Wraight on his way.

She thought of all the times she'd been frustrated with Wraight, and with the other slow learners in her class. How wrong she'd been about him! Perhaps different students learned in different ways. It was her job to find the door that would allow each one into the place where Wraight had just ventured.

When he was done, she applauded. "That was amazing, Wraight. Absolutely amazing."

"Ain't nothin'. You just sound 'em out, one at a time. Low notes are down at that end. High ones up yonder." He shrugged. "It's easy enough."

"Tell that to my old piano teacher." Christy laughed. "You have a real gift, Wraight. I was wondering . . . if I could locate some piano instruction books, how would you like to come over to the mission house after school and practice? I could teach you what I know, which isn't much. But then you'd be pretty much on your own."

To her shock, Wraight shook his head firmly. "Can't," was all he said.

"But I thought you'd . . ." Once again, Miss Alice's words about the donations came back to her. *There's a strong mountain code, you see. No one wants to owe anyone for anything. These people don't respect anyone who can't earn his own way.*

"Wraight," Christy said, "suppose you did odd jobs around the mission to pay for your lessons? It would be a way to pay us back for the damage to the piano, too. We'll need to replace that wire. I know David's got a lot of work around here left to do. He wants to build a better barn for Goldie and Prince and Old Theo, to start with. And one of these days, he may have a telephone he needs help hooking up."

Wraight scratched his chin. "So it'd be fair and square-like? I'd be working for the time I spent on the piano?"

"Fair and square."

"I s'pose I could manage that," he said casually, but Christy could see the excitement in his eyes.

"Good. It's a deal, then. And Wraight?"

"Yes'm?"

"If you feel angry like that again, will you come to me and talk about it?"

"No'm."

Christy sighed. "But why not?"

"Don't need to talk with you, if'n I got this here piano to talk to." He looked up at her hopefully. "You reckon I could play real quiet-like for another minute or two? I was hopin' maybe I could practice up to play for Lizette."

"I have an even better idea," Christy said. "Wait here."

She went upstairs. Zach was asleep on the landing. Ruby Mae and Bessie had gone back to bed. But Lizette was sitting on the top step, wide awake.

"Have you been listening?" Christy asked.

"Oh, no, Miz Christy. I ain't no eavesdropper."

"Of course, you might have *accidently* overheard a thing or two."

Lizette gave a sheepish grin. "Well, maybe just a wee bit."

"If you're in the mood for a concert," Christy said, "I happen to know a fine piano player who's in the mood to give one."

Lizette ran down the stairs. A moment later, Christy heard the slow, careful strains of "What a Friend We Have in Jesus" coming from the parlor. There were a few missed notes and some awkward pauses, but she'd never heard the old hymn played with more love.

About the Author

Catherine Marshall

With *Christy*, Catherine Marshall LeSourd (1914–1983) created one of the world's most widely read and best-loved classics. Published in 1967, the book spent 39 weeks on the New York Times bestseller list. With an estimated 30 million Americans having read it, *Christy* is now approaching its 90th printing and has sold over eight million copies. Although a novel, *Christy* is in fact a thinly-veiled biography of Catherine's mother, Leonora Wood.

Catherine Marshall LeSourd also authored *A Man Called Peter*, which has sold over four million copies. It is an American bestseller, portraying the love between a dynamic man and his God, and the tender, romantic love between a man and the girl he married. *Julie* is a powerful, sweeping novel of love and adventure, courage and commitment, tragedy and triumph, in a Pennsylvania town during the Great Depression. Catherine also authored many other devotional books of encouragement.

THE CHRISTY® JUVENILE FICTION SERIES

You'll want to read them all!

Based upon Catherine Marshall's international bestseller *Christy®*, this new series contains expanded adventures filled with romance, intrigue, and excitement.

VOLUME ONE
(ISBN 1-4003-0772-4)

#1—The Bridge to Cutter Gap
Nineteen-year-old Christy leaves her family to teach at a mission school in the Great Smoky Mountains. On the other side of an icy bridge lie excitement, adventure, and maybe even the man of her dreams . . . but can she survive a life-and-death struggle when she falls into the rushing waters below?

#2—Silent Superstitions
Christy's students are suddenly afraid to come to school. Is what Granny O'Teale says true? Is their teacher cursed? Will the children's fears and the adults' superstitions force Christy to abandon her dreams and return to North Carolina?

#3—The Angry Intruder
Someone wants Christy to leave Cutter Gap, and they'll stop at nothing. Mysterious pranks soon turn dangerous. Could a student be the culprit? When Christy confronts the late-night intruder, will it be a face she knows?

VOLUME TWO
(ISBN 1-4003-0773-2)

#4—Midnight Rescue
The mission's black stallion, Prince, has vanished, and so has Christy's student Ruby Mae. Christy must brave the guns of angry moonshiners to bring them home. Will her faith in God see her through her darkest night?

#5—The Proposal
Christy should be thrilled when David Grantland, the handsome minister, proposes marriage, but her feelings of excitement are mixed with confusion and uncertainty. Several untimely interruptions delay her answer to David's proposal. Then a terrible riding accident and blindness threaten all of Christy's dreams for the future.

#6—Christy's Choice
When Christy is offered a chance to teach in her hometown, she faces a difficult decision. Will her train ride back to Cutter Gap be a journey home or a last farewell? In a moment of terror and danger, Christy must decide where her future lies.

VOLUME THREE
(ISBN 1-4003-0774-0)

#7—The Princess Club
When Ruby Mae, Bessie, and Clara discover gold at Cutter Gap, they form an exclusive organization, "The Princess Club." Christy watches in dismay as her classroom—and her community—are torn apart by greed, envy, and an understanding of what true wealth really means.

#8—Family Secrets
Bob Allen and many of the residents of Cutter Gap
are upset when a black family, the Washingtons,
moves in near the Allens' property. When a series of
threatening incidents befall the Washingtons, Christy
steps in to help. But it's a clue in the Washingtons'
family Bible that may hold the real key to peace and
acceptance.

#9—Mountain Madness
When Christy travels alone to a nearby mountain,
she vows to discover the truth behind the terrifying
legend of a strange mountain creature. But what she
finds, at first seems worse than she ever imagined!

VOLUME FOUR
(ISBN 1-4003-0775-9)

#10—Stage Fright
As Christy's students are preparing for a school play,
she reveals her dream to act on stage herself. Little
does she know that Doctor MacNeill's aunt is the
artistic director of the Knoxville theater. Before long,
just as Christy is about to debut on stage, several
mysterious incidents threaten both her dreams and
her pride!

#11—Goodbye, Sweet Prince
Prince, the mission's stallion, is sold to a cruel
owner, then disappears. Christy Huddleston and her
students are heartsick. Is there any way to reclaim the
magnificent horse?

#12—Brotherly Love
Everyone is delighted when Christy's younger brother,
George Huddleston, visits Christy at the Cutter Gap

Mission. But the delight ends when George reveals that he has been expelled from school for stealing. Can Christy summon the love and faith to help her brother do the right thing?